CONFIDENTIAL MEMO— FILES OF SGT. NATE McCALL, OCPD

Badge No. 1197: Joshua McCall

Rank: Sergeant, Sex Crimes Division, OCPD

Skill/Expertise: A maverick with a passion for seeing justice done, known to bend the rules to get what—or *who*—he wants.

What We Know: Currently ending a leave of absence, the cop in McCall is intrigued by the gorgeous newcomer working at his favorite watering hole. And the man in him won't be able to ignore the allure of her dangerous beauty.…

Subject: Regan Ford

Current Profession: Bartender, Person of Interest

What We Know: This sexy newcomer is tight-lipped about her past, and jittery as hell around cops. Whatever she's hiding, McCall is jeopardizing his already-endangered career—and his heart—by getting closer to the enigmatic bartender.

Dear Reader,

What a glorious time of year—full of shopping, holiday cheer and endless opportunities to eat baked goods. For your shopping list I suggest this month's stellar lineup of Silhouette Intimate Moments books—romances with adrenaline.

New York Times bestselling author Maggie Shayne delights readers with *Feels Like Home* (#1395), an emotional tale from her miniseries THE OKLAHOMA ALL-GIRL BRANDS, in which a cop returns to his hometown and falls for a woman from his past. Will a deadly threat end their relationship? In Maggie Price's *Most Wanted Woman* (#1396), from her miniseries LINE OF DUTY, a police sergeant is intrigued by a bartender with a dark secret and an irresistible face. Don't miss it!

You'll love Karen Whiddon's next story, *Secrets of the Wolf* (#1397), from her spine-tingling miniseries THE PACK. Here, a determined heroine seeks answers about her past, which leads her to a handsome sheriff with his own secrets. Can she trust this mysterious man and the passion that consumes them? Michelle Celmer's story is *Out of Sight* (#1398), a thrilling tale in which an embittered FBI agent searches for a missing witness and finds her…in his bed. Will she flee before helping bring a killer to justice?

So, take a break from the nonstop festivities and get engrossed in these fabulous love stories. Happy reading!

Sincerely,

Patience Smith
Associate Senior Editor
Silhouette Intimate Moments

Please address questions and book requests to:
Silhouette Reader Service
U.S.: 3010 Walden Ave., P.O. Box 1325, Buffalo, NY 14269
Canadian: P.O. Box 609, Fort Erie, Ont. L2A 5X3

MAGGIE PRICE

Most Wanted Woman

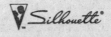

INTIMATE MOMENTS™

Published by Silhouette Books

America's Publisher of Contemporary Romance

 SILHOUETTE BOOKS

ISBN 0-373-27466-1

MOST WANTED WOMAN

Copyright © 2005 by Margaret Price

This edition published by arrangement with Harlequin Books S.A.

® and TM are trademarks of Harlequin Books S.A., used under license.
Trademarks indicated with ® are registered in the United States Patent
and Trademark Office, the Canadian Trade Marks Office and in other
countries.

Visit Silhouette Books at www.eHarlequin.com

Printed in U.S.A.

Books by Maggie Price

Silhouette Intimate Moments

Prime Suspect #816
The Man She Almost Married #838
Most Wanted #948
On Dangerous Ground #989
Dangerous Liaisons #1043
Special Report #1045
  "Midnight Seduction"
Moment of Truth #1143
Sure Bet #1263
Hidden Agenda #1269
The Cradle Will Fall #1276
Shattered Vows #1335
Most Wanted Woman #1396

*Line of Duty

Silhouette Bombshell

Trigger Effect #47

The Coltons
Protecting Peggy
Wed to the Witness

MAGGIE PRICE

is no stranger to law enforcement. While on the job as a civilian crime analyst for the Oklahoma City Police Department, she analyzed robberies and sex crimes, and snagged numerous special assignments to homicide task-forces.

While at OCPD, Maggie stored up enough tales of intrigue, murder and mayhem to keep her at the keyboard for years. The first of those tales won the Romance Writers of America's Golden Heart Award for Romantic Suspense. Maggie is also the recipient of *Romantic Times* Career Achievement Award in series romantic suspense.

Maggie invites her readers to contact her at 416 N.W. 8th St., Oklahoma City, OK 73102-2604, or on the Web at www.maggieprice.net.

For Debbie Cowan, my esteemed pal and "mediator,"
for bucking me up and bailing me out more
times than I can count.

Chapter 1

The instant the stranger stepped through the tavern's front door, a weight dropped on Regan Ford's chest, pressing against her heart so hard she could hear the panicked beat of it in her ears.

In his denim work shirt and worn jeans he looked tall, tough and sinewy. He stood with his feet wide, chest a bit forward for balance. His right leg was slightly back, as if keeping an invisible holster out of reach.

Cop! her senses warned.

The quick, instinctive fear of cornered prey had her swiveling toward the cash register. Fear barreling in like a locomotive, she rang up the pitcher of beer she'd just served to the pair of grizzled regulars gossiping about the day's catch. Keeping her back to the man, she focused her gaze on the mirror that spanned the length of the bar. Her breathing grew shallow as she studied him through the gray haze of smoky air.

His thick, black hair brushed the wrinkled collar of the shirt that was rolled up at the sleeves to reveal muscled, sun-bronzed

forearms. The faded jeans molded powerful legs. Dark stubble
shadowed his jaw. There was a ruggedness about his tanned
face that reached all the way to his eyes. Eyes that looked as
sharp as a stiletto while he studied his surroundings.

Was he here for her? Had her flight from the law—which
had begun exactly one year ago today—come to an end?

While a country song about the misery of lost love crooned
from the jukebox, Regan did a quick survey of the patrons who
sat shoulder to shoulder at every table and overflowed the
booths. Except for a few stools at the bar, the only vacant seats
belonged to the people crowded onto the dance floor. The panic
sizzling through her made her want to cut and run, try to lose
herself in the crowd, then slip out the back door where her car
was parked. But if the cop was here for her, he'd be armed with
more than just an arrest warrant. He would have a gun, and be
within his legal rights to pull it while pursuing a wanted mur-
derer. Her trying to make a break right now could get an innocent person hurt. Killed.

Regan reminded herself that people in this cozy, out-of-the-
way town wouldn't just stand by and watch him drag her away.
She thought of Howie Lyons, the night shift cook working in
the kitchen. Mindful of trouble that sometimes broke out when
alcohol mixed with rowdy customers, Howie kept a Louisville
Slugger stashed beneath the grill. Then there was Deni Graham.

Regan swept her gaze around the tavern's dim interior until
she spotted the blond waitress. Dressed in a snug red tank top
and tight jeans, Deni stood at a table, laughing and flirting with
six men while she jotted their orders on her pad.

Regan conceded she didn't know her coworkers all that
well. Wouldn't let *them* get to know *her.* But she felt sure they
would help her if the cop slapped a pair of cuffs on her. She
would demand they call Sundown's police chief, remind him
it was within her rights to be locked up in his jail while she
fought extradition to New Orleans. During that time, she could

maybe figure out a way to escape and run. Again. For the rest of her life, she had to run.

Hands unsteady, she tidied the liquor bottles lining the bar's mirrored shelf while she watched the cop through her lashes. A not-so-subtle masculine power drifted with him as he strode toward her across the peanut-shell-scattered wooden floor.

A faint, liquid tug in her belly had Regan blinking. For a year she had been dead inside. No laughter, no warmth, no feeling. That some sort of primitive awareness of this man, *this cop,* could spark something inside her had her spine going as stiff as a blade.

"Josh McCall!" Deni squealed then engulfed the stranger in a hug and gave him a smacking kiss on the mouth. "It's about time you came back to Sundown."

Regan eased out a breath. The waitress's familiarity with the man went far toward assuring her he wasn't there at the devil's bidding.

Still, she was positive he carried a badge. Knowing that kept the prickles of fear at the back of her neck. She knew better than anyone there was no one more capable of treachery than a cop.

With the jukebox now between selections, the crack and clatter of pool balls drifted from the back room. Regan rolled her shoulders, attempting to ease her tension and turned in time to see the man send Deni a grin that was all charm.

"Long time no see, angel face." They stood close enough to the bar for Regan to hear his voice, which was as smooth as the move he made to extract himself from Deni's embrace.

"I swear, Josh, it seems like an eternity since you've been here." She tugged him the few remaining steps to the bar while giving him the once-over. "You look as good as always."

"So do you."

Deni slid a palm up and down his arm. "When'd you get to town?"

"Just now. I wasn't sure what I'd find in the cabin's pantry so I decided to stop here first."

She fluttered her lashes. "Maybe you'll stay in Sundown long enough this time for us to get together?"

When he eased a hip onto one of the bar stools, his gaze met Regan's. For the space of a heartbeat, his eyes focused on her so completely it was as if she were spotlighted on an otherwise empty stage.

That one searing look, along with the whispers of awareness already stirring her senses, made Regan's throat go even more dry.

He gave her the merest fraction of a nod, then shifted his attention back to Deni.

"I'll be here about three weeks."

Just then, Howie's voice bellowed an order number through the open wall hatch between the kitchen and the bar.

"That's my cue," Deni said. "You want your regular for dinner, Josh?"

"You bet."

While Deni sauntered toward the kitchen's swinging door, Regan steeled her nerves and slid a napkin onto the bar. She couldn't exactly ignore a customer.

"What can I get you?"

"Corona." When he shifted on the stool, light fell on the thin scar winding out of his collar and up the right side of his neck. "I'm Josh McCall."

"Nice to meet you."

"You're new to Sundown."

She turned to the cooler, met his gaze in the mirror. His eyes were intent on her face. Too intent. "Right."

"Been here long?"

"A few months." She retrieved a bottle, twisted off its cap.

"Have relatives around here?"

"No." She topped the bottle with a lime wedge. "Do you?"

"More like extended family." His eyes were so deeply brown it was impossible to see a boundary between pupil and iris. "So, where's home?"

What should have been a simple question was as loaded as a shotgun that had been primed and pumped. "Here. There. Everywhere. I'm a gypsy at heart." Regan had rehearsed the response so many times it now sounded normal.

She settled the bottle onto the napkin, then wiped a cloth across the bar, its gleaming wood nearly black with age.

"Sounds like you've known Deni awhile," she commented.

"My family owns a cabin here. We used to spend every summer in Sundown. Mostly now we make it here for holidays." He took a long sip of his drink. "The South."

"The South what?"

"You've spent time in the South. There's a trace of it in your voice."

Regan kept her face blank, her hands loose while her insides clenched. "I've been in that part of the country a few times," she improvised. She'd practiced endless hours to lose her native Louisiana accent. The fact he'd pegged it within minutes had her nerves scrambling.

"What about you?" She placed a plastic bowl of unshelled peanuts beside the beer bottle. Despite her inner turmoil, her voice remained steady. "Where are you from?"

He eyed her while he snagged a peanut, cracked it. "Oklahoma City. Ever pass through on your way to here, there and everywhere?"

"No. Is your family's cabin on the lake?"

"Yeah. It sits just to the west of your boss's house." He popped a peanut in his mouth, chased it with a swallow of beer. "You know it?"

"Yes." Since just standing there had her wanting to jump out of her skin, she plunged her hands into the warm soapy water in the small metal sink and began washing glasses. "I wouldn't call it a cabin. It's one of the biggest houses on the lake. And sits on the lot with about the best view of the water."

"Point taken." He palmed more peanuts, began shelling them

onto the cocktail napkin. "When my grandfather bought the land and built the house, he made sure the place was roomy enough for all his kids, then later the grandkids. The entire Mc-Call clan's descending here for the Fourth of July. I volunteered to come down ahead of time and make repairs."

"The holiday's weeks away. Is the house in bad shape?"

The shot glass she was currently rinsing had Regan glancing at the big bear of a man seated at one end of the bar. Seamus O'Toole owned several used car lots in Dallas and was an avid participant in Paradise Lake's annual fishing derby. He'd been here an hour and already had empty shot glasses stacked in a pyramid before him.

"No, there's just a lot of minor repairs that need to be done."

McCall's comment had her looking back at him. She saw that his gaze had followed hers to O'Toole.

"Maybe you'll have time to get some fishing in," she said.

"Maybe." He glanced toward the kitchen door. "I spotted Etta's car parked in the back. If she's in the office slaving over the books, I'd like to stick my head in and tell her hello. Give her a kiss."

"You're a friendly neighbor."

"More than. Etta's like a second mom to me and my brothers and sisters." He took another drink. "To tell you the truth, I'm crazy in love with your boss."

Regan arched a brow. Etta Truelove was a vibrant sixty-something widow with ten grandchildren, two great-grandchildren and a fiancé. "Does Etta know how you feel about her?"

"I tell her all the time." His mouth curved in a wide, reckless grin. "One taste of her apple pie, the woman owned my heart. If she would dump A.C. and run off with me, I'd die a happy man."

Regan was sure that glib talk and grin tumbled women like bowling pins. There had been a time in her life Josh McCall would have had the same effect on her. And, yes, she admitted, there was something about him that, despite her panic, her fear, had her heartbeat kicking hard. But she would ignore that something—*easily ignore it*—because she'd learned too well that you never knew, not for certain, what was under a cop's smooth words and smiles.

With the glasses washed, she retrieved a rag and began drying. "I guess you haven't heard about Etta's accident."

He set his beer aside while what looked like genuine concern settled in his eyes. "What accident?"

"She broke a bone in her foot when she slipped and fell at the marina."

"Is she okay?"

"Well enough, considering she has to stay cooped up in her house with her leg in a walking cast. She can hobble around using a cane, but the doctor doesn't want her on her feet for any length of time. He's banned her from work because he knows she'd start tending bar the minute she got here. Just to make sure she follows the doc's orders, I confiscated her car. That's why it's parked out back."

"I'll stop by her place when I leave here. Find out if she needs anything."

"It'll be dark out by the time you finish dinner," Regan said. "Sundown's got a prowler running around, so people are nervous. I'll call Etta to let her know to expect you."

He frowned. "What kind of prowler?"

"Beats me. He wears black and creeps around at night." She brushed her bangs out of her eyes. "Etta mentioned him the day she hired me, so he's been at it awhile."

Regan felt a rush of relief when Deni stepped to the bar with a tray heaped with empties and a pad of orders. She'd spent enough time talking to McCall. Far too long in his presence that was unsettling on numerous levels. She planned to spend the rest of her shift—and his entire time in Sundown—avoiding him.

She glanced at him over her shoulder. "Let me know if you need a refill."

"Sure. Before you go, tell me one thing."

"What?"

"Your name."

She hesitated. "Regan."

"Nice name. Unusual."

She'd thought the same thing when she saw it on a tomb-stone. She scooped a bag of peanuts from beneath the counter. "I've got work."

"Okay. Nice to meet you, Regan."

With dusk melting into darkness and the mellow notes of a guitar sliding from the stereo, Josh steered his red Corvette convertible along the road that ringed Paradise Lake. His mind wasn't on the night air that flowed like warm water across his face, the soothing music or the shadowy groves of oaks and glimpses of shoreline that zipped by.

His thoughts centered on the bartender.

Although a booth had opened up just as Deni served his hamburger and fries, he had remained at the bar. While eating, he watched Regan draw beers, mix drinks and refill bowls of peanuts with single-minded intensity.

She was petite, slim and sleek. The white blouse she wore had been tucked into the waistband of jeans snug enough to whet a man's appetite.

Her hair was as black and shiny as the lapel of a tuxedo, and it hung straight to her shoulders. She had wispy bangs that ended just above brown, gold-flecked eyes. Eyes that had reminded him of a cat's—watching and waiting.

For what? he wondered.

When a yellow warning sign blipped in the high beams of the car's headlights, Josh downshifted. Seconds later, the 'Vette reached the razor-sharp bend in the road the locals had dubbed Wipeout Curve.

He felt the 'Vette's raw power as it whispered through the

treacherous turn. Any other time he would have cleared his mind, eased back and savored the ride. Tonight, his thoughts remained on a slim, dark-haired stranger.

He had noticed her the instant he walked into the tavern. Noticed, too, that while she worked the register and straightened liquor bottles, she surveilled him in the mirror behind the bar. He was used to feeling a woman's gaze, but instinct told him Regan's study of him had nothing to do with hot-blooded attraction, and everything to do with cool-eyed suspicion.

"Interesting," he murmured while the guitar's soothing notes mixed with the night air. It was also of interest that she'd failed to give him her last name, nor had she revealed where she was from. It hadn't been lost on him that every question he'd asked about *her,* she'd turned back on him.

Just because he'd been on suspension didn't mean he'd gotten rusty when it came to spotting some nifty evasion tactics.

His mood darkened as the reminder of the past month threw a mental switch, rerouting his thoughts. The bitterness over having been accused of planting evidence in a rapist's apartment was still there, simmering with a foul taste he'd almost grown used to. What he would never get used to was how his nearly losing his badge and the job that defined him had hurt his family. A law enforcement family, in which cops were the majority and wearing a uniform was a matter of pride.

He respected the badge and the law. He had just found it sometimes necessary, while coming up through the ranks, to circumvent the letter of the law in order to get what he needed to take down a guilty bad guy. No harm, no foul…until he'd been at the right place at the wrong time, and his reputation for stretching the rules had gone far in having a hell of a lot of cops suspect the worst of him.

And, yeah, he *had* looked guilty—who knew better than a sex crimes detective what evidence was needed to score a slam-dunk conviction on a rape? The whole squad had known he'd spent uncountable off-duty hours trying to track down the vicious six-time rapist. And stretching the rules innumerable ways just to get the bastard's scent wasn't something he'd shy away from—but crossing the line wasn't one of those ways. The finger-pointing in Josh's direction, the insinuation that he'd planted evidence had him close to quitting the force in a rage. And then he'd thought about his family and what the badge meant to him. So he'd swallowed back that rage and in the end managed to clear himself.

Now that he was back in the department's good graces, he intended to toe the line a little closer when he reported back to duty.

Another mile down the road Josh steered into the drive of what he'd considered his second home for his entire life. The three-story structure was an architectural masterpiece. Built on a sloped, heavily wooded lot and made entirely of cedar and glass, it had a broad wraparound porch and a wide chimney built of local rock that had been weathered to a soft gray. Beyond the lush back lawn lay Paradise Lake, its rambling shoreline coiling like a snake across the Oklahoma-Texas border.

Josh climbed out of the car. Instead of heading for the house, he strode across the drive and skirted the hedge that separated McCall and Truelove property.

Although only a single porch light glowed beside Etta's front door, Josh knew from memory that the two-story house was painted a pale blue with white shutters. A wooden swing suspended on chains dangled from the porch's ceiling.

The air around him sparked with fireflies as he headed up the walk lined by plants that formed shadowy shapes in the night. By the time he reached the porch, the front door had swung open.

"Joshua McCall, if you aren't a sight for sore eyes."

The woman standing behind the patched screen door, soft light glowing behind her, was tall and lean with a helmet of iron-gray curls framing a square-jawed face. She wore a short-sleeved yellow cotton dress that hit her midcalf.

"So are you." Frowning at the snow-white cast on her right leg, he jogged up the porch steps, gripped the screen she held half open and dropped a kiss on her forehead. He couldn't remember when he'd actually met the gregarious tavern owner and her late husband. They had just always been permanent fixtures during his summers at the lake. As had their two sons who had wreaked havoc with the McCall brothers.

"How's your foot, Etta?"

"Healing too slow for my liking." Her scowl emphasized the network of lines around her eyes and mouth. "Come in and sit, Joshua. I can use the company."

"You're sure it's not too late?"

"Not for this night owl." Leaning on a cane, she limped across the living room filled with furniture positioned on an earth-toned rug. Colorful candles and crocheted throws added to the room's sense of comfort.

"Who's this?" Josh asked, pausing to stroke a finger over the jet-black kitten curled on the recliner.

"Anthracite. She's a stray who wouldn't leave."

"Especially after you fed her, I bet."

"What else was I supposed to do? Poor thing was starving."

Josh scratched behind one furry ear, and was rewarded with a purr. "You named her after coal?"

"Scotty did," Etta said, referring to her youngest grandson. "When he saw the kitten, he decided she looked like the coal he'd learned about in science class."

"Good call." Leaving the kitten sharpening its claws on the recliner, Josh followed Etta along a hallway. When they neared the kitchen, he raised his chin. "Do I smell apple pie?"

"You do. I decided to bake tonight and just took the last of the pies out of the oven. Could be I had a premonition you'd show up, looking too thin for your own good."

Blame that on his suspension, he thought.

He followed her into the kitchen, painted in soft yellow, its white-tiled countertops sparkling beneath the bright overhead light. "Have I told you I'm crazy about you?"

"Every time you want pie." She waved him to the small metal table. "Have a seat and I'll cut us some."

"You sit." Placing a hand on her bony shoulder, he nudged her to a chair. "Everything still in the same place?"

"Nothing's changed." Etta shifted a stack of mail to one corner of the table. "There's tea in the refrigerator."

Minutes later, he had slices of pie and glasses of iced tea on the table. Josh settled into the chair across from hers, lifted his fork and dug in. The warm pie tasted like heaven.

"How's the family?" Etta asked before taking her first bite.

"Mom and Dad are rocking along. Everybody's married now, except Nate and myself. He's fallen for a gorgeous ex-cop from Dallas. He and Paige just moved in together." Feeling a tug on his sock, Josh looked down in time to see Anthracite attack his shoe. Chuckling, he scooped her up, settled her onto his lap and went back to his pie. "I figure it's only a matter of time before Nate calls and tells me to rent a wedding tux."

Etta regarded him over the rim of her glass. "Think it's time you found a girl of your own?"

"I got tons of 'em," he drawled.

"You'll settle down when you find the right woman."

"She'll have to find me because I'm not looking for her." The simple fact was his life had always run more efficiently solo. After Nate moved out of the house they'd shared, Josh had discovered how much he savored living alone. Made things less complicated. Just like women whose idea of the perfect relationship was a good time, a fast ride and a friendly parting.

As he popped the last bite of pie into his mouth, his gaze

settled on the stack of mail on the corner of the table. "Is that a digital recorder?" he asked, plucking up the long silver piece of metal that sat on top of the stack.

"Michael bought me that gadget," Etta said, referring to her eldest son. "I use it to record reminders. Like when to take my medicine. I call it my memory box."

"Smart."

"The thing tends to startle me when my own voice comes out of the blue, telling me to take my pills. There's already enough going on around Sundown to make a person nervous."

Josh set the recorder aside. "I heard about the prowler."

"Whoever it is has been peeping in windows for months now. Chief Decker hasn't had any luck catching him."

Josh frowned. From working sex crimes, he knew that prowlers sometimes turned out to be Peeping Toms, who had the potential of escalating to indecent exposure, then more serious sex crimes. Like rape. His own career problems had been due to one man's zeal to take down the six-time rapist.

"How were things at my tavern tonight?"

Etta's question diverted his thoughts. "The place was packed." Leaning back, he watched the kitten climb up his chest, wincing when her razor-sharp claws stabbed through his shirt. "Howie's burgers are still gold. Deni's as big a flirt as ever. Your new bartender is…interesting."

"Regan's a pretty little thing, isn't she? All that dark hair and those big brown eyes."

Cat's eyes, he thought again. Watching and waiting. For what?

"I baked an extra pie for her," Etta added, sliding her plate aside. "The girl's way too thin. She hardly ever sits still and she eats like a bird."

"And brings to mind a raw nerve."

"How so?"

"Cops get used to people getting fidgety around them—goes with the job. But what I do for a living didn't come up, so it wasn't that." He sipped his tea. "I can't put my finger on why I made Regan nervous. Yet."

Chuckling, Etta patted his hand. "Joshua, men who are all rakish charm and promise of trouble to come have given women the jitters since the beginning of time. You're no exception."

"You think that's it? My *charm* made Regan itchy?"

"What else could it be?"

"Yeah, what else?" He thought about how effectively she had evaded his questions, divulging next to nothing about herself. "Does Regan have a last name?"

"Doesn't everyone? Hers is Ford."

"Regan Ford," he said, trying it out. Regan Ford, hailing from no particular place, yet sounding to him more like the deep South than anywhere else. "I take it you checked her employment record and references before you hired her?"

"I didn't need to. My instincts told me to take a chance on her. She's living in the apartment over the tavern."

With the kitten now propped on his shoulder, Josh crossed his forearms on the table. "You gave her a job and a place to live without running a background check? That's not wise, Etta."

"My late husband had a philosophy about the tavern business. Never water down the whiskey and, when it comes to employees, follow your heart." She raised a shoulder. "I had a good feeling about Regan, so I offered her the job. The apartment over the tavern was empty, so why not let her live there?"

"Why not check her out first?"

"Like I said, I had a good feeling about her. Anyway, I had her work the same shift I did the first month she was here. Time has proven me right about Regan. She works like a trooper. The register has never come up short on her shift. Now that I'm stove up, Regan adds up all the receipts, makes the bank deposits and balances the books. She handles the ordering. You think either Howie or Deni, or any of my day workers could do that without making a mess of things?"

"I doubt it." Like most cops, he had a healthy distrust of all mankind. Knowing that Etta had turned over her bank account to a woman she hadn't checked out didn't sit well. At all.

"Regan's got a caring soul," Etta continued. "The day cook makes me lunch and Regan brings it here. She takes the time to sit with me on the porch and visit. She runs the vacuum and dusts. Does my marketing. And cooks dinner for A.C. and me here every Sunday on her night off."

"You ever ask Mystery Woman where she's from? Where she's worked?"

"No."

He settled his hand on Etta's. "You're letting a woman you know nothing about handle your money and basically run your business. Who's to say she won't empty your bank account and disappear? Let me look into her background. Check her references. I can call Nate, have him run her through the national crime database."

Etta's blue eyes met his squarely. "Joshua McCall, do you own a part interest in my tavern?"

He sighed. "No, ma'am."

"Then leave my business to me. I may not know everything about Regan, but I know what matters."

It was all Josh could do not to remind Etta of the drifter she'd trusted a few years ago. The guy had tended bar only a week before he cleaned out the safe then disappeared.

Etta pointed a long, sturdy finger his way. "While we're on the subject, I want you to understand that I'm fond of Regan. I don't expect she needs to get all stirred up over a man who goes through women like water."

"I don't plan on doing any stirring in that area." He glanced at the pies cooling on the counter. "I forgot to stop by the mini-mart, so I need to drive back into town. How about I drop off Regan's pie while I'm at it?"

"Sounds good."

He set Anthracite on the floor, gathered up the plates and carried them to the sink. What he did intend to do was look after Etta's best interests. Which meant finding out all there was to know about Regan Ford.

Chapter 2

"C'mon, Regan. Let's you 'n me go upstairs to your place 'n have some fun."

"Not interested." Regan stood at the tavern's front door, staring up into Seamus O'Toole's bloodshot eyes. The beefy Dallas used-car dealership owner's breath smelled like a brewery.

He leaned in. "There's lots of women mighty glad they said yes to old Seamus."

"Not interested, Mr. O'Toole. *At all.*"

When Regan shifted to open the door, he lunged, thrusting a finger in her face. "Whas' wrong with you? Don'cha like men? You one of them flamin'…"

As quick as a snake, her hand lashed out, grabbed his outstretched thumb, and forced it back into his wrist.

Howling, O'Toole dropped to his knees.

Behind her, Regan heard the kitchen door swing open.

"Need some help?"

Keeping a grip on O'Toole's thumb, she glanced across her

shoulder. Howie Lyons stood with the door propped open, a metal mop bucket behind him. After six months of working together, Truelove's night cook knew Regan could hold her own with an obnoxious drunk.

"I've got this covered." She looked down at O'Toole. His face was beet-red, his forehead beaded with sweat. "I said *no*. Got it?"

"Yeah. Sweet Jesus, I hear ya."

She let go of his thumb and stepped back two paces.

With his knees creaking in protest, he lurched to his feet. "Ya' crazy broad! You tried ta' break my thumb."

"If I intended to break it, you'd need a cast right now." She didn't add that due to her paramedic training, she could also apply that cast. "Did you drive or walk tonight, Mr. O'Toole?"

"Can't 'member," he mumbled while massaging his bruised thumb.

Regan shoved the door open. A gleaming silver Beemer sporting a dealer's tag sat in the parking lot beneath one of the mercury vapor lamps.

"You drove, but you're walking home." She held out a hand. "Give me your keys. I'll put them behind the bar. You can pick the car up when you're sober, like you did last week."

When he continued glaring at her, she wiggled her fingers. "Keys. You try to drive, you could wind up in a cell."

"Maybe." Wobbling, he dug into a pocket of his khakis. Keys jangled as he slapped them into her palm. "Somebody oughta do something 'bout man-hatin' women," he sneered as he lurched out the door.

"Idiot," Regan said under her breath. After setting the lock, she wove her way around the tables, then stepped behind the bar. She dropped O'Toole's keys inside a drawer, then hesitated.

Still wearing his grease-smeared apron over his black T-shirt and jeans, Howie gave her a considering look while overturning chairs onto the tables on the far side of the dance floor. "Something wrong?"

"What if that moron staggers in front of a car and gets mowed down?"

"You nearly ripped off O'Toole's thumb. Now you're worried about him stepping in front of a car?"

"I'm thinking about Etta. If O'Toole gets hurt, Truelove's could get sued because he got drunk here."

"Right," Howie said. "When I leave I'll drive the route to his house. Make sure he hasn't stumbled and hit his head."

"Thanks."

Since she had already washed the pitchers and glasses, restocked the cooler, wiped down the bar and locked the night's receipts in the safe, Regan was free to head upstairs. Instead, she began overturning chairs onto the tables.

"You don't have to do that," Howie reminded her. "My job."

"I've got time," she said, hefting another chair.

Snagging an oversize broom, he began sweeping up peanut shells. "I guess neither of us have someone waitin' at home," he commented, his voice now harsh and bitter. "Regan, you ever know anyone who claimed to have found religion? Someone who went off the deep end, preaching fire and brimstone?"

"No." Etta had told her she suspected the night cook's motive for taking on the tavern's janitorial duties after his wife left him was to delay going home to an empty apartment.

"It's hard defending yourself when someone gets certain ideas into their head." Howie shook his head. "There's battles a person just can't win."

Regan pulled her bottom lip between her teeth. She wasn't trying to win a battle. She was trying to stay hidden.

After a few minutes of their working in silence, Howie raised a shoulder as he wielded the broom. "I expect havin' Josh McCall in town'll make Etta happy, being they're close."

Regan felt another stab of unease as she pictured McCall sitting at the bar, watching her just a bit too closely with those dark eyes. Eyes that had made her shiver as she fought their hypnotic pull. She had become so accustomed to the numb bleakness inside her that feeling even a slight attraction to any man unnerved her.

With all the chairs overturned, she walked to the jukebox, its light painting her arm gold as she reached to flip off the power. "Do you know McCall?"

"Sure. His family's been coming to Sundown long as I can remember. Josh and Etta's oldest boy were forever getting into mischief." Howie nudged the mop bucket toward a corner. "Those two caught hell one summer when they raided the Camp Fire Girls overnight jamboree." He chuckled as he put his back into mopping. "Now Etta's oldest is a minister and Josh is a cop. Who'd have thought?"

"I figured out the cop part on my own," Regan muttered.

"What'd you say?"

"Nothing." She slid the key to her apartment out of her jeans pocket. "I'm going upstairs. Lock up when you leave."

"Will do."

Giving the area a last check, she headed toward a door on the opposite side of the barroom. After dealing with the lock, she reached in and flipped on the light. The narrow staircase was as straight as a ruler, with no shadowy nooks or crannies in which someone could hide.

At the top of the stairs she paused, making sure the dead bolt she'd installed on the door was still latched. A study of the door-jamb revealed no notches or pry marks. Everything appeared undisturbed.

Even so, she felt a twinge of apprehension as the lock snicked open. She would continue to feel uneasy until she checked the French doors leading to the balcony that spanned the rear of the building.

As she stepped inside what had been her safe haven for six months, the familiar sense of grief and loneliness hit her. Memories flashed toward dangerous places as her mind formed a picture of Steven's house in New Orleans, filled with antiques and furniture covered in rich fabrics. It had been a home where gleaming tables were crammed with framed photographs. Where rare old books filled floor-to-ceiling shelves and expertly lit paintings hung on silk-covered walls.

She had planned to live the rest of her life in that house with the man she loved. Raise their children and grow old.

Her dream had ended over a year ago when she found Steven dead from what everyone believed was suicide. Weeks later, after another man died on her account, she'd learned the truth.

Since the moment I met you, you've disappointed me, cher. *I shared that disappointment with your fiancé. And your partner. How many more times are you going to disappoint me?*

Because Detective Payne Creath's voice played all too clearly in her ears, because the words filled her with guilt and remorse she would never be free of, she wrenched her thoughts from the past. She had to think about now. Make sure she was safe for another night.

Her gaze swept the small living area, skimming across the orange-and-brown plaid sofa, matching chair and watermarked coffee table Etta had scored at a garage sale. The latest copy of the *Sundown Sentinel* lay on the table at the same angle she'd left it beside the vase of daisies that had just started to fade. She stepped into the kitchenette tucked in an alcove. Her coffee mug still sat on the cork coaster placed exactly two inches from the edge of the chipped sink.

She headed across the living room, noting the lamp she'd left on in the bedroom still beamed light through the doorway. The pair of mullioned French doors were locked, with no discernible notches or pry marks on the jamb. The glass panes covered by sheer white curtains presented a possible safety hazard. Still, she considered the doors a necessity since they afforded an alternate escape route. And the balcony faced the lake, providing a peaceful spot on her evenings off to sit and watch the dazzling yellow-and-red sunsets over the water.

She clenched her fingers as she stepped into the bedroom. The twin-size brass bed looked tidy and inviting with its pink chenille spread. The only thing lying on the spread was her plump throw pillow.

The closet door stood open. She habitually left it that way to eliminate a hiding spot. The few clothes she owned hung as she'd left them. Her suitcase sat on the closet floor, its lid open for quick packing.

Although it increased her sense of security, Regan knew her nightly check of doorjambs and locks was futile. Creath had once disabled the high-tech alarm on her apartment. She'd known he'd been inside solely because of the peppermint candies he left strewn across her bed.

The cop who had methodically stalked her, killed because of her, then set her up to take the fall for Steven's murder had wanted her to know how effortlessly he could get to her.

Her gaze went to her reflection in the wavy-surfaced mirror hanging over the vanity painted a garish yellow. Sometimes when she looked in the mirror she still got a jolt. The dark-haired woman she saw wasn't *her,* couldn't possibly be Susan Kincaid, who had spent six years saving lives and wearing her auburn hair in a short cap of curls. Now, her hair was midnight black and board straight, and belonged to a bartender named Regan Ford. But the nightmares that still woke her up in an icy, terrified sweat were Susan's.

She swallowed back a sudden rush of tears. She was so tired—physically drained, emotionally exhausted, sick of feeling out of control.

Because she had learned the uselessness of tears, she scrubbed a hand over her eyes, grabbed her laptop off the rocking chair angled in one corner, then returned to the living room. Nudging the newspaper aside, she plugged the computer into the phone jack. That done, she toed off her shoes, then settled onto the couch. While the computer booted up, she rested her head against the wall. Was it sick to consider celebrating, since Creath hadn't found her after an entire year?

Not yet, anyway.

Listening to the modem connect to the Internet, her thoughts centered on Dan Langley, the private investigator who was her one link to the life she'd left behind. Not just for safety's sake, but her own peace of mind, she'd *had* to ensure Creath hadn't followed her when she disappeared. No matter how sly and patient the monster inside him, he couldn't personally track her if he stayed on the job.

Langley had no idea where she was or what names she used. All he had was her e-mail address to which he had sent messages for the past year to let her know Creath was still in New Orleans.

Regan accessed her e-mail account, saw she had no message from Langley. That meant the P.I. still had Creath in his sights.

Even as relief rolled over her, a sharp rap on the French doors brought her chin up. Through the sheer curtains she saw a man's shadowy form on the balcony beyond. He stood just outside the light fixture's pool of illumination. Purposely?

Panic fizzed through her. Had Creath slipped out of New Orleans without Langley knowing? Somehow found her? Was it Creath waiting for her on the other side of the door?

Regan pressed a hand between her breasts to hold in her frantic heart while she fought a short, ferocious battle to pull herself together. Creath's style wasn't to announce himself. He would slide into the apartment like smoke, and grab her before she knew he was there.

Closing her laptop, she rose. Because she believed in evening the odds, she moved into the kitchenette and pulled a knife out of a drawer. Her breath shallowed as she neared the door. Fingers clenched on the knife's hilt, she used her free hand to edge back one side of the sheers.

When she saw Josh McCall, the flood of adrenaline in her veins became a full-blown tsunami. In the dim light, the prominent planes of his stubbled face looked sharp as glass. The cop eyeing her through the door's pane in some ways presented as great a danger to her as Creath.

She lowered her gaze to the pie carrier in his hand. Since he'd planned to drop by Etta's after he left the tavern, Regan knew exactly what had happened. It was bad enough that Etta had been on her injured foot long enough to bake pies, but she was ferrying them via cop.

Having no choice, Regan undid the dead bolt, opened the door a few inches. "You moonlighting as Etta's errand boy?" she asked smoothly.

His smile flashed charmingly. "Making deliveries gets you access into places you might not be otherwise invited to."

Before she could react, he'd nudged a shoulder against the door, forcing her to take a step back. A slick move, she thought as he stepped past her. She narrowed her eyes. "Uninvited places like my home, you mean."

"Exactly." His gaze dropped to her hand. "You're as pasty as Etta's biscuit dough and that's one hell of a grip you've got on that knife. Something wrong?"

You. "Yes, you pounded on my door at one o'clock in the morning." When she reached for the pie, he shifted.

"If you try to juggle the pie and that knife, you might cut yourself," he said as he headed to the kitchenette. "Wouldn't want that."

Teeth clenched, she remained at the open door, struggling for calm. "If anyone gets cut, it won't be me."

He set the pie on the counter, then turned, studying her with unconcealed interest. "You're a tough customer, Ms. Ford."

She felt her throat tighten. "I didn't tell you my last name."

"That's right, you didn't. I asked Etta."

"Why?"

His gaze swept the room before returning to her. "You wouldn't tell me."

Sweat pooled on her palm against the knife's handle. "You didn't ask."

"True." He raised a dark brow. "Aren't you going to offer me a piece of pie?"

"Etta never bakes just one of something. I'm sure you've already had your fill."

"You'd make a good detective, Ms. Ford."

"Like you?"

He crossed his arms over his chest. "I didn't tell you my profession."

"Howie mentioned it."

He angled his chin. "You asked Howie about me?"

"No, he commented you used to be a wild kid who wound up a cop." Regan knew she had to act with confidence or blow her cover. So, she forced her mouth into a slight upward curve. "He mentioned something about you and Etta's son raiding a Camp Fire Girls jamboree."

Josh stroked a finger along his stubbled jaw. "Now there's a great memory. During the raid I stole a kiss from Mary Beth Powers. That was the first time I'd kissed a girl and it was a moving experience. For my part in the raid, Chief Decker made me pick up trash along Sundown's roadsides for a week." He wiggled his dark brows. "After I served my sentence, I went back and kissed Mary Beth again."

The wicked amusement in his eyes sent the primitive sensation Regan had felt before seeping over her, heating her flesh and making her stomach jitter.

"Doesn't sound like you're a man who learns from his mistakes," she said, hoping the nerves jumping inside her didn't sound in her voice.

His finger shifted from his jaw to the thin scar on the side of his neck. "If I wasn't, I'd be long dead." He wandered to the sofa, glanced down at her laptop, the fading daisies. "I'm worried that Etta doesn't learn from the past."

"How so?"

His gaze slowly lifted, locked with hers. "She takes in strays. That kitten she has? Etta probably hasn't had her checked for rabies."

Knowing he was talking about more than just the kitten had Regan's stomach burning like acid. "One look at Anthracite and you can tell she's okay."

He moved to her bedroom door, glanced in before looking back at her. "What about you, Regan Ford?"

"I don't have rabies."

His gaze traveled down, all the way to her bare feet, then back up again. "You do look good on the surface."

His intimate scrutiny seared Regan like a blast, an almost palpable force that made her knees weak. God, she had to get away from him.

Clenching her fingers on the knob, she jerked the door open wider. "It's late, McCall, and I want to go to bed."

He stepped to her, curled a finger under her chin and nudged it up. "That an invitation?" he murmured.

"For you to leave." She slapped his hand away while her pulse thrummed. He was all but standing on top of her. Close enough that she could smell him. No cologne, just soap— something that brought the woods to mind one moment and dark, intimate nights the next.

She didn't want to *feel*. It was safer that way, easier; if she hadn't been numb over the past year she couldn't have survived. Two men were dead because of her. Their murders were an internal wound she didn't dare touch because it was still bleeding. She wanted to keep the bleak ice inside her frozen.

She took a step back from the man whose hot gaze threatened to crack that ice. "Since you're apparently Etta's self-designated watchdog, you might want to stick your nose in an aspect of her life where she *is* at risk."

"That would be?"

"Her health. She baked tonight, meaning she spent a lot of time on her feet, which is exactly what she shouldn't be doing. She broke a bone, she has to keep her weight off her foot as much as possible or complications could set in."

His eyes were now crimped with concern. "What sort of complications?"

"Are you aware she's a diabetic?"

"Yeah. Has been since I've known her."

"A diabetic's immune system isn't top-notch. That means slower healing. Possible infections." Regan paused when she heard the emotion begin to break through her voice. She owed everything to the woman who'd given her a job, a place to live. *To hide.* "I try to get Etta to follow the doctor's orders, but she's stubborn."

His gaze narrowed on her face and Regan could swear she felt it penetrate through her. "You sound like you know a lot about medicine."

She clenched her fingers tighter on the knife. "I'm just repeating what Doc Zink told me."

"I'll talk to Etta tomorrow. Try to get her to behave."

"Good."

He stepped out on the balcony. Even as he turned back toward the door, Regan shut it and shot the dead bolt into place.

She walked to the kitchenette, laid the knife on the counter and waited. When she heard his footsteps clatter down the outside staircase, a shiver ran through her, like icy fingers slicking her flesh.

He was curious about her, *too damn curious.* Like any cop, Josh McCall had numerous law enforcement networks available. Her Regan Ford identity could pass a cursory check, but what if he dug deeper? Standing there, she could almost feel the cold steel of handcuffs lock onto her wrists.

Panic clawed at the base of her throat. It would take mere minutes to cram her clothes into her suitcase, grab her running money and drive away from Sundown.

And go where? a voice inside her asked. Drift through a blur of towns and cities as she'd done when she first went on the run, forever looking over her shoulder to see if Creath was there?

Allowing herself a moment of despair, she dropped her head into her hands. Her life might as well have a sign posted: Danger Behind. Danger Ahead. What the hell should she do? Just the thought of taking off again, of giving up the tenuous life she'd begun in Sundown made her feel physically ill.

So, she would stay, at least for a while. Until she had time to think. To work out a plan.

She looked back at the French doors. It hadn't been just a cop she feared who'd just walked out of them but the man whose warm touch she could still feel against her flesh. She thought her sensuality had died with Steven, but Josh McCall had proven her wrong.

A vivid premonition of disaster swept over her. "Stay away from me, McCall," she said, her voice a thready whisper. "Just stay away."

Payne Creath sat alone in the Homicide detail's dim squad room amid a maze of steel desks the color of dirty putty. The air carried a stale edge of tobacco. If he concentrated, he could hear the raucous sounds of the French Quarter seeping in through the building's grubby windows. The computer monitor holding his attention flooded his sharp-angled face with an eerie unnatural hue as his agile fingers worked the keyboard.

He possessed an innate ability to hunt. Combined with a fixed persistence, he could locate anything and anyone, no matter how long it took.

He would find her—it was fated.

Susan. She had smooth skin and liquid brown eyes, small breasts and a slender waist. From his first glimpse of her, he had loved the look of her, the sound of her, the scent. She'd been his one magic person. Only her. He had dealt with his rivals. All of them. That she'd run from him, *left him,* had been a dagger to the heart. As quick as that, love turned to hate. One year later, his wound still oozed blood.

Was she feeling safe, burrowed in her hiding place? Had she fooled herself into thinking he would fail to keep his promise to share his disappointment with her in the worst way imaginable? Would she feel a shiver race beneath that smooth skin if she knew how much the passage of time had honed his resolve to find her?

"Just got us a homicide call. Gonna be a long night."

Looking up, Creath met the gaze of the short, stocky man who strode into the squad room, cell phone in hand. Creath had no friends on the police force, just acquaintances. His partner was no exception.

He dipped a hand into the plastic bag on his desk, pulled out a peppermint while his mouth formed the polished smile that pulled people in, making them believe anything he said. "What'd we do, *cher,* snag us a mass murder?"

"Triple. Two male college tourists and a pimp named Lo-Vell. Lots of blood."

Creath unwrapped the peppermint. "Well, hell, guess we'll have to put off eating breakfast."

"Guess so. I'll get the car, pick you up out front."

Creath began shutting down the computer, feeling a tic of regret over interrupting the night's search. She was smart—not once since she'd run had she used her real name, nor did he think she would. Numbers were something else. The passage of time increased the likelihood she would let down her guard. It was easier to slip back into using one's real date of birth, maybe risk using her actual social security number a time or two. So, he watched. If any cop radioed in a check to the National Crime Information Center computer, or checked an ID or made any other type of documented contact with a female matching her description who used her *real* date of birth or social security number, his off-line search would turn it up.

His hunt didn't stop with law enforcement. Using his home computer, he had hacked into the database of hospitals and ambulance services, searching for new hires. She'd have to work. By now, the amount of money she could make in her chosen profession might outweigh the peril of exposure.

And if anyone—from cop to job recruiter—ran her prints, they'd get a hit on the murder warrant.

Then she'd be his.

He would see she paid for rejecting him. For the pain she'd caused him. He would take pleasure in being the ultimate victor in this struggle.

He felt the power rise inside him as the computer clicked off and the monitor's single eye went black. The image of him locking handcuffs around her delicate wrists crouched darkly in his brain. For him, it would be the ultimate twisting of the knife to escort her to prison, knowing she'd be spending the rest of her life locked in a cell.

Thinking of him.

Chapter 3

Josh woke the following morning with a picture in his head of Regan Ford standing at her French doors, gripping a knife. Not your normal small town response when greeting a visitor.

Of course, he had no clue if the woman who'd looked willing to wield that knife hailed from the country or a big city. No idea of where she'd come from. What, or who was in her past.

No idea *yet*.

Deciding to get his morning run over with before the heat set in, he pulled on shorts and a T-shirt with the sleeves torn out, then snagged a pair of crew socks and his running shoes from the duffel bag he'd yet to unpack. Halfway down the broad oak staircase a rich, heady scent greeted him. Thankful he'd taken time last night to program the coffeemaker, he headed for the kitchen.

The room was big and cluttered and, despite the gleam of snazzy appliances and shiny tiles, homey. Tossing his socks and shoes beside the granite-topped cooking island, he pulled a

mug from a cabinet. While pouring coffee, his thoughts returned to Regan. Since he couldn't shake her, he bowed to the
inevitable and took a shot at analyzing what it was about the
enigmatic bartender that had her clinging like a burr to his brain.

His mouth formed a cynical arch. Her sexy, slim-as-a-reed
build had a lot to do with it. Females with nifty little bodies had
always drawn him like…well, a cop to a crime scene.

He toasted a bagel before heading out of the kitchen. Steam
billowed from his mug as he walked along the paneled hallway
lined with a pictorial history of the McCall family. There'd be
new photos soon, he thought. His three sisters had recently married. His oldest brother had reconciled with his wife and they'd
renewed their vows. His parents had taken a boatload of pictures during the Valentine's Day quadruple wedding ceremony.

Josh stepped out onto the front porch, narrowing his eyes
against the already intense morning sunlight. With his thoughts
centered on the dark-eyed bartender, he was only vaguely aware
of the sweet scent of the yellow roses spilling out of the clay
pots lining the porch rail.

Regan Ford had more attributes than just a body built to star
in his fantasies, he conceded. There was that fox-sharp face,
made even more compelling by a frame of thick, midnight-
black hair he wouldn't mind plunging his fingers into. And
those auburn-flecked eyes. Watchful. Waiting. Intriguing.

On a physical level, she wasn't a woman he could easily rid
his mind of.

Then there was the challenge she presented. Last night at her
apartment she'd been a package full of nerves and hostility. The
nerves she tried to hide. She hadn't bothered with the hostility.

No problem—as a cop he was used to being where he wasn't
wanted. As a man, he savored the prospect of digging through
whatever layers made up Regan Ford.

Granted, it was her right not to tell him where she was from.
And keep her last name to herself. A woman tending bar was

smart to withhold information while engaged in a conversation with a stranger. People had all sorts of reasons for holding back personal information. One being privacy. Another, they had something to hide. Problem was, secrets sometimes held a nefarious edge, causing innocent people to get hurt.

Finishing off his bagel, he strolled to the end of the porch. Etta's blue two-story house sat bathed in sunlight, its white shutters gleaming.

Like most cops, he believed in being thorough and covering every base. He had learned in both his personal and professional lives never to take anything or anyone at face value. Which was what Etta had done when she hired a stray off the street without checking her out.

A stray who was damn prickly about questions.

He did a mental replay of Regan's small apartment. There'd been no photographs, letters or other personal items in sight. A lone vase of daisies was the only indication the woman who'd lived there half a year had done anything to transform the apartment into a home. The woman who'd answered the door looking pale as chalk, and gripping a knife. During his years on the force, he'd never met an abused woman who hadn't been systematically isolated from friends and alienated from family. Was Regan Ford hiding from an abuser?

Josh sipped his coffee. That was just one of many questions his gut told him needed answers, for Etta's protection. And to satisfy his own curiosity, which he conceded had transformed overnight from idle to intense.

The whispering slap of footsteps against pavement brought his chin up. Turning, he caught movement on the road. Raven-black hair bobbed in a ponytail as Regan, looking wasp slim in a black crop top, gray shorts and running shoes, jogged by at an impressive clip.

"Speak of the devil," he murmured then dumped the remainder of his coffee onto the lawn. No time like the present to start working on satisfying his curiosity, he decided as he swung back into the house to grab his shoes and socks.

Ten minutes later, he jogged around a curve on the patchy asphalt road and had Regan in his sights. His gaze slid over the black crop top, down a long feline arch of spine to a small, shapely bottom in snug shorts.

One hell of an inspiring view.

Even this early, heat and humidity turned the air thick as syrup, forcing his lungs to work like a bellows. Sweat pooled on his flesh, soaked into his clothes as he focused on his target. She kept her speed steady. Her pace disciplined.

Up to this point he had held back his own speed, letting the muscles he hadn't taken time to stretch soften and warm. Now he quickened his pace, lengthened his stride as a mindless rhythm orchestrated his movements.

He watched as Regan reached the turnoff for the marina. Traffic on the road had picked up so she had to pause and jog in place while a pickup pulling a boat on a trailer took the turn, grit popping beneath its tires. When she dashed off, she took the fork rimming the lake, heading in the direction of the tavern. He knew from previous runs that Truelove's was five miles from his family's house. Ten miles, round trip. If Regan made a habit of jogging from her apartment to Etta's and back each day, she had to be in great shape.

His gaze slid from her waist down to her trim bottom, then to her tanned, coltish legs. Amazing legs. Yeah, that sexy little body was in primo shape.

After waiting at the turnoff for a break in traffic, he increased his speed. Since Regan gave no indication she was aware of his presence, he figured the heavy traffic muted the sound of his footsteps. By the time he closed in on her, all he could hear was the drum of his own pulse echoing in his ears.

He reached out, touched her elbow. "How's it going?"

The next instant she rounded on the balls of her feet. Her

arm swept up. He saw the Mace canister just in time to lock a hand on her wrist, twist her arm behind her back and turn her into the solid restraint of his body.

"Sweetheart," he murmured in her ear. "You need to work on your friendship skills."

With her locked against him he felt the outrage—and something more—shoot through her stiffened frame. Then his words must have penetrated and she began to squirm.

"Let go!"

He took a moment to savor the warm, salty smell of woman. Another to acknowledge that the tightening in his gut was raw and purely sexual. Then he dropped the arm he'd locked around her waist, but kept his hand clenched on her wrist. She instantly whirled to face him while trying to jerk from his hold.

"Let me go." Her voice sounded far away. Hollow.

He pried the cylinder from her grasp, then gave her a long, speculative look. Her face was flushed, her eyes wide. "Do you Mace every jogger you meet?"

Regan's heart slammed against her rib cage; she took choppy breaths, trying to control the adrenaline rushing through her system. "You snuck up on me. Put your hand on me. What the hell did you expect?"

"A friendly hello?"

Cars whizzed past while she glared up at him. The hand gripping her wrist was hard and strong. Like his face, his voice. "Just…let…go."

"If I do, you going to try to Mace me again?"

She clenched her jaw. "That would be hard to do, since you're holding the canister."

"Good point." He released his hold, studying her with those dark eyes that seemed to see everything at once. "I didn't sneak up on you. Not intentionally." He used his forearm to swipe sweat off his brow. "The traffic's heavy—the sound of it must have kept you from hearing me come up from behind."

"Right. Okay." Panting, she walked in small circles to keep her muscles from locking up. "I...overreacted."

"You're prepared, I'll give you that." He held out the canister. "For a tiny thing, you pack a punch."

Cursing herself inwardly, she grabbed the Mace from his hand and shoved it into her pocket. She'd barely heard his voice over the sound of traffic and her pounding pulse. Had known only that it was male, that the fingers on her elbow were rock hard and filled with strength. The mix of paranoia and fear that shot through her mind told her it was Creath who'd come up behind her.

The man staring at her with open curiosity was almost as bad.

For the first time, she allowed herself to take a good look at him. He looked sweaty and incredibly sexy in tattered gray shorts that revealed long, firmly muscled tanned legs. His white T-shirt was wrinkled, ragged and sleeveless. Shoulders, she thought. The man had amazing shoulders.

And, dear Lord, when she'd been locked against him his body had felt like solid muscle. When she realized it was McCall, not Creath, who controlled her struggles, fear had rocketed into searing need. It was as if her body had been starved for a man's hardness, the hunger buried beneath her grief. And now the feel of McCall's body had unleashed that hunger.

Her heart hammered painfully against her breastbone as she shoved an unsteady hand at the damp tendrils escaping her ponytail. "Well, see you around, McCall."

He stepped into her path. "Wait a minute."

"What?"

"We're headed in the same direction. Why not run together?"

Her mouth was so dry it was hard to speak. "I prefer to jog alone."

The grin he sent her was quick and careless. "You're from a big city, right? A big *Southern* city?"

Her fingers curled into her palms. "What makes you think so?"

"You answer your door armed with a knife. You just told me to get lost. Not the usual mindset of someone who hails from a small town."

"Look, I came out this morning to run. Not get analyzed."

"Just making an observation. And issuing a friendly invitation. We're headed in the same direction so we might as well jog together. You ready to go?"

She swiped her hand across her damp throat while she felt her raw nerves stretch razor-sharp. Instinct told her the more she protested, the harder he would push. And dig. The sooner she cooperated, the faster she'd get away from him.

"Try to keep up," she said, then sprinted off.

He caught up, matched the cadence of his pace with hers. "You run every day?" he asked between breaths.

"Yes." A prophetic question, she thought, watching him out of the corner of her eye. "You?"

"I try never to miss."

They continued for several minutes in silence, then he said, "How about heading into town for breakfast at the café?"

"I don't eat breakfast."

"Lunch then."

"Can't."

Her warmed muscles moved as fluidly as oiled gears by the time Regan topped the next rise. She caught sight of the narrow wooden bridge that spanned a small stream snaking off the lake. A few yards past the bridge, the road bent like a crooked finger, then narrowed into Wipeout Curve. One mile to go, and she'd be back at her apartment over the tavern. Then she could sort out her thoughts. Work to tighten her hold on her self-control even though she could feel it crumbling beneath her.

"You *can't*, or you *don't* eat lunch?" he persisted.

"I take lunch to Etta every day." Her words came out in a staccato that matched the rhythm of her run. "I eat with her."

"Dinner, then?"

"I work nights."

"Not every night."

"Most."

"I get the feeling I shouldn't plan on sharing a meal with you."

"Trust your feelings."

"You're hell on a man's ego, Regan."

"Plenty of women at the tavern last night gave you the eye. Ask one of them to dinner."

He shot her a smile, a quick flash of teeth that was unexpectedly charming. "Should I be flattered you paid me so much attention?"

God, he was smooth. Too smooth. "I noticed only because Deni was one of those women. More than once I had to tell her to keep her mind off you and on her job."

"Another bruise to my pride."

"I'm sure you'll recover."

Her words were nearly drowned out by the engine roar of a green Chevy with heavy metal pumping from its radio. The car shot past them, the bridge's wooden planks clattering in the wake of speeding tires. Regan caught a glimpse of the driver—a male teenager with dark hair and an insolent grin. A laughing teenage girl with flowing blond hair leaned out the passenger window, a beer can clutched in one hand.

"Beer this early in the morning," Regan commented. A sick feeling welled in her stomach as the car careened out of sight. "There's an accident waiting to happen."

"No kidding," Josh said as he sidestepped a pothole. "Signs are posted, warning about the narrow bridge and the curve ahead. Does that kid have the sense to slow down? Not when ninety-five percent of his brainpower is in his pants."

Regan opened her mouth to agree, her thoughts spinning off as she heard the high squeal of brakes and rubber against pavement. She and Josh had already picked up speed when the crash of glass and horrendous rending of metal exploded through the air.

Above the roaring of her heart Regan heard the pounding of her feet against the bridge's wooden slats as she and Josh raced toward the sound of the crash. Yards past the bridge, the road transformed into the treacherous curve.

Halfway through the curve, she got a whiff of burning rubber. Fresh skid marks veered off onto the shoulder, tearing ridges into ground already rutted like a washboard. From there, the green Chevy had hurdled into a clearing rimmed with massive oaks. From what she could tell at this distance, it had crashed head-on into a thick tree trunk. The car's hood was buckled; smoke spewed from the engine. Half of the back window was gone. The remaining glass was cracked, resembling a massive spiderweb that glinted like diamonds in the sun.

Dread settled in the pit of Regan's stomach as she and Josh dashed toward the car. She knew from experience speed was a major predictor of severity of crash injuries. The sedan had shot across the bridge like a bullet, probably taken the curve at the same speed. Chances were, both teens were gravely injured, if not dead.

"The impact knocked out the engine," Josh said as they neared the car. "At least we don't have to worry about a fire."

"Probably the only thing."

"Yeah."

In her peripheral vision, Regan spotted a black van skid to a stop. Its doors flew open. A bald man and a woman with a blond beehive piled out and started toward the carnage.

Metal scraped against metal as the driver's door on the wrecked car slowly opened. The teenage boy angled his legs into view, then pushed himself unsteadily up. Blood poured out of his nose, streamed down his chin. Already, the front of his white T-shirt was stained crimson.

As if the last twelve months had never happened, Regan slid seamlessly into the paramedic she'd been in another lifetime. She felt the familiar adrenaline spike that came with knowing lives might be at stake.

What she was about to do carried consequences, but she couldn't let them matter right now. What mattered were the two teenagers in the car.

She flicked Josh a look. "Do you know anything about emergency medicine?"

"What I've picked up working traffic accidents and crime scenes." His gaze sharpened. "You have some training?"

Years of it. "I know what needs to be done."

He gave her a curt nod. "I'll follow your lead."

Gripping the top of the car's open door, the teen raised his head. His eyes were saucer wide and had a feral look. "Help us." He staggered forward. "Help. Please, help."

Josh snagged one of his arms, Regan the other, her mind going cold, analytical. "Don't move," she ordered, wrapping her hand around his wrist. His pulse was jumping, his heart rate off the chart. He was talking, breathing, which omitted the possibility of an airway obstruction. "What's your name?"

"I… Easton." Josh held him in place when he made a feeble attempt to turn back toward the car. "Amelia's hurt. Bad." He used his shoulder to wipe at the blood streaming from his nose. "She's hurt. Please…"

"We're going to help her," Regan said, then looked up when the bald man and blond woman reached them. The man was sweating profusely and the woman's face was chalk-white. She hoped to hell neither of them passed out. "Do you have a phone?"

"I do." The man dug his cell phone out of his shirt pocket.

"Call 911 and give the dispatcher our location," she ordered, then looked at Josh. "I don't know Oklahoma codes. They need to be advised this is life threatening and to use lights and sirens en route."

"Tell dispatch this is a Code 4," Josh instructed the man.

"Have the dispatcher connect you to the nearest EMT," Regan added. "I need you to stay on the line with the EMT so I can relay conditions of the victims."

"Got it," the man said.

Regan looked back at the injured boy. "Easton, I want you to lie down. Slowly."

"No. Gotta help 'Melia." He was sobbing. Tears mixed with the blood on his face, dripped in rivulets onto his T-shirt. The adrenaline shooting through his veins had him straining, fighting against their hold. "Let me go. Gotta help—"

"We're going to help her." Regan tightened her grip on his arm. An air bag had probably protected him, but he could still have spinal injuries. His head needed to be immobilized.

"Josh, we have to get him down." Beneath her hand, the boy's pulse hammered. "Gently."

"All right." He stepped in front of the teen, locked his hands on his shoulders. "Easton, I'm Sergeant McCall. Do what we tell you so we can take care of Amelia. Lie down. Now."

A sob cut off his words as he shivered uncontrollably. "Okay."

The instant they got Easton on the ground, Josh looked at Regan. "I'll check on the girl."

"I'll be there as soon as I can."

He dashed for the car while Regan waved the blond woman over. "What's your name?"

"Helen."

"Helen, I need you to hold Easton's head like this."

Gulping, the woman dropped to her knees. Regan positioned the woman's trembling hands on either side of Easton's head. "His spine has to be kept as straight as possible. Keep his head still."

"I'll do my best."

Still crouched, Regan shifted. "Easton, look at me. Look

up at my face." Using her palm, she shaded his eyes from the
sun, then moved her hand while watching his pupils react to
the light.

Rising, Regan snagged the bald man's arm and pulled him
toward the car. "What's your name?"

"Quentin."

"Tell the EMT the male victim is equal and reactive to light,"
she instructed. After Quentin echoed her words into his cell
phone, Regan added, "Stay close to me."

"Okay."

She reached the gaping driver's door just as Josh slid out.
She'd seen his same grim, flat stare on the faces of uncountable cops at accident scenes.

"She's alive, but bad," he began in a detached voice that
Regan knew came with the job. "Wasn't wearing a seat belt."
He gestured a blood-smeared hand at the car. "There's an im-
pression of her face imbedded in the windshield."

Like an instant replay, Regan again saw the girl as the car
sped by. A pretty smiling girl, her long blond hair blowing in
the wind. Carefree. Happy.

Not anymore, Regan thought as she leaned in through the
door and shoved the deflated air bag aside. Her throat tightened
at the devastation.

"Amelia?"

The girl's face was an unrecognizable bloody mass, her long
hair dripping crimson. Using her middle three fingers, Regan
pressed against the pulse-point on the girl's neck. She watched
Amelia's chest rise and fall in labored, sporadic heaves while
counting her breaths. At that instant, Regan would have given anything for some medical equipment. "Amelia, can you hear me?"

The girl's eyelids fluttered open. She moved her head, ex-
pelled a feeble moan.

"Hang on, Amelia." Regan checked her pupils. They were
small, with sluggish reaction to the light. At this point, at least,

her brain was still functioning. "I need to leave you for a second, but I'll be back. You're going to be okay."

Scooting out of the car, Regan snagged the phone from Quentin. "This is a load-and-go situation," she told the paramedic on the other end. "One patient critical, one stable. Critical patient is an approximately seventeen-year-old female with a severe head injury. Glasgow coma scale is seven. Pulse slow at fifty, respirations ten and signs of Cheyne-Stoking. Possible punctured lung."

She exchanged a few more details with the paramedic, then handed the phone back to Quentin. "Stay on the line."

He gave her an impressed look. "Sure, Doc."

Regan shifted her gaze to Josh. "I need you sitting behind her. We've got to stabilize her head and spine."

"The back doors are jammed. I'll go in over the front seat."

She glanced at his bare legs. She had glimpsed the broken glass littering the backseat. Angling to give him room to get past her she said, "Be careful of the glass."

"Least of our problems." He went over the seat like a shot. Regan dived back in beside Amelia.

"Wedge your elbows on top of the seat so your arms won't get so tired." As she spoke, Regan positioned Josh's hands on either side of the girl's head. Beneath her palms, she was aware of the firmness in his long fingers, the steadiness. The type of man you'd want around in a crisis.

"Right now she's breathing on her own, but we've got to make sure her airway stays open," Regan explained. "Use your fingers to push her jaw forward." She adjusted her hands on Josh's, moving his fingers beneath hers into position for a modified jaw thrust. "You've got to keep her head absolutely still."

"All right."

"She'll probably vomit. Head injury patients almost always do, so get ready. When it happens, I'll deal with cleaning her airway. You keep her motionless."

"Yeah."

Already, Amelia's breathing had slowed, become even more irregular. The pinkish cerebral spinal fluid that bathed and suspended the brain and spinal cord now seeped from the girl's ears and nose, indicating serious brain injury. An empty helplessness tightened Regan's chest. If only she had some equipment. "Amelia?"

Nothing.

Pinching the girl's arm got no response. "Amelia, can you hear me?" Regan knew that unconscious patients could still hear what was going on around them. "Hang on," she said, keeping her voice calm and soothing as she rechecked the girl's pulse. "Easton's okay, Amelia. You're going to be okay, too. Hang on."

Despair engulfing her, Regan met Josh's gaze. She knew the girl's chances were as bleak as the look in his eyes.

An hour later, Josh stood in the clearing with Jim Decker, Sundown's police chief. A few yards away, the coroner wheeled a gurney over the baked grass toward a hearse. The body bag on the gurney glistened like a mound of wet, black clay beneath the sun's blazing rays.

"A shame the girl didn't make it." The navy-blue uniform that hugged Decker's tall, lean frame had creases sharp enough to carve rock. Signaling his rank, silver eagles nested on each collar point of his tapered shirt. Mirrored aviator sunglasses completed the look. Josh knew that the man was in his sixties, but his dedication to keeping fit—along with a head of thick, black hair that was only now showing threads of gray—made him look a decade younger.

"Amelia was here for the summer, visiting her grandparents," Decker continued. "They're good folks. Now I have to go tell 'em she's dead. And for what? A beer and a fast ride."

Josh scrubbed a hand over his face. He'd been at the scene less than two hours, but it felt like twenty-four. "Death notices are one of the downsides of our profession."

"That they are."

When Decker shifted his stance, Josh's gaze followed the chief's across the clearing to where Regan sat in the shade of a massive oak. Her knees were up against her chest, her arms wrapped around her legs as she stared toward the road where a cop directed traffic.

Decker dipped his head. "Etta's bartender. There's an interesting young woman."

The undertone of guarded curiosity in his voice told Josh the chief wasn't referring to Regan's physical attributes. "What's interesting about her?"

"From what I heard when I got here, Regan Ford knows a lot about taking care of injured folks. A hell of a lot. When I asked her about it, she said she took a couple of first aid classes."

Decker's comment underscored what Josh now knew for certain—there was a lot more going on with Regan than met the eye. "I'd say she took more than a couple."

Decker crossed his arms over his chest. "I drop into Truelove's now and then, sometimes when Regan's tending bar. She sure doesn't have a lot to say. Now that I think about it, she does a good job of detouring around me." Josh didn't need to see past the dark lenses of Decker's glasses to know the cop's eyes held a look of narrowed speculation. "Can't help but wonder if it's me, or the fact I'm the law."

"Maybe you're just not charismatic enough?" Josh ventured.

Decker dipped his head. "Maybe you've forgotten that night about fifteen years ago when I happened upon you and Etta's oldest boy with your dates out by the lake? As I recall, the four of you had made a lot of headway getting your clothes off. You were underage and had beer. I could have run the lot of you in, but I didn't. I figure I was pretty damn charismatic that night."

Josh chuckled. "Forget what I said, Chief. You're the most magnetic guy I know."

"Yeah." Decker glanced back at the hearse, let out a breath. "Suppose kids'll ever learn booze and speed don't mix?"

"Wouldn't count on it."

"I'm not. See you later."

Josh watched Decker climb into his sky-blue cruiser with the gold police chief's badge on the door. So, it wasn't just him. Regan had an aversion to other cops, too.

Why? he wondered as he headed across the clearing. Did she have something to fear from the law?

She looked up when his shadow slid over her. The paramedics who'd arrived with the ambulance had given them alcohol wipes to get the blood off their skin, but that hadn't helped their clothes. Her crop top, shorts, even her socks sported numerous bloodstains and smears.

Up close, her skin looked pale. Sallow. Her eyes still held the devastation that had settled in them when Amelia died while they worked to save her.

"Decker talked to the hospital," he said quietly. "The doc expects Easton to recover fully."

Her gaze tracked the hearse as it crept toward the road. "Wish we could say the same about Amelia."

Josh crouched, settled a hand on her shoulder. "It's not because we didn't try."

She instantly tensed, leaned away, forcing him to drop his hand. Okay, she didn't want to be comforted. He didn't have her full measure yet, but he would.

"Regan, are you a doctor?"

She kept her gaze focused on the road. "No."

"A nurse?"

"No. I've taken some first aid classes."

"I'd say more than a few." When he shifted closer, he felt the tension thicken around them on the hot air. "I spent a lot of years riding a black and white and I've seen plenty of EMTs in action. It's obvious you have a lot of training and experience.

You're damn good at the job. So, here I am, wondering what a woman with your skills is doing tending bar instead of riding with an ambulance crew. Or working at a hospital."

She surged up. "I have to go."

He rose as she did, locked a hand on her upper arm. "That couple who stopped first to help saw you in action. They'll tell people what you did for those kids. Hell, I already heard Quentin tell one of the cops you're a *doctor*. Word of what happened this morning will spread like wildfire across Sundown. Every time you turn around someone's going to ask how you know what you know. Where you learned your skills. Why you're not using them. You think telling them you've had a couple of first aid classes is going to cut it?" He stepped closer. "Doesn't do it for me. Don't you know that the less you tell someone, the more they want to know?"

She jerked from his touch. "I have to pick up some things at the market for Etta before I take her lunch."

"I'll run with you as far as your place."

"No." Her face was flushed now from either the heat or emotion. Maybe both. "I told you, I prefer jogging alone."

"What is it about cops that makes you nervous?"

Something flickered in her eyes, then was gone. "I don't know what you mean."

"Then I'll explain. Chief Decker says when he stops by Truelove's, you make a point to avoid him. I have to wonder why, since he's a decent guy. You sure as hell didn't want him to know you list 'skilled in emergency medicine' on your résumé. Then there's me. I come around, I get the impression you check for running room."

She sent him a cool smile. "Cops aren't my favorite people. Nothing personal, McCall."

"Sorry to hear that. Some of us can be real charming if we put our mind to it."

"Charming men don't impress me. Now I've got to go."

He stepped forward, blocking her retreat. "I watched your face while you worked on that girl. You're not just good at emergency medicine, you've got a passion for it."

"You have no idea how I feel," she shot back. "About anything."

"You're right. I have no clue what stopped you from being out there, helping people. Saving lives. Or why you've stuck yourself in an out-of-the-way, small-town tavern."

"I'm not *stuck*. I tend bar now." Her hands clenched. "That's what I do. What I want to do. There's nothing wrong with that."

"Didn't say there was." He dipped his head. "I don't know you well enough to have you figured out. Yet. But Etta does—or thinks she does. She cares about you. Her feelings matter to me. If whatever is going on with you harms her, you'll have me to deal with."

Her eyes went hot. "I love Etta. She gave me a job, a place to live. I *owe* her. I would never hurt her."

"I'm sure you'll understand if I don't just take your word for it. I intend to keep an eye on you."

"Do it from a distance." He saw the tremor in the hand she used to shove her bangs out of her eyes. "I don't want to jog with you, McCall. I don't want to eat breakfast, lunch or dinner with you. Is that clear?"

He kept his eyes cool and steady on her face. "Crystal."

"Fine. So please leave me the hell alone."

He watched her dash toward the road, her tanned legs pumping, ponytail bouncing.

"Not a chance, sweetheart," he murmured.

Chapter 4

Five minutes into that evening's shift, Regan knew Josh Mc-Call's prediction had been right—word of what happened that morning had spread like a wildfire across Sundown. Every customer seated at the bar had commented on the accident and her part in aiding the teenage victims. Even the pair of grizzled regulars whose usual topic of conversation was the catch of the day had shifted their focus to the wreck at Wipeout Curve.

While she poured drinks, washed glasses and filled bowls with peanuts, Regan had made sure to shrug intermittently and comment she'd taken a few first aid classes. That had satisfied some of the questioners. Others had given her a skeptical look, but hadn't pushed for additional details.

At two hours before closing time, most of the talk had shifted to which fisherman had racked up the most points so far in Paradise Lake's fishing derby. That, and the fact McCall hadn't darkened the tavern's doorstep, had Regan hoping she'd weathered the storm. If she could just fade back into obscurity and keep her distance from McCall for however long he spent in Sundown, her luck might hold.

That feeble hope went up in flames when Burns Yost, owner of the *Sundown Sentinel,* settled onto a stool at the bar.

"I need a beer and an interview, Regan."

Icy panic jabbed through her while the balding, middle-aged man pulled a pen and small notebook from the pocket of his gray shirt. Yost had been only second to the police chief in people she'd made a point to avoid during her six months in Sundown. Especially after Etta told her Yost had once been an investigative reporter for a major newspaper and had gained fame by sniffing out a huge corruption-at-the-Pentagon story. A few years later, Yost had been fired when a high-profile exposé of his turned out to be fraudulent. He'd come home to Sundown and bought the *Sentinel.*

As far as Regan was concerned, a reporter was a reporter, no matter what was in his past. And this one apparently smelled a story.

She filled a frosted mug, set it in front of him. "Here's your beer. You want one of Howie's hamburgers to go along with that?"

"No, I want to interview you about what you did today."

"I witnessed an accident and watched a young girl die, Mr. Yost. That's not something I want to talk about."

"Amelia's death was unfortunate," Yost said over the clatter of pool balls, loud talk and blare of a boot-scootin' boogie from the jukebox. "I've just come from her grandparents' house and they're beyond grief." He sipped his beer. "When I told them I planned to interview you, they asked me to give you their thanks for helping Amelia."

"I did what anyone else who'd taken a few first aid classes would have done."

Yost's mouth curved. "I also talked to Helen and Quentin Peterson. They're the couple who stopped at the wreck the same time as you and Josh McCall. The Petersons think you're a doctor."

"People tend to get impressed when someone checks a pulse while tossing out a few medical terms. That doesn't mean they have M.D. after their name."

"Okay, so you're not a doctor. What are you?"

"A bartender."

"That's what Josh McCall said."

The bands around her chest tightened. "You interviewed McCall?"

"Tried to. He wouldn't even invite me in, just stood on his front porch sipping a beer and saying the same thing as you. He doesn't want to talk about the young girl who died."

For an instant Regan was back in that twisted, glass-strewn car with Josh, working feverishly to save Amelia. And when the girl died, Regan had looked into his dark eyes and felt a connection snap into place. A searing, wrenching link. Now, it wasn't just her body reacting to him, it was her emotions, too.

For a woman wanted for murder to allow herself to feel any sort of connection with a cop was ridiculously reckless. As was talking to a reporter.

"Neither McCall nor I want to comment about Amelia," Regan said. "Looks like you struck out all the way around, Mr. Yost."

"More like I'll have to wait until the next inning to score." He took a long drag on his beer. "McCall also refused to comment about what he'd witnessed you do while the two of you were in that car, tending to Amelia. Since he's a cop, I don't take his stonewalling personally. The boys in blue trust the press about as much as they trust politicians and lawyers."

Yost grabbed a handful of peanuts out of the nearest bowl, began shelling them. "Besides, you're the story, not McCall. There might not be a lot of people in Sundown, but the ones who are here have a right to know what's going on in their town. At present, you're what's going on."

The dread inside Regan built. There was no way she could

get away from Yost as long as he chose to sit at her bar. She was going to have to deal with him, the same way she'd dealt with McCall. Which, in retrospect, had only heightened his curiosity.

"All right, Mr. Yost, I'll give you a comment. First, my heart goes out to the families of those two teenagers. Second, it's time the Sundown city council does something about Wipeout Curve. You should research how many accidents have occurred there, find out how many people have been injured and/or died in those accidents. Your running articles on that in the *Sentinel* could prevent more deaths."

Yost made a note on his pad, remet her gaze. "An exposé on Wipeout Curve won't appease the curiosity of my readers, Regan. They want to know about you—where you're from. How you wound up tending bar in Sundown. *Why* you're doing that instead of working in the medical field."

In a finger snap of time her thoughts shot back to Josh. *Don't you know that the less you tell someone, the more they want to know?*

Until this moment, she hadn't realized, not fully, the repercussions of what she'd done today. Having the attention of both a cop and a reporter focused on her was the last thing she needed. Both had the potential to discover she was using a fake identity. If that happened, the next logical step would be to try to find out her real name. Armed with that, the murder warrant would pop up on some computer run.

She took a slow, deep breath to try to control the adrenaline spewing through her system. She could almost feel Payne Creath's hot breath on the back of her neck.

"You've got my comment." She tightened her unsteady fingers on the rag in her hand and wiped it across the bar's scarred, polished wood. "It'll have to do."

Yost tossed a couple of bucks beside his mug, flipped his pad closed and slid off the stool. "We'll talk again soon, Regan."

* * *

At closing time Regan dealt with her duties, then said good-night to Howie. If the cook wondered why this was the first night she'd declined to help with his janitorial chores, he didn't comment on it. He just kept sweeping up peanut shells while assuring her he would lock up when he left.

Upstairs, she went through the motion of checking the doors and windows, then booted up her computer to see if she had an e-mail from Langley. There was nothing in her inbox from the P.I., which told her Creath was still in New Orleans.

For a year that had been enough to assure her, to afford her breathing room. Over the past twenty-four hours, she'd lost even that small comfort. She had McCall and Yost curious about her. *Watching her.* She could maybe get by with one or the other, but not both.

She flipped off the lamp beside the couch. The weak light from the fixture on the balcony seeped in through the French doors and her bedroom window, guiding her way into the bedroom.

There, she changed into a camisole and silky boxers. The way she'd exposed her background at the accident scene—topped by Yost's visit to the tavern—convinced her she had to leave Sundown. Had to turn her back on the small apartment that had begun to feel like home. Say goodbye to the people she'd come to care about.

Etta, she thought, her throat tightening. She couldn't just pack her meager belongings tonight and leave without saying goodbye to Etta.

First thing in the morning, Regan resolved. By this time to-morrow night, Sundown would be just a memory for her.

With exhaustion and despair overwhelming her, she didn't bother to pull down the pink chenille spread, just toppled onto her bed.

Seconds later, she dropped off the edge of fatigue into sleep.

* * *

With a scream stuck at her throat, Regan shot up in bed. She sat unmoving in the inky darkness, her heart hammering.

Her trembling fingers clenched into fists, she gulped in air. Thinking she must have clawed her way up through the slippery slope of a nightmare, she tried to pull back some memory of it.

Nothing. She remembered nothing.

If she hadn't had a nightmare, what had woken her? She shoved her hair away from her face, then glanced down. Her watch didn't have a luminous dial, but she should be able to see the hands.

The realization hit her that she was shrouded in total darkness. When she'd fallen asleep, there'd been light seeping in the window from the fixture out on the balcony. There was no light now, just darkness.

From somewhere came a creaking sound.

Her pulse rate shot into the red zone. *Downstairs,* she thought, straining to hear past the roar of blood in her head. Had someone broken into the tavern? *Creath?*

No, she countered instantly, shoving back a wave of paranoia. Langley was watching him. If the homicide cop had left New Orleans, Langley would have sent her an e-mail.

Another creak had her swallowing a lump of fear. She slid out of bed, her knees almost giving out as she groped her way into the pitch-black living room. She felt her way to the couch, grabbed the phone on the end table. The dial wasn't lighted; she didn't want to waste time fumbling for buttons, so she stabbed redial.

After three rings, Etta answered, her voice thick with sleep.

"Etta, it's Regan," she said, keeping her voice whisper soft. "Someone's broken into the tavern. I need you to call the police."

"Lord, child, where are you?"

"Upstairs. If I try to leave, I might run into whoever it is."

"You stay where you are and keep the doors locked. I'll get the police there."

* * *

In less than ten minutes, a car pulled to a stop at the rear of the tavern where Etta's car and Regan's Mustang sat parked. Inching back the sheer curtain that covered one of the French doors, Regan narrowed her eyes when she realized the vehicle wasn't the Sundown police car she'd expected.

In the bright headlights that reflected off the tavern's rear wall, she made out the sleek lines of a convertible. And the tall, lanky form of the driver who climbed out without bothering to open the driver's door.

"McCall," she murmured as the headlights went out, plunging the building's exterior back into darkness. Her hand moved up to rub at her throat where her nerves had shifted into overdrive. *Great. Just great.* If she'd thought Etta would have called him instead of the Sundown PD, she'd have opted to take her chances with the burglar.

She could almost picture McCall keeping his back snugged against the wall as he moved soundlessly up the wooden staircase. When he gained the top step, he clicked on a flashlight, swept its beam toward the far end of the balcony.

She waited to unlock the French doors until he reached them. "What are you doing here?" she whispered.

He slipped through the door as silent as smoke, the edgy violence in the set of his body making her mouth go dry. The knots in her stomach tightened when she saw the automatic gripped in his right hand.

For a moment, no more than a blink of the eye, the image of him coming for her, arresting her for murder clawed in her brain.

"The Sundown cop on duty is on the other side of the lake, handling a domestic disturbance that involves a shooting," he said, keeping his voice low. "Chief Decker's there, too."

In the beam of the flashlight the rugged lines of his face looked as if they were set in stone and he had a cop's intensity in his dark eyes. "When the dispatcher told Etta it'd be at least

an hour before a Sundown cop could get here, Etta called me."
He took a step closer. "Tell me what you heard."

"A creaking noise. Footsteps. I heard them twice." Fear
crimped her voice, but she couldn't help it, not when she was
afraid of so much more than just the sound she'd heard.

"From downstairs?"

"I think so," she said, brushing her bangs aside.

His gaze ranged across the small living room. "Is that the
door to the interior staircase that goes down to the tavern?"

"Yes. The door at the base of the stairs is locked. I've got
the key."

"Give it to me. I'll check things out."

She moved to the coffee table, retrieved her key ring, found
the key in question. "It's this one."

He stepped to her, his fingers brushing hers when he accepted the key ring. "Lock this door behind me."

"All right." She struggled to steady her heartbeat. It took all
her control to keep her voice low and even. "This isn't your job.
You don't have to do this."

Pausing, he flicked the flashlight's beam over her, his gaze trav-
eling the length of her. "Seeing you in that outfit makes up for any
inconvenience," he said, then turned and strode toward the door.

Realization came with a quick jolt, followed by a rush of
heat into her cheeks. Her brain had been so muddled by sleep,
then fright, it hadn't occurred to her to grab a robe. From the
gleam she'd glimpsed in Josh's eyes, she had a good idea what
she looked like, standing there in an air-thin camisole and silky
boxer shorts.

She watched him unlock the dead bolt, then shift to one side
before he eased the door open. In one smooth move, he aimed
his weapon and the flashlight's beam down the steep staircase.

He glanced at her across his shoulder. "Lock this behind
me," he repeated, then slipped like a shadow into the stairway
and pulled the door shut.

Swallowed again by darkness, Regan moved to the door and engaged the dead bolt. Closing her eyes, she leaned against the door while the look that had flashed in Josh's eyes replayed in her brain. In that heartbeat of time, it hadn't been a cop gazing at her, but a man. And the rapid surge in her pulse that she felt even now had everything to do with hot-blooded desire and nothing to do with fear.

She pressed her shaking hands to her lips. She was walking a tightrope between passion and danger, but the knowledge didn't lessen the need.

If she'd wanted any convincing that her decision to leave Sundown the following day was the right one, her own body's response to Josh McCall was it.

Ten minutes later, Josh had completed his check of the tavern's interior and had done a full sweep around the outside of the sturdy brick building. The night was pitch-black, the humid June air warm against his face as he reached the wooden staircase at the building's rear.

In addition to his 'Vette, there were two other cars parked there. One was Etta's. The older model Mustang with its trunk held shut by wire clearly belonged to Regan.

Convinced that any intruder was long gone, he reset the safety on his automatic and reached behind him. The weapon slid snugly into the holster clipped inside the waist of his jeans at the small of his back. As he'd already done once that night, he followed the sharp slashes of his flashlight's beam up the wooden staircase. This time he didn't bother keeping his footsteps quiet.

Pausing at the French doors, he rapped lightly while aiming the beam at his face so Regan would know it was him.

When she pulled open the door, he acknowledged an instant flare of disappointment when he saw she'd changed into jeans and a white T-shirt. "You can turn on the lights now," he said, stepping past her.

He kept the flashlight on until she walked across the room and clicked on the table lamp beside the sagging plaid couch.

"Was there anyone downstairs?" Her face was pale, tight with strain.

"No." He laid his flashlight on the coffee table. "The front and back doors to the tavern were locked. I couldn't find any sign of forced entry on the windows."

"It wasn't my imagination," she said, shoving her hand through her hair. "I know I heard something. *Someone.*"

He gave her a mild look. "Since preservers of the law aren't your favorite people, I doubt you'd have reported this if there was any question in your mind about that." He pulled his cell phone out of his pocket, stabbed buttons. "I need to get some details from you, but first I want to call Etta. Tell her you're okay."

Regan rubbed a fingertip against her right temple, as if a headache had settled there. "I should have thought to do that."

"You've got other things on your mind." More, he thought, than just what had happened tonight. Something that put a haunted look in those gold-flecked eyes.

While he spoke to Etta, Josh watched Regan step into the small alcove that served as a kitchen. She pulled a bottle of aspirin out of a cabinet, shook out a couple, washed them down with water. Then she mixed two mugs of instant coffee, and slid them into the microwave. As she moved, he could almost feel the nerves crackle inside her.

He ended his call to Etta just as Regan carried both mugs into the living room. "Is Etta okay?"

"She is now that she knows you're all right."

"I wish I hadn't had to call her. But it was pitch black in here, and I didn't want to fumble around trying to dial 911. I just hit redial."

"Understandable." He lifted a brow. "Is one of those mugs of coffee for me, or do you plan to drink both?"

She blinked. "Sorry. It's instant," she warned as she handed him a mug.

"That just means it'll be fifty percent better than the sludge that gets brewed in the squad room." He waited until Regan settled on the couch, then he lowered onto one arm of the chair.

He sipped his coffee. It was strong enough to cause a nosebleed. "Tell me exactly what you heard."

"Creaking. Footsteps." She cradled her mug in both hands as if savoring the heat. "At first I wasn't sure what woke me. I thought maybe I'd had a bad dream, so I waited. Then I heard the noise. Twice."

"Coming from downstairs?"

"Yes. At least that's where I thought it came from."

"What time did you wake up?"

"I don't know. I tried to check my watch, but the bulb in the light fixture on the balcony must have burned out and my bedroom was pitch-black."

Josh frowned. "When did the bulb go out?"

"I don't know." She raised a shoulder. "It was on when I went to sleep."

He glanced at the French doors, then looked back at her. "How long has that bulb been in the fixture?"

"It was there when I moved in six months ago."

"I need to check it."

"Why?"

"Just a hunch. Do you have a plastic baggy?"

"Yes." She carried her mug into the kitchen, rummaged through a drawer. "Here."

Josh set his mug on the coffee table on top of the latest edition of the *Sundown Sentinel* and snagged his flashlight.

"I'm going to need your help."

"With what?"

She met him at the French doors where he traded her the flashlight for the baggy. "Aim the beam at the light fixture."

Outside, the night air was leaden with heat and as still as death.

While Regan aimed the beam as instructed, he slid the baggy over his hand and touched the lightbulb. It was loose. Two twists, and it came on. Almost instantly, an air force of small bugs swarmed around the light.

He looked over at Regan. "I've got an idea who you heard."

"Who?" Her voice was barely a whisper on the still air.

"Sundown's infamous Peeping Tom." While he spoke, he unscrewed the bulb, then pulled the edges of the baggy over it, sealing it in plastic. He had no idea if the local cops would get any useful prints off the glass, but it was worth a shot.

"Why do you think it was the peeper?" Regan asked as they stepped back into her apartment.

"Because that light fixture is right outside your bedroom window. With it on, he wouldn't have been able to see in."

She handed him the flashlight. "The curtains are lacy. With the outside light off, he could see…everything."

"Basically."

She wrapped her arms around her waist. "I hate knowing someone was out there. That he stood there, watching me sleep."

Her words touched a chord in him. He'd dealt with a lot of victims of sex crimes. Although voyeurism wasn't on the same scale as physical rape, the victim was still violated.

"That image, the feeling of being watched, is going to stay in your head for a while," he said quietly as he followed her back into the apartment. "Why don't you pack a few things, let me drop you by Etta's before I hook up with Chief Decker?"

"I don't want to wake Etta up again. And I doubt I could go back to sleep, no matter where I am. Anyway, there are some things I need to do around here."

He heard the tension in her voice, saw it in the way she held her shoulders, the strain about her eyes. She'd had a bad day, he thought, his mind returning to the young girl who'd died that morning.

He angled his chin. "Did Burns Yost come here after he left my place and hit you up for an interview? Ask you what sort of medical training you've had?"

Something flickered in her eyes, then was gone. She walked to the kitchen, picked up her mug and dumped her coffee into the sink. Keeping her back to him, she said, "He came in a couple of hours before closing time."

"Did you talk to him about the wreck?"

"No. I told him he should do an exposé on Wipeout Curve."

Shift the subject away from you, Josh thought as his gaze swept the small apartment void of pictures, knickknacks and personal items. Even the vase of daisies had disappeared. The place had no more personality than a motel room.

He stepped into the kitchen, laid the baggy and flashlight on the counter. "Regan."

"It's late," she said, keeping her back to him. "You should go."

"First off, things go smoother if people look at each other when they talk." He settled his hands on her shoulders, felt them stiffen beneath his palms when he turned her to face him. "Second, there's a look I've seen in your eyes—"

"It's called fatigue." She pressed a palm against his chest. "It's been a long day, McCall. Like I said, you need to leave."

"In a minute." She smelled of lemony soap. Clean, fresh and simple. "This morning in that car, while you worked on Amelia, I could almost see whatever it is inside you that you want to keep hidden. All day, I've been thinking about what that might be. Wondering where you've been. Where you're going. Asking myself how many pieces do I have to find to solve the puzzle that's Regan Ford."

"I'm not a damn puzzle."

"To me you are." He was suddenly aware of how quiet the building was, how dark the balcony outside had been, and how the two of them were alone in a tiny alcove in a very small apartment.

It was crazy, he thought. He had no business forgetting that something about her hadn't felt right since the first time he'd talked to her. Or that he'd resolved to keep an eye on her to make sure Etta's best interests were protected. Still, there was no law that said he couldn't enjoy the proximity while he was at it.

And, crazy or not, he wanted to feel her mouth on his. Find out if she tasted as good as she looked.

He lifted a hand, trailed his fingers down her cheek, along her jaw, then down so that he felt the pulse in her throat beat hard and erratic. He lowered his mouth toward hers, stopping an inch before contact. He watched her eyes darken, heard her long intake of breath. He waited, while his already hot blood surged and he knew they were both suffering.

His lips brushed over hers, and he felt her tremble. Keeping his gaze locked on hers, he settled one hand at the bend of her waist, cupped his other palm against the side of her throat.

He closed his mouth over hers, teased her lips apart with his tongue and tasted the arousal on her first shaky breath.

He'd known her mouth would taste like this—hot and tempting. Known her flesh would feel as smooth as soft butter. Had that been why he'd lain awake in bed for hours tonight thinking of her? Had that been why, beneath the urgent concern he'd felt a tug of pleasure when Etta called and asked him to come check on Regan? As his blood burned and time bled away, he found that the reasons didn't matter. Not while his mouth was pressed against hers.

When a soft moan slid up her throat, it took all of his control not to bring her closer, to deepen the kiss. Instead, he kept it a slow, long glide, full of erotic promise.

His kiss was ravaging, not in force but in effect. Desire poured through Regan like heated wine, and she had to tether her body's instinctive need to mold to his. She struggled to breathe. Her lungs weren't working properly, only drawing in fast, shallow breaths. Her palms were still braced against his chest and she felt the incredible heat of his body through his shirt. Her skin was on fire, too, almost painfully sensitive. She couldn't think while her heart thudded and need slammed into her like a velvet fist. And she *had* to think.

"No." She pulled back as far as she could with his hand gripping her waist. Her head was spinning while her breath came in ragged gulps. "I...don't want this."

He arched a brow. "That's not the message you're sending, Regan."

"You got dragged out here because Etta called you. Because there wasn't a local cop available." She closed her eyes for an instant. "I appreciate you coming."

"I didn't get dragged here. And I don't want your thanks."

"That's all I can give you."

Her skin was no longer pale, but flushed. The heat of it pumped her soft, lemon scent into his lungs. Watching her, he slid his fingers around her hand, brought it up and pressed his lips to her wrist. He felt her pulse jerk, scramble. "Our stopping won't change anything. I'm still going to want you. You're still going to want me."

Her hand trembled against his palm. "We're still stopping. I want you to back off."

It cost him, but he dropped his hands, stepped back. "Want to tell me why we're stopping?"

She moved into the living room, putting as much space between them as possible before she turned to face him. "I was wrong to let things between us go this far." She wrapped her arms around her waist. "It's not what I want."

He angled his chin. Holding her, he'd felt her burning as hot for him as he had for her. Even now, traces of a sultry yearning glinted in her eyes and her awareness of him showed plainly in her face. He was a man who knew how to wait, to choose his time and his place in order to get what he wanted. And she was the woman he wanted.

"Then I'll be going." He retrieved his flashlight and the baggy holding the lightbulb, then strode to the French doors. With his hand on the knob he paused, taking her in. She stood in the center of the living room, alone and defiant, her chin angled like a sword.

He'd known her just over twenty-four hours. In that time, they'd felt a young girl's life slip between their fingers. Then shared a kiss. Each event had evoked far different emotions, but emotions all the same. Something was tugging at his insides—whatever it was, it was as big a mystery as the woman who'd demanded he keep his distance.

As a cop, he was skilled at solving mysteries, step by step.

"Till next time, Regan," he said, then stepped out into the heated night air and closed the door behind him.

Clicking on the flashlight, he descended the wooden staircase, then climbed into the 'Vette. His gaze lifted, settled on the French doors with soft light glowing behind them. He wanted another taste of her. A long, slow, deep taste that didn't stop at just a kiss.

While he worked on that, he was going to start peeling away the layers and find out exactly what was going on with Regan Ford.

Chapter 5

Regan flipped down the Mustang's visor as the sun inched upward, misting the early-morning air with hints of gold. She wouldn't allow herself even one glance at Paradise Lake's vivid blue water. Refused to admit this was the last time she would drive along the patchy asphalt road between Truelove's Tavern and Etta's house. Didn't want to acknowledge the deep-seated ache that came from knowing it had taken less than fifteen minutes to retrieve her running money from its hiding place, then pack everything she owned into the single suitcase that sat on the backseat.

First rule of a wanted killer on the run: keep your cash handy and travel light.

Nothing lasted forever, Regan reminded herself when tears blurred her vision. Good times or bad, they passed. Which meant the nightmare she now starred in would end eventually. She only had to get through it, one day at a time.

What a load of bull, she thought as a dreadful emptiness

opened inside her. Payne Creath's obsession to have her had seeped like a stain into her life, tainting everything. He might be hundreds of miles away, yet she could *feel* him using the sweeping computer access available to law enforcement to hunt her with the perseverance of a rabid wolf. The nightmare that had become her life would continue as long as Creath's sick, hateful heart continued to beat.

And even if something happened to him, there'd still be the arrest warrant hanging over her head.

She had no way to prove her innocence. No evidence to back up her claim that a decorated homicide cop had murdered the man she loved, then killed her best friend. And when she refused to become his, he framed her for her fiancé's murder. That left her two very narrow options: keep running, or turn herself in and wind up in a cell with no hope of ever getting out. So, she would run. For the rest of her life.

Dragging in an unsteady breath, she blinked away the tears. She didn't want to think about Creath. Doing so only brought the fear back, which clouded her mind.

Right now, she needed to keep her wits about her and her thoughts sharp. Because she faced a more imminent danger than even Creath catching her scent: Josh McCall.

In one hammer-beat of her heart, her thoughts careened back to the previous night as she stood in her tiny kitchen, staring up into those steady, measuring eyes.

This morning in that car, while you worked on Amelia, I could almost see whatever it is inside you that you want to keep hidden. All day, I've been thinking about what that might be. Wondering where you've been. Where you're going. Asking myself how many pieces do I have to find to solve the puzzle that's Regan Ford.

Josh's words had sent fear slithering along her nerves. She could have sworn a cold hand had clamped onto her heart. Yet, what had she done a half second later? Kissed the man.

Kissed him *back* to be more precise. And found herself fighting off a brushfire inside her that had been close to flaming out of control.

After he left, she'd spent the rest of the night making excuses for her behavior. Telling herself if she hadn't been alone for so long she wouldn't have felt such a searing, seductive need to be held. To just be held.

And kissed. God, the man could kiss!

She shoved her sunglasses higher on the bridge of her nose, then clenched her fingers around the steering wheel. Just the thought of stepping into his arms again shot a lightning-fast thrill of desire through her.

Regan set her jaw against the hot need. Letting down her guard with the man—the cop—had been idiotic. Wrong and risky and dangerous. Too dangerous. But it was over and done, and she would never see him again.

When the Mustang topped the next hill, Etta's pristine blue house came into view, its white shutters shimmering in the sunlight. Regan felt a hitch under her ribs. She didn't want to say goodbye to Etta. But she had no choice, not with a former investigative reporter demanding an interview while a cop who eyed her with unrestrained curiosity kissed her blind.

Then there was the matter of the bulb Josh had unscrewed from the light fixture and dropped into the plastic baggy.

It hadn't been thoughts of the peeper leering at her that had misted her skin in a cold sweat. It was knowing that if she'd done something so benign as replacing that bulb after she moved in, the peeper's fingerprints wouldn't be the only ones that might pop up in the Sundown PD's computer.

She had ducked that close call. No way could she hang around and risk her luck again.

Although she told herself not to, she glanced at the three-story house next door to Etta's. The McCall family's lake home was all cedar and glass, wrapped in the embrace of a porch where yellow roses spilled from a multitude of planters. In the driveway, the pristine cherry-red Corvette that glinted in the sunshine looked as though it belonged in a showroom.

Giving silent thanks she saw no sign of the 'Vette's owner, she steered into Etta's driveway.

Regan gathered up the tavern's account book off the passenger seat, then climbed out of the Mustang's air-conditioned comfort into heat that was already edging toward oppressive. North, she thought idly. She should head north, then veer west. Not only would that route take her away from the worst of the summer heat, it would put more distance between herself and Creath.

And Josh McCall.

She caught movement out of the corner of her eye and turned in time to see Josh step out of the house onto his porch. When his gaze settled on her, his mouth curved. Thinking about the erotic glide of that mouth on hers rocketed a missile straight to her libido. She could have sworn the air's heat index spiked by twenty degrees.

Damn. Damn, damn, *damn.* All she'd wanted was to slip in and say goodbye to Etta, Regan thought as she watched Josh stride across the lawn toward her. Now, she'd be forced to deal with the main reason she had to turn her back on the only home she'd known during the past year.

"Morning, Regan." He wore a black T-shirt with a white OCPD logo across the front and a pair of worn jeans. The shirt's snug fit emphasized the contours of his strong shoulders and broad, solid chest. His dark hair was rumpled and the stubble shadowing his jaw heightened his rugged look.

With the ledger cradled in the crook of one arm, she slid her car keys into one pocket of her jean cutoffs. "I thought you might be out jogging this morning." She had *hoped.*

"I ran early." His gaze flicked past her to the Mustang, then settled back on her. "And I thought I might catch you jogging again."

"I took a pass on today. See you later." Regan turned and headed up the walk, bordered by a colorful riot of flowers.

"Get any sleep last night after I left?" he asked, falling into step beside her.

"No." Feeling a tug on her conscience, she slid him a look. He had, after all, gone out of his way to check out the tavern when the local cops weren't available. "I hope you didn't have to spend all night at the police station when you dropped off the lightbulb."

"The only person there was the dispatcher, so I was in and out. I'll touch base with Decker this morning, see if they can lift the peeper's prints. I'll let you know what happens."

"Thanks." She had no intention of telling him she was leaving. Didn't want him asking why. Or give him reason to look any deeper into her than he already had.

She took the porch steps two at a time; the instant she reached the top, his hand locked on her elbow, halting her. She looked at him across her shoulder. "McCall—"

"Question," he said, nudging her around to face him. He stood two steps below her, which lined them up eye to eye. "What's with the suitcase in the backseat of your car?"

"What's with you asking?" she countered, lifting her chin.

She hadn't realized that small movement had put her mouth in direct line with his until he leaned in. That sudden closeness had the breath backing up in her lungs and her pulse throbbing hard and quick. She could feel the heat of his body, smell his woodsy cologne, something virile and strong.

"I got a taste of you last night," he murmured, his breath warm across her jaw. "I want another. That won't happen if you're not around."

"I told…" When her voice went raspy, Regan cleared her throat. The need whispering through her made it impossible to draw in more than a shallow breath. "I told you nothing's going to happen between us. I thought you were listening."

"I heard every word," Josh said, his breath a warm wash against her flesh.

"Good. That's settled."

"I also felt you tremble in my arms. What went on between us last night was mutual, Regan. We both wanted it."

She closed her eyes against the fireball need to feel his hot, demanding, tempting mouth on hers one more time. "Yes," she managed. "It was mutual."

"So, I wouldn't say things between us are settled." His hands skimmed down her sides to rest at her waist. "That's because I tend to deal with most things in an untraditional manner."

Her pulse was drumming. She couldn't stop it. "I said 'no,' McCall." But holy heaven, she wanted to say yes. "I make it a rule never to change my mind."

He gave her a long, level look. "Funny you mention rules. I've spent a lot of time figuring out how to work around them."

Regan diverted her gaze to the scar winding out of his collar and up the right side of his neck. She wasn't dealing with some pretty boy, but a man with hard, handsome features who looked as though he'd lived through some rough times, crossed a few lines and wouldn't mind crossing a few more.

"I'd think a cop would have a different view of rules," she said evenly.

Something flickered in his dark eyes, then disappeared. "We're talking rules, not laws." He tilted his head as if to gain a new perspective. "Have you broken any laws, Ms. Ford?"

She forced herself to breathe. Forced herself to keep her eyes locked on his. "Not a one," she said, hoping like hell he couldn't feel the unsteadiness churning inside her.

"Look, McCall, I need to talk to Etta." Her body trembling, her emotions tangled, she pulled from his hold. When he stepped alongside her onto the porch, she rounded on him. "Dammit, McCall, your trailing after me isn't going to change things." She swept her arm in the direction of his house. "Go do some of those repairs you said you came here to do."

He gave her a mild look. "Is Etta expecting you?"

"She doesn't require me to make an appointment." Regan strode across the porch, jerked the screen door open.

"Turns out, Etta *is* expecting me," he said as he moved in behind her and pulled the screen open wider. "Last night when I called to tell her you were okay, she invited me to breakfast. Guess that's her way of thanking me for going to the aid of a woman at risk." He stepped around her and into the house, then turned, giving her a patronizing smile. "I don't mind you trailing after me, Regan. You play your cards right, Etta might even invite you to join us."

Regan tightened her grip on the ledger and glanced across her shoulder at her Mustang. She was one desperate step away from leaving before she had to spend another minute with this man who stirred her blood and pulled at something deep inside her.

But, dammit, she couldn't leave without saying goodbye to Etta. And she had no intention of doing that in front of Josh.

Patience, she told herself, jabbing a hand through her hair. What the hell did it matter if she stayed in Sundown another hour or two? It wasn't as if she had a firm destination. Or anyone waiting for her.

Shoring up her resolve, she looked back at Josh. "Etta shouldn't be on her feet cooking," she said, stepping into the house behind him. "So I'll stay and give her a hand."

"I planned on doing that myself." Pausing, he sniffed the air. "It smells like she's already cooking. There's nothing better than Etta's biscuits."

The warm, yeasty scent of baking bread settled a dull ache in Regan's belly. She was going to miss the scents, the cozy feel of home. "There's not," she agreed quietly.

She heard the hitch in her voice, saw the curious look in Josh's eyes just as a ball of black fur skittered into view.

"Attack cat," he chuckled, scooping up the scrawny kitten. "Hey, Anthracite."

Grateful for the diversion, Regan stepped into the living room, pausing for an instant to lay the ledger on the coffee table. She moved down the hallway, then into the cheery yellow kitchen, its white-tiled countertops sparkling beneath the bright overhead light.

Dressed in a red shirtwaist dress, Etta sat at the small metal table, sipping from a glass of iced tea. Regan frowned. Etta swore by her morning coffee.

"Morning, Etta," Regan said, crossing to the table. "Can I stay for breakfast if I help cook?"

"Always happy to have an extra mouth to feed." Etta smiled but the usual glint was missing from her eyes. "Child, I've worried about you since you called last night. You sounded so scared."

"I was." Resting a hip against the table, Regan glanced up when Josh strode in with Anthracite cupped in one palm. "I'm sorry I had to wake you," she said, looking back at Etta. "Thanks for sending the cavalry."

"The tavern and all who are in it are my responsibility." Etta shifted her gaze to Josh. "It makes me sick to think about that Peeping Tom setting foot on my property, staring in the window at Regan. Is there anything I can do to the building to make it safer?"

"The door locks are sound," Josh said. "So is the one on the apartment's window. The curtains are thin, so you need to have a blind put up. Sometimes peepers lose interest if there's nothing to look at."

"I'll call the hardware store and order a blind today," Etta said.

"Let me know when it's in and I'll pick it up and install it for you," Josh said. In his hand, the kitten purred like a little motorboat.

"I appreciate that," Etta said, regarding him. "Anthracite sure has taken a shine to you."

Grinning, he planted a hip on the table. "Well, she *is* a female."

Regan studied Etta while she and Josh talked. Her gray hair wasn't brushed in its usual tidy shape, and her color was off. "You look a little flushed," she said, laying her hand on Etta's. "Do you feel okay?"

"It's hotter than an oven at Thanksgiving in here. I need to turn on the air conditioner before the morning gets warmer."

"It's more than that." Beneath Regan's palm, the woman's skin felt hot. Clammy. "You have a fever."

"When I woke up, I felt a little sluggish. Like I might be coming down with a cold."

Regan didn't look at Josh, but she could feel the intensity of his dark gaze on her, as if trying to gauge her true intentions toward Etta. Fine, he could analyze that aspect of her all he wanted.

"Did you check your blood sugar level this morning?" Regan continued. "And take your insulin?"

"Heavens, Regan, I've been doing that nearly all my life." Etta slid a hand into the pocket of her dress and pulled out the long, silver recorder. "And if I did somehow forget, you've got my memory box programmed to remind me."

"True." Regan kept her voice light, but Etta's flushed skin and spike in temperature had her deeply concerned. "I think we need to have Doc Zink come over and take a look under your cast. Just to make sure everything's all right."

Etta blew out a breath. "Doc's got his hands full right now. Mildred England called a while ago to let me know her daughter-in-law went into labor. They're all at the clinic."

"Then that's where we'll go," Regan said.

"I hate to bother Doc Zink when he's got Jenny's baby to deliver," Etta said.

"Well, I don't want to have to face Doc Zink if he finds out I knew you had a fever and didn't bring you by the clinic," Regan said. She met Josh's concerned gaze over Etta's head.

"What about you? Are you willing to face the heat from the doc if we don't get Etta in to see him?"

"No way am I going one-on-one with Zink," he said. "Man's got syringes with six-inch-long needles."

Josh settled Anthracite on the floor, then placed a hand on Etta's shoulder. "Here's the deal, doll face, when it comes to medicine, Regan knows what she's talking about. She says you need to go to the clinic, that's where you'll go." He dipped his head when Etta started to protest. "Don't make me take you into custody, ma'am," he drawled.

Etta gave him a stern look. "Over the years, I've taken a switch to your backside once or twice, Josh McCall. I can still do it."

"I'll just have to risk it." He slid his palm beneath Etta's elbow and helped her up. "Let's go."

"What about breakfast?"

Regan checked the oven to make sure it was turned off. "We'll get around to that later," she said, handing Etta her cane. "Josh, if you'll help Etta to my car, I'll take things from there."

His eyes flashed with impatience. "I'm going to the clinic."

"I just thought—"

"I know what you thought," he said levelly. "And we'll talk about it later." Keeping his eyes locked with Regan's, he wrapped an arm around Etta's waist. "My car only holds two people so we'll all go in yours."

Regan's muscles tightened. Why did her every attempt to get away from Josh McCall just bring him closer?

"Fine," she said evenly, knowing any protest on her part would just heighten his curiosity about her. She tugged the keys out of her pocket. "I'll drive."

With a shoulder propped against the wall of the exam room, Josh studied Etta. Seeing her lying on a padded exam table while wearing an oversize hospital gown had him realizing just how fragile she'd grown over the years. The tube feeding antibiotics into her via a needle in her arm just added to the look.

His stomach knotted. He felt useless standing there, unable to do anything to help the woman he'd always thought of as robust. He'd experienced the same sense of futility yesterday in that car while he watched Regan work with methodical efficiency to try to save a young girl's life.

His gaze shifted. Regan looked just as efficient now as she adjusted the clear bag hanging from the portable IV stand. He appreciated the white T-shirt that hugged her breasts, the worn cutoff jeans that molded to her slim hips and showcased her tanned legs. Still, he suspected some sort of health care uniform would suit her better. She should be working in the medical field, he thought. *Belonged* there.

Instead, she'd chosen to tend bar in an out-of-the-way watering hole. And this morning, she'd shown up at her boss's house with the tavern's account book, and her suitcase on the backseat of her car. He figured if it hadn't been for this detour to the clinic, she'd have already left Sundown for good.

Why? Had she all of a sudden felt the need to get the hell out of Dodge because she'd revealed too much of herself yesterday at the accident scene? Or had he spooked her last night when he told her he was curious about her? Had the kiss they'd shared gotten through one of the defensive walls she'd put up, and had her worried he might get through more? The kiss, he conceded, that had rocked him like no other had before.

"Doc Zink isn't keeping me here one minute longer than it takes to dose me with this stuff," Etta said, flicking her wrist in the direction of the IV pole. "I'm not sick."

"You got a sore under your cast and it got infected," Regan said as she propped up the pillows behind Etta's head. "And you have a fever. That's called sick."

"Maybe." Etta lifted a thin shoulder. "Doesn't mean I intend to let the doc keep me here."

At that instant, the door swung open and Doctor Orson Zink stepped into the exam room. He was in his early fifties and fit, his wiry, athletic frame clad in black pants and a baby-blue shirt. The lines fanning out from his dark brown eyes deepened when he smiled at Etta.

"Jenny England just gave birth to a seven-pound, ten-ounce daughter. Thought you'd want to be one of the first to know."

Etta beamed. "Well, that's good news. How's Mildred doing?"

"As calm as a first-time grandmother is expected to be." Zink crossed his arms over his chest. "How are you feeling now?"

"I'm fit as a fiddle," Etta stated. "Regan and Josh are ready to take me home."

"If Doc Zink says we can," Regan added, then shifted away from the exam table to give the doctor room.

With her standing only inches away now, Josh picked up her scent—warm lemony soap and skin. Every hunger he'd ever known stirred while he took in the stiffness of her spine, the rigid set of her shoulders. She was wound as tight as an addict in withdrawal. *Panic,* he sensed suddenly. Beneath all that tension was quietly desperate panic.

Over what? Etta being sick?

He glanced at the older woman, now in deep conversation with her doctor. Already Etta's color had improved, so he didn't think that was the source of the distress he could almost feel emanating from Regan.

He studied her profile, her thick, straight hair a dark contrast against the high sweep of one pale cheekbone. His need to hold that nifty body against his while he took another long, slow taste of her had only intensified over time.

Yet, something more than physical was going on, he admitted in a shadowed corner of his mind. Something more than just an intense curiosity about her had hooked him. At this point he wasn't sure whether he wanted to pry himself loose or be reeled in. It would take time to figure that out. Figure *her* out. Time he wouldn't have if she left Sundown.

Watching her, he felt something inside him shift, something he was hesitant to acknowledge, much less want to understand. All he knew was the last thing he wanted was for her to disappear from his life.

"I can't afford a hospital stay," Etta said, pulling Josh's attention back across the exam room. "Can't you just send me home with some pills?"

"If you weren't a diabetic, probably," the doctor said. "In your case, you need bed rest, the dressing on your foot changed four times a day and IV antibiotics every eight hours."

"For how long?"

"Depends on how you heal."

"No hospital," Etta said, her lips trembling. "People go into those places alive and come out dead."

Having seen Regan in paramedic mode, Josh figured it'd be a snap for her to change dressings and administer IVs. The temptation to point that out faded when he flicked her a look. Her hands were clenched and her dark eyes swam with emotion. It was as if he could see the battle raging inside her. Dammit, why the hell did she feel such an urgent need to leave Sundown?

When Regan remained silent, he stepped to the exam table. "Doc, what about your nurse here at the clinic? Could we hire her come by Etta's house a couple of times a day to change her dressing and give her the IV?"

Zink shook his head. "Irene could probably use the money, but she's got three kids at home and a baby on the way. I doubt she'd have time."

Josh nodded. "Okay, is there a visiting nurses' association around here? They might have someone we can hire."

"The closest nurses' group is in Dallas," Zink replied. "That's a two-hour drive. Four hours, round trip."

"Let me make a call," Josh said. "The mother of one of the cops in my unit is a retired nurse. She might—"

"I can do it."

He turned as Regan moved to Zink's side. Her skin had gone ice pale.

"I know how to change a dressing. Administer IVs." She gestured toward the IV pole. "You can send Etta home with a heplock in her arm, right? Prescribe bags of Unasyn or some other antibiotic that I can pick up at the pharmacy?"

Zink studied her. "You know news travels fast in Sundown. I heard about how you took care of that girl yesterday. A couple of people have already asked why I haven't hired you to help out around here."

"I already have a job." Regan shifted her gaze to Etta. "And since my boss is also the patient, I bet she'll let me adjust my work schedule at the tavern."

"Regan, I'm like the doc," Etta said. "I heard about what you did for Amelia. But I figure if you wanted to do a job like that, you'd be doing it. So don't think you have to tend me."

"I want to." Reaching out, Regan squeezed Etta's hand, then looked back at Zink. "I imagine you'll want to see for yourself I can do what needs to be done for Etta."

"That's right." Zink gestured toward Josh. "Mind keeping Etta company while Regan and I discuss some things?"

"Always happy to spend time with my favorite girl." Easing one hip onto the padded table, he tracked Regan out the door.

"That poor child must have been through some terrible times."

He looked back at Etta. The worry he'd heard in her voice swam in her eyes. "Why do you say that?"

"The day I met Regan, her car had broken down in the middle of Main Street. She saw my card on the corkboard at the garage advertising a bartender's job, so she walked over to the tavern. She looked as fragile as glass. Had a hollowness in her eyes. And probably weighed ten pounds less than she does now. All that's changed in the months she's been in Sundown."

Not enough, he thought. Because whatever had put the hollowness in her eyes still had a hold of her. Still had the power to make her toss her belongings in a suitcase with the intention of leaving town.

He cupped Etta's hand in his. "Have you asked Regan about her past? Why she's here?"

"Asked, no. Wondered, yes. For reasons of her own, she's chosen to keep things to herself. I respect that." Etta met his gaze, her face taut with worry. "As private as she is, it must have been hard yesterday to let folks see how much she knows about medicine."

"Yeah," he agreed quietly. Just as it must have been hard as hell to offer to stay in Sundown and do nurse duty for Etta. Which in his mind was slam-dunk proof Regan had Etta's well-being at heart.

Josh scrubbed a hand over his stubbled jaw.

Have you broken any laws?

Not a one.

Standing on Etta's porch with his hands on Regan's waist, he'd felt her tremble when he'd turned their conversation to the law. Yet there'd been something in her tone, in her eyes that had every instinct he'd developed after years on the force sending the message she'd been telling the truth.

He thought again about the starkness of her apartment. The total absence of personal items that would give a hint of her past. What the hell kind of life had she left behind her? And who? A husband? A lover?

Just the thought of her belonging to another man, no matter what the circumstances, scraped at him like tiny claws. He'd never experienced jealousy over any woman and he didn't much care for it now. Just as he damn well didn't like the fact that every time he laid eyes on Regan, he felt himself sink a little deeper into a woman who was a walking enigma.

Rules, he thought. He'd been serious when he told Regan he was adept at bending them. As a cop, his infinite knowledge of how to skirt rules and slice red tape came in handy when digging into someone's past.

The direction of his thoughts brought his suspension to mind. His willingness to bend rules and cut corners had been one of the reasons so many cops had been quick to believe he'd stepped over the line.

Josh set his jaw. He would never forget what the brush with losing his job had done to him. His family. He had no intention of letting history repeat itself.

Still, that didn't change the fact it was more than just her clothes that he wanted to peel off Regan. It was also all those layers of secrets.

He was just going to have to figure out how to stay on the straight and narrow while he peeled.

Chapter 6

"Etta's going to be okay, right?" Deni Graham asked from across the island topped with butcher block in the tavern's kitchen. "She'll get over that infection and be as good as new?"

"That's the plan." Regan shifted her gaze to Howie Lyons. He'd sent the day cook home early and had the sauce for that evening's spaghetti special simmering on the stove. The air was filled with the spicy aroma. Regan marveled over how the man stayed as thin as a thermometer while eating his own culinary masterpieces.

"Howie, at the end of each shift I need you to make a list of food items we're low on so I can get the orders turned in."

"All right." Wearing a white apron lashed over his dark T-shirt and jeans, Howie pulled open the refrigerator's door. "I'd have done that all along, if you'd asked."

"I know. But with me living upstairs it was easy to run down and check the pantry. I can't do that while I'm at Etta's."

Deni eased her order pad into the back waistband of her snug jeans. Her mouth was glossed taffy pink to match her T-shirt. "Are you moving in with Etta permanently?"

"No," Regan replied, thinking permanence wasn't a concept she'd ever again have in her life. "Just until Etta's well. Don't forget, she and A.C. are getting married soon and he'll move in. They aren't going to want company."

Regan checked her watch. It was nearly six, the time their shift started. "After we got home from the clinic, Etta called Frannie Tays. I understand she used to bartend here?"

"Yeah." Howie retrieved a knife from the holder on the island and began slicing a softball-size onion. "Frannie had to quit when she was pregnant 'cause of some medical problem."

"She's going to tend bar each evening so I can go check on Etta." Regan avoided any mention of her administering their boss IVs. She felt shaky enough over how much she'd divulged to Doc Zink about her medical training. "Then I'll come back and work to the end of my shift," she added.

"All that running's going to wear you out." Deni fluffed her blond hair while studying Regan. "You already look tired."

"I didn't get much sleep last night." Regan gathered up the order list she'd prepared for the liquor distributor. "The peeper showed up outside my bedroom window."

The long-bladed knife halting midchop, Howie jerked his attention from the onion. "Did you see the guy?"

"No, I just heard him on the balcony." She rubbed at the headache that had settled in her right temple. "I thought someone had broken in down here."

"That would have scared the liver out of me," Deni breathed.

Regan lifted a brow. "Good way to describe how I felt. I called Etta and she phoned the police."

"They find anything?" Howie asked.

"The cops didn't show up," Regan said, then explained about the domestic shooting on the far side of the lake. "Etta called Josh McCall. He checked things out."

"Well." Deni leaned a hip against the island. "It'd be worth getting scared if Josh was who showed up to protect me."

Before Regan could switch off her thoughts, her mind clicked to the kiss she and Josh had shared. And the blast furnace of desire it had ignited in her.

"I could have done without the entire experience," she said.

"Etta'll have a fit if the doc won't let her go to the derby fish fry," Howie said. "Excepting Christmas and Thanksgiving, that's the only night Truelove's closes."

"I'd forgotten about the fish fry." From the chatter Regan had heard from the locals, everyone in Sundown attended the event at the marina where the winner of the annual fishing derby was announced.

"If Etta's fever stays down, Doc Zink should let her go," Regan said, her mind working on a solution. "I just have to keep her off her feet. Is there a place nearby that rents wheelchairs?"

"The chair my ma used is up in my attic," Howie said. His expression clouded. "Guess it won't be *my* attic after my ex gets through with me."

Deni patted his shoulder. "I'll call Cinda and ask to borrow the wheelchair for Etta."

"That'd be good. Woman's gone overboard with religion. Every time I see her, she accuses me of being a heathen." He shook his head. "You expect to live out your life with someone, then look what happens."

Regan closed her eyes. She'd done nothing more than join a group of colleagues for coffee after delivering a gunshot victim to the E.R. What would her life be like now if Detective Payne Creath hadn't been in that group?

"Hey, Regan, looks like you're in for it."

Deni's comment scattered Regan's thoughts. She glanced across the kitchen. Deni now stood near the swinging door, peering through the cutout in the wall.

"What am I in for?" Regan asked.

"Burns Yost just bellied up to bar," Deni answered. "I heard him last night pestering you for an interview. He never gives up when he smells a story. Bet he's back for round two."

"Great," Regan said, and felt her headache crank into high gear. "Just what I need."

After her shift ended, Regan drove back to Etta's. Slipping noiselessly into the dimly lit bedroom, she was relieved to find her patient fast asleep and her temperature hovering near normal.

Despite the late hour and the fatigue that weighed on her, Regan felt too unsettled to go to bed. Wanting fresh air and solitude, she changed into shorts and a tank top. After pouring a generous glass of merlot, she stepped out the back door to the wooden deck that nestled against the lake's bank.

The night air was a still, warm caress against her flesh. Moonlight poured down, mingling with the soft glow of the lights affixed to the back of the house. Settling on a padded lounge chair, Regan stretched out her legs and sipped wine while taking in the stars that twinkled against the dark sky.

She had thought she'd be spending this night somewhere other than Sundown. Regan didn't lament her decision to stay and take care of the woman who'd given her so much. She could, however, regret that by staying she'd had to deal with another barrage of Burns Yost's determined insistence that she give him an interview. The owner of the *Sundown Sentinel* had finally given up and left, but Regan had the feeling she hadn't seen the last of the former investigative reporter.

Closing her eyes, she savored the warmth the wine had begun infusing into her system. With her muscles loosening like molten wax, she concentrated on the sounds around her. Cicadas sawing a scratchy tune. The croaking of far-off bullfrogs. The bumping of the sleek, high-powered speedboat moored against the dock next door.

McCall's boat.

Her forehead furrowed. She was going to have to be careful around Josh. Limit her contact with him.

Pressing her fingertips against her eyelids, she struggled to block the remembered feel of his mouth against hers, the strength of his hands when they'd curved possessively at her waist. Suddenly—distressingly—close to tears, she swallowed around the lump in her throat. Why, of the men she had met since she'd begun her new life, did only Josh McCall have the potential to reach her? And why was she allowing herself to even acknowledge that fact when getting involved with him would have so many far-reaching consequences? The least being his somehow finding out her true identity, slapping her in handcuffs and arresting her for murder. The worst—Josh could become a target for Payne Creath's vengeance.

That sudden realization had Regan going still on the inside. The New Orleans homicide cop had killed Steven and Bobby because he perceived them as standing in his way. For the past year, she'd been so filled with grief and fear that the last thing she would have done was turn to any man for protection, much less for comfort. Then Josh walked into Truelove's, and she'd felt the earth move. And, despite her best intentions, every encounter since then had brought them closer together. If Creath found out, if he even *sensed* that, he would deal with Josh as he had Steven and Bobby.

"You're quite a picture, Regan Ford, sitting there in the moonlight."

Gasping, she lunged forward on the lounge chair. Wine sloshed onto her thigh.

"Dammit!" Josh's sudden appearance while her thoughts had been focused on Creath's black-hearted revenge had panic beating wings in her stomach. *He's not here,* she reminded herself. He had no way of knowing Josh even existed.

"Careful," Josh cautioned softly, handing her a white hand towel. "You don't want to waste good wine."

Wiping the towel against her wet thigh, she shot him a look, and the retort on the tip of her tongue slid away. He was standing in a wash of dim light, big and wet and naked except for a pair of low-slung black swim trunks.

Oh, my. "You're dripping," she managed, and returned the towel. It wasn't fear or panic that had her pulse thudding now.

"That usually happens after I go for a dip in the lake," he said as he began toweling off.

Despite his leanness, there was a sense of power and endurance in the breadth of his chest and shoulders, the streamlined waist. In the silver moonlight his body looked like polished rock.

He watched her watching him. "You interested in a swim, Regan?"

She sank back into the cushions and tightened her fingers on the stem of her glass. "I don't have a swimsuit."

His mouth curved. "I'll take mine off so you won't feel overdressed."

"Not interested." She closed her eyes in defense. Why did those broad shoulders and hard muscles—the entire package—have to look so good, so *tempting?* She set her jaw against a rush of arousal, rendering it a distant throb she could control. "Don't let me keep you from going back in the water."

"Things are more inviting here on the dock. How's Etta?"

"Her fever's down and she's sleeping like a baby."

"Good."

Regan heard wood creak as he moved closer. His clean, musky male scent had her breath going shallow.

"This boat dock holds a lot of memories for me," he said.

She kept her eyes closed. "I'm guessing women were involved."

"No, at least not in the way you're thinking. One of those memories has to do with my sister Carrie. I pierced her ears right about on the spot where you're sitting."

Regan opened one eye, gazed up at him. "Is that a fact?"

"It is." He looped the towel around his neck, then sat down beside her, his thigh resting against her left hip. "Carrie was about four years old, which would have made me ten," he added, apparently oblivious that the contact had started Regan's nerves jumping like cold water on a hot griddle.

She pointed to the padded lounge chair a few inches from hers. "We'd both have more room if you'd sit there."

"Carrie kept whining to mom about getting her ears pierced," he continued without missing a beat. "Mom vetoed that, saying Carrie was too young." He shrugged. "We all put up with Carrie's pouting for about a week, then I decided to do something about it. So I pilfered a couple of clothes pins, sat Carrie down out here and stuck the pins on her earlobes until they went numb and then used a needle to pierce her ears."

Regan had both eyes open now. "Did you at least sterilize the needle?"

"No, and my dad pointed that out before he blistered my butt with his belt." Grinning, Josh snagged the glass from her hand, his fingers gliding over hers. "Good merlot," he commented after taking a sip.

Regan studied his strong, chiseled profile as he took another drink from the glass. She knew she should excuse herself. Go inside and get away from the man who presently had her system jangling and could make her throat click shut with just one slow, lazy grin.

Just for a while, she promised herself. Would it really be so awful if she stayed for a little longer? Listened to stories about people who had normal lives, as she'd once had.

Reclaiming her wineglass, she took a slow drink while she met his gaze over the rim. "You said this dock has memories. Plural. What's another?"

"It's the first place I got arrested."

"Arrested?"

"That's right."

Taking another sip, she settled back into the cushion. "I'm all ears, Sergeant McCall." Much better to talk about his criminal history than hers.

"I must have been fifteen that summer. My sisters had gone to a sleepover and my parents were at a dance at Truelove's Tavern. They left my oldest brother, Bran, in charge. Which was a mistake because he'd just gotten engaged and his fiancée was staying here, too. So, Bran and Patience were otherwise occupied instead of keeping an eye on Nate and me, and Etta's son, Mike."

"Three teenage boys with no restrictions on a summer night," Regan said. "Sounds like a recipe for trouble."

"We weren't looking for trouble, just a little fun," Josh said, raking a hand through his damp hair. "After it got dark, Mike and I decided to do some slalom skiing. Nate said he'd drive, so we piled into our boat and headed out. Somebody called Chief Decker. He busted Mike and me, and hauled us in."

Regan frowned. "For skiing at night?"

"Actually it was our *style* that someone took exception to. We called it full body barefootin' slalom."

Regan sent him a wary look. "I never heard of that."

"Not surprising." He slid the glass from her fingers, sipped, then handed it back. "Mike and I invented the technique."

"Okay, I'll bite. Why did Decker bust you for your style of skiing?"

"Because it's also known as 'buck naked, full body barefootin' slalom.'"

Regan didn't mean to smile, it just happened. "You skied naked?"

"As jaybirds. Decker was waiting on the dock when we got back. He loaded Mike and me, still wearing our birthday suits, into the back of the patrol car and drove to the station. The only person there was Ula Reynolds, the dispatcher. She had five boys of her own, all hell-raisers, so her seeing Mike and me bare-assed didn't faze her, but it sure did us. Decker paraded us into a cell, then called our parents. They had to leave the dance, go home and get us some clothes and come pick us up. I was grounded for about a year."

Laughing, breathless, Regan shook her head. "What about Nate? Didn't your brother get hauled in, too?"

"No, he kept his trunks on while he drove the boat. Mr. Law and Order just sat on the dock, giving us a shit-eating grin while Decker hauled us off."

"Mr. Law and Order?"

"Nate's a cop, too. So are Bran and my three sisters. All on the Oklahoma City PD."

"So, there are six cops in the McCall family?" Regan asked, remembering he'd said the entire clan planned to descend on Sundown over the Fourth of July holiday.

"More. My dad and granddad are both retired from the OCPD. And Morgan, Carrie and Grace are all married to cops."

The thought of living next door to so many people who had the power to lock her in a cell brought all of Regan's nerves swimming to the surface—and reminded her just how dangerous the man was who presently had his thigh snugged against her hip. "Sounds like you have your own miniprecinct."

"We could probably handle a minor riot all on our own."

She pulled her legs up to her chest, breaking the contact. "You said this dock was the *first* place you were arrested. Was there a second?"

His dark gaze dropped to her legs, then lifted. "There was."

"Arrestees don't usually wind up becoming law enforcement officers."

"I almost didn't, but that wasn't due so much to the trouble I constantly got myself into. It was more because my brothers and sisters were always going around saying how they wanted to be a cop when they grew up. Nobody ever said fireman or doctor or lawyer. It was always just cop. Then they'd give me this we-expect-you-to-pin-on-a-badge look. I got the feeling I had no say in the matter."

"So you rebelled?"

"Big-time. Back then, I was hellbent on making my own mark. Cops' and preachers' kids are a lot alike when it comes to thinking there's a certain enticement to living life on the edge. So I took up with some disreputable types and for a couple of years surfed just above the law. I knew my pals stole cars and were into other criminal activities. I even saw them committing various petty crimes. Miraculously, I never got involved."

"Do you think that was due to an inborn sense of right and wrong?"

"Could have been. Sometimes circumstances kept me from tripping up. A sibling's birthday party or an encounter with a girl or something along those lines would keep me from meeting up with my supposed friends. My dad always made sure to let me know whenever one of them got picked up. And he'd point out that if I'd been with them I'd have been nabbed, too. Looking back, I figure I missed becoming a felon by a matter of minutes."

"What got you arrested that second time?"

"All the hell I raised got me into a lot of brushes with cops, but they'd routinely call Dad instead of hauling me to juvie hall. Then one night a party I was at got raided and I got picked up for public drinking. The patrol cop knew me and called my Dad. The problem was, he'd reached his limit and refused to intervene. So I wound up in juvie hall lockup with a pissed-off cokehead who had a knife hidden in his shoe." Josh raised his hand, rubbed a fingertip along the scar that snaked up the right side of his neck. "I mouthed off to the dude and he nearly severed my carotid artery. If a counselor hadn't been nearby, I'd have bled to death."

Regan resisted the urge to reach out and slick her fingers across the scar. "Did that brush with death convert you?"

"It was more like changing sides than a conversion." Keeping his gaze on hers, he cupped his palm against her right calf. "Living life on the edge will always have a certain appeal for me," he added. "You've got soft skin, Regan."

The warmth of his palm against her flesh had her breath shallowing. "So…the former bad boy is a cop. One who admits he has no respect for rules. How does that work, McCall?"

"I didn't say I don't respect rules. What I said was rules complicate things, so I work around most of them." Keeping his gaze on hers, he slid his hand up to nest behind her knee. "Not all rules, though. I have a short list of unbreakable ones."

Heat crept up her neck into her face. "For instance?"

"Getting involved with another man's woman. That's something I won't do." He leaned closer, his bare chest brushing her knee. "So, I have to ask you, Regan, are you married?"

She tore her gaze from his and focused on the still lake, its surface shimmering with a dozen silver shades of moonlight. "My status didn't seem to matter to you last night when you kissed me."

"I've been doing some thinking since then."

"About?"

"You." He hooked a finger under her chin, tugged her head back, forcing her to meet his gaze. "I don't know why, but I can't seem to lock you out of my head."

She pulled her chin from his touch. His thumb was skimming up and down her calf, spreading heat through her entire body. "You need to work harder at locking me out, McCall." And she him.

"Why?"

"I'm not free."

"Does that mean you're married?"

She hesitated. By necessity, she had lied to everyone she'd encountered over the past year. Doing so was second nature to her now. Yet, something inside her wanted to tell Josh the truth, or at least a version of it. "Marriage isn't the only thing that puts a person off-limits."

"So, you're not married?"

"No. Look, just—"

"Relax," he said, his fingers tightening on her leg when she began to pull away. "Do you know tonight's the first time I've heard you laugh?"

"Lately, I haven't found a lot that amuses me."

"That's a shame because you've got this rippling, smoky laugh that flows across the skin." He slid the glass from her hand, set it on the dock, then edged closer on the padded cushion. "It's not a sound a man forgets."

"Don't." She lifted a hand, splayed her fingers across his chest. His warm, bare, hard-as-a-rock chest. Beneath her palm, she felt his heartbeat. How could his be so even and steady while hers had launched into orbit? "I can't do this."

"You said you weren't married."

"I don't *want* to do this."

"I might believe that if I couldn't see the way your pulse is pounding in your throat." His hand eased up to her thigh. "Or feel it jumping."

The air around them went very still, very suddenly. The night sounds echoed off the water and surrounded them as if she and Josh were on some small island, all alone. Regan's gaze dropped to his mouth, and her breathing went uneven. Heaven help her, she wanted to feel his lips against hers again even more than she wanted to drag in her next ragged breath.

Lust crept over her skin, as searing and heady as the wine she'd consumed. She wanted her hands on him, all over him. Wanted him, knowing how temporary it would be, how fleeting. How agonizing that there could be nothing for them in the future. She forced herself to ease back.

"No," she said, but the denial wasn't as strong as she would have wished. "I don't—"

"I think you do," he murmured. With one hand, he cupped the back of her neck, his fingers warm and strong. For an instant the urge to retreat continued to hammer at her. And then need surged inside her. Overwhelmed, she slid her hand up the muscled planes of his chest to his shoulder, gripped there.

His mouth lowered, roamed over hers in warm, lazy seduction. She tasted the wine on his lips, dark and potent as she eased closer until her breasts fit snug against his chest.

She felt those hard, seeking fingers run up and down the back of her neck, filling her mind with images of them making a long, mesmerizing journey over her entire body. While she was distracted by them, his mouth became more greedy, pulling response from her before she was aware of the demand.

Blood thundered in her head; she couldn't breathe, or think. All of the wariness and fear she carried in her vanished. In their place, rioting sensations sprinted. The tensed ripple of muscle under her fingers, the hot and demanding taste of his mouth, the thunder of her heartbeat that raced with dizzying speed. She wrapped her arms around him, her fingers digging in, her body straining, her mouth as urgent and impatient as his.

The sheer power of her desire ripped through her. She moaned, a low, throaty sound that was as much demand as surrender.

She felt the change in him: the violent tremor in the hard body, the tightening of his arm, locking her against him. His free hand slid up the inside of her thigh, his fingers nudging beneath the fabric of her shorts.

"Let me," he murmured against her mouth. "Let me have you, Regan."

Overwhelming heat rolled over her. There was nowhere to run from the onslaught. Nowhere to hide. To escape to.

Her eyes slowly opened on the realization. Then reason broke through the smothering desire, bringing a sharp clarity about what was happening. What she was doing. *Risking.*

It didn't matter that the lounge chair was on the outer edge of the dim lights. Or that they were behind Etta's house on a secluded cove of the lake. What mattered was that Creath was hunting her. And if he tracked her here, chances were he'd also find out she'd taken a lover. Another man who Creath would perceive blocked his way to her.

Since the moment I met you, you've disappointed me, cher. I shared that disappointment with your fiancé. And your partner.

Creath's face loomed up before her, vicious, taunting. *How many more times are you going to disappointment me?*

Fear burst inside her heart like a bomb. She clamped her fingers on Josh's wrist, stilling his hand against her inner thigh. "No. Stop."

He went still. Absolutely still. Against her breasts, she felt his heart pound. "Regan—"

"I can't do this."

He shifted his head back and she saw desire, the dangerous burn of it in his dark eyes. When she felt the same desire stab inside her, she shoved from his touch, pushing up off the lounge chair.

"I'm sorry," she said, her voice hollow. Ragged. "I just… I can't."

Still seated, he grabbed the wineglass, downed its contents, then set it aside. "Why can't you?" he asked, his voice a cold snap on the heated air.

"It's just…" She curled her fingers into her palms. "It's not the…right thing for me to do."

"Try telling that to someone who didn't just feel you tremble against him," he said, his dark eyes locked on her face. "It felt as right to you as it did to me."

"Yes. Yes, it did." She closed her eyes, opened them. "I'm sorry, Josh."

He stood, walked to her, towering over her. "Exactly what are you sorry about?"

Everything. "For letting things get out of hand. I just…" She shoved a hand through her hair. "I should go."

When she started to turn, he clamped a hand on her arm. "Want to know what I'm sorry about?" He loomed over her, a muscle clenching in the side of his jaw.

"What?"

"That you won't trust me enough to tell me who you're afraid of. I want you to tell me who you're running from."

A sick trembling settled in her stomach. "I'm not—"

"You are." He locked his hands on her shoulders. "I'm a cop, I've seen plenty of women who've been abused. Isolated from friends and family. Most of them just stay and get used as punching bags over and over until the beatings kill them. Others—the smart ones—get the hell away, even if it means going on the run. Like you."

"Let go." Fear crimped her voice; sweat slid down her back as she struggled against his grip. "Let me go, Josh."

"Tell me," he insisted. "Tell me so I can help you."

"Dammit, give me some air," she said. "Some space."

"All right." His eyes narrowed. "But I warn you, if you try walking into Etta's house without giving me some answers, I'm coming in after you."

She raised her chin. "I'll give you the answers I can give," she said evenly. "You'll have to settle for that."

He stared at her for a long moment, then gave her a curt nod.

When he released her, she backed out of range. *Abused,* she thought weakly. He thought she'd been beaten, that she was on the run from an abuser.

Her legs unsteady, she turned her back on him, clamped one hand on the lounge chair for support. And, oh God, he was right, she realized. Creath hadn't physically assaulted her, but he'd battered her mentally. Killed two men she'd loved and set her up to take the fall for one of those murders. He'd stolen her life, robbed her of the simplest of joys. Yes, she'd been abused.

Turning slowly, she faced Josh. It might be crazy, she thought, but she felt a sudden easing of the pressure in her chest just knowing that what she was about to tell him wouldn't be all lies.

"You're right," she said quietly. "I'm running. Hiding from a man who abused me. Because of him, I've given up my friends, my job, my home, the life I had." She dragged in a ragged breath. "People I loved."

"Were you married to him?"

"No. God, no." As she spoke, she watched the moonlight dance on the lake's surface. "We were never lovers, although that's what he wanted. I didn't even know him all that well. But that didn't matter—having me was an obsession for him. *Is* an obsession. An endless one."

"Tell me his name."

She closed her eyes a moment, then made herself open them and meet his. "The important thing for you to know is that if he finds me, it won't be just me he'll come after. It will be any man he perceives is blocking his way to having me."

Despite the dim light, she saw the glint of battle settle in Josh's eyes. "I can take care of myself."

Steven and Bobby had felt the same way. And they'd both died because of Creath's obsession. Without warning, grief washed over her. The pressure in her chest was so strong she had to consciously school every breath.

She gazed at Josh, so strong, so sure of himself. And in danger of dying simply by being with her.

"I know you're trained." Despair worked its way to the surface and made her tone sharp. "But the man who wants me is...dangerous." She would go as far as she could with the truth, yet still keep her secrets. "I can't be with you. It's too big a risk."

"Taking risks is a part of my job. My life. If the bastard who's abused you shows up, I know how to deal with him." His eyes locked intently on hers, probed. "You're afraid. That's understandable. I won't let him lay a hand on you."

"No." She took a step back. "I'll say again how sorry I am that I let things get out of hand between us."

"I don't want a damn apology. You're under my skin, Regan, in a way no woman has ever been. I want to find out why." He angled his chin. "Don't you?"

She dropped her gaze. More than anything she wanted to explore the hot, greedy need for him that churned inside her. But what she wanted could get Josh killed.

He took a step toward her. "We can't figure things out if you turn your back."

"I have to."

"That's it? You're going to let some abusive bastard continue to play games with your life?"

"I win as long as he doesn't find me."

"Running scared doesn't sound like winning to me."

It was enough to keep her out of prison for a murder she didn't commit. And alone for the rest of her life.

The thought of that, just the thought, had her fighting another swell of tears. "There can't be a repeat of what happened between us tonight. I'm asking you to accept that. And I'd like your word that you'll keep your distance."

His mouth pressed into a thin line. "You want *my word* I'll stay away from you?"

She wanted it, because she wasn't sure she was strong enough to resist him if he kept coming around. "Yes. You strike me as a man who, once he gives his word, keeps it."

His eyes narrowed on her face. Now, he studied her with a cop's scrutiny that had her nerves screaming. "You figure if I give you my word, I won't view this as the equivalent of some *rule* I can figure out how to get around?"

"Basically."

"I'm not in the habit of forcing women, so you don't need to worry about me keeping my damn distance," he ground out. He slicked his gaze toward the house at her back. "This morning you had your suitcase packed. You came here, intending to quit your job and say goodbye to Etta. I'm right, aren't I?"

"Yes."

"Were you leaving Sundown because you think whoever this guy is knows you're here?"

"No. It's just that…" *You're a cop and I'm wanted for murder.* Her stomach knotted with fear, with longing. How was it possible to be swept away so quickly, to want so desperately what you knew you shouldn't have? "It's harder to find someone who moves around," she said. "I've been in Sundown for six months. That's too long. It's time I leave."

"Which you'll do as soon as Etta gets well." It wasn't a question.

"Yes."

"And go where?"

"I won't know until I get there."

"Dammit, Regan—"

"I don't have a choice."

"Wrong. You could choose to stay." The heat in his eyes was so intense it could have thawed ice. "I can help you. All you have to do is let me."

"You can't. No one can."

Turning her back on him, she walked away on legs that felt like glass, ready to shatter.

Chapter 7

"Did this Regan Ford name the guy she's supposedly running from?" Nate McCall's voice came over the phone mixed with a backwash of noise from the Oklahoma City PD's homicide squad room.

"There's no 'supposedly' to it." Phone tucked between his ear and shoulder, Josh tilted his chair back and propped his battered running shoes on the front porch rail. It was barely past eight; already heat hung in the still-as-death air. The sweet scent of the yellow roses tumbling from the clay pots lining the porch cloyed in his lungs.

"And, no, she didn't give me his name," Josh added. "She's scared down to the bone. The only info she gave up is that he's dangerous. And might not view my interest in her in a positive light."

"Exactly what is your interest, bro?"

Josh shifted his gaze to Etta's pale blue house. Before he'd left on his morning run, he'd lingered on his porch, hoping

Regan would appear so they could jog together. Now, he'd finished jogging and here he was, back on the damn porch. He'd
never before watched and waited for a woman. The fact that he
did now made him scowl.

"I'll tell you what it is when I figure it out," he said.

"Has it occurred to you that the story she gave you might be
a load of bull? That she's hiding because she's got more to con-
ceal about herself than she let on?"

Have you broken any laws?

Not a one.

Something about her was niggling, bugging him, something
Josh couldn't pin down. But his sixth sense still sent the same
message: she'd told the truth.

"If Regan Ford's a criminal, I'll eat my badge," he said.

"That'd be tasty," Nate remarked. "Since you have no idea
what your interest is in her, why don't you just back off?"

"Can't. I'm compelled to keep my eye on her."

"Sounds like you've had more than just your eye on Etta's
secretive bartender."

You've got that right. He pictured Regan as she'd looked last
night, sitting in the moonlight, her eyes closed, a glass of ruby-
red wine in one hand. Raw lust had slammed into him the instant he'd seen her. Followed closely by the urge to get her
naked and bury himself inside her.

Josh shoved his fingers through his hair, still damp from his
run. "You know me, Nate. I'm a hands-on type of guy."

"I also know there's nothing wrong with getting up close and
personal when both parties are free and consenting. But you've
answered enough domestic calls to know they're like dry kin-
dling—takes one spark to set things off. You could wind up in
the center of the inferno if this dangerous dude Regan Ford
claims she's hiding from tracks her to Sundown."

"I'm not going to get myself into a bind."

"This coming from the guy who just came off suspension."

Josh's eyes narrowed. "I didn't plant that evidence. Internal Affairs cleared me, remember?"

"They cleared you *after* they put you through a month of hell. And I never thought you planted the evidence. But a lot of cops were willing to believe it was you. Don't forget how close you came to losing your badge, *Stretch*."

Josh set his jaw at Nate's use of the nickname Josh had earned while coming up through the department's ranks. He was known for stretching rules, but never the law. Internal Affairs had ignored that distinction while investigating him.

"Look, Nate, I'm not stretching anything here. I'm doing what any cop does when he encounters a 'person of interest.' I need you to run a simple 28/29 check on Regan's Mustang. Are you going to do that, or not?"

"Chill, bro, I'll run the car. Any idea what you'll do if it's registered to someone else? Or comes back as stolen?"

Josh scrubbed a palm over his face. He'd spent the entire night thinking about Regan. Cursing her. Wanting her. Around dawn, it had taken every ounce of self-control not to stride across the lawn, walk into Etta's house and demand Regan give him more answers. About her past. And her present feelings for him.

It wasn't as if what was between them was all one-sided, he thought dourly. He knew when a woman was interested. And when Regan had been in his arms last night, trembling and kissing him back like there was no tomorrow, she'd been damn interested. He *knew* that, so why for the first time in his life did it matter that a woman *confirm* she was on the same wavelength as him?

"You still there?"

"Yeah," Josh muttered. "Whatever info comes back on the Mustang, I'll deal with it." And because his mood was still raw from the way Regan had melted in his arms one minute, then as good as told him to get lost the next, he changed the subject. "How's Paige?"

"Ms. Carmichael is as sexy and gorgeous as ever."

Josh heard the unmistakable warmth in his brother's voice. Oh, yeah, he was hooked like a marlin. "Sounds like your moving in together was the right thing to do."

"An understatement. As a matter of fact, I was going to call you later today. When you get back to Oklahoma City, you need to get measured for a tux."

Josh grinned. "So, you and Paige are making things legal?"

"You got it."

"Congratulations. Although I can't figure out why a smart woman like Paige would tie herself down to the likes of you."

"It's the McCall charm. Too bad you didn't inherit any."

Josh voiced a short, explicit curse while honing in on the sound of an engine. He glanced at the road just as a car came into view. Squinting against the sunlight glinting off its windshield, he made out the gold badge on the patrol car's door.

"Decker just drove up," Josh said when the cruiser pulled into the driveway behind his 'Vette.

"Have you been skiing naked again?" Nate asked.

Josh chuckled. "Hell, no. Doing time in my birthday suit cured me of breaking the law in Decker's town." He glanced at Regan's Mustang. "Nate, get back to me on that run."

"Will do. Just remember, the last thing you need is to get in the middle of a domestic battle that's out of your jurisdiction. If things get dicey, let Decker handle them."

In other words, Josh thought as the call disconnected, don't stretch the rules as you did before when it nearly cost you your badge. He settled his chair onto all four legs with a thump, rose, propped a shoulder against a porch column and watched Decker approach.

As usual, the chief's navy-blue uniform had creases as sharp as razor blades. Sunlight reflected off his mirrored sunglasses. In one hand he carried a bulging manila envelope.

"Morning, Chief."

"Josh."

Decker paused at the porch steps. "You getting ready to jog?" he asked, taking in Josh's shorts and gray T-shirt.

"Already been. What's up?"

Decker placed one foot on the bottom step and leaned against the banister. "That damn Peeping Tom."

"Did you get prints off the lightbulb from Regan's balcony?"

"Partials covered with dust, so they're probably from whoever put the bulb in the fixture before she moved in. There were some fresh smudges from gloves. I figure the peeper is smart enough to cover his tracks."

"Too bad," Josh said.

"Yeah." Decker scrubbed a hand over his jaw. "This guy is escalating. If I don't catch him, there might be some rapes down the line. I know you're on vacation, but you work sex crimes and I'd be in your debt if you'd look at the reports. View things with a fresh eye. See if there's anything I've missed."

Josh gestured toward the envelope in Decker's hand. "Is that the file?"

"Copies of everything in it."

"Come up and have a seat in the shade."

"Appreciate it." Decker slipped off his glasses, hung them by the earpiece in the pocket beneath his badge.

After they settled in chairs, Josh said, "Why don't you tell me about this guy? I'll take a look at the file later."

"Late last year we started getting reports from ladies who heard noises outside their bedroom windows at night. In every instance, the suspect unscrewed the bulb in any outdoor fixture he could reach."

"Cuts down on the chance of a witness getting a physical description of him," Josh commented.

"The reports died down, so I figured he'd stopped or left Sundown. Then he started up again this month." Decker batted a fly away. "The night before the peeper showed up on Regan's balcony there was another incident. It's what makes me think the guy's getting braver."

"What'd he do?" Josh asked.

"If my theory's right, he unscrewed the back porch light on Virginia Nash's house then went in through an unlocked door, which opens into the laundry room. There was a basket of clean clothes sitting on the dryer. It looks like he helped himself to a pair of black panties. Thongs, they're called."

"Thongs?" Josh scowled. "Virginia Nash is eighty. Are you telling me she wears black thongs?"

"Lord no, and that's an image I don't need in my head. Virginia's granddaughter is staying with her. Karen's twenty, has red hair, nice looking. She swears her thong was in the basket that evening when she left to meet friends at Truelove's. That's the same night you were there."

The image of a shapely redhead who'd shared a booth with two other women slid through Josh's mind. "I noticed her." Which was amazing, he thought, since his attention had been riveted on the tavern's sexy, dark-haired bartender with secrets in her eyes. Now, he knew one of those secrets. Thinking about the way Regan had melted against him, about how her heated mouth had yielded to his solidified his determination to learn the rest.

With Decker sitting beside him, Josh broke away from that thought and shifted his mind to business. "Anything else missing from the Nash house?"

"Just Karen's thong."

"Could be a case of 'if you can't get the candy, steal the wrapper,'" Josh murmured. "Do you think Karen being at Truelove's had something to do with the burglary?"

"It's possible. Do you know Seamus O'Toole?"

"The name doesn't sound familiar."

"He was also at the tavern. On the nights he goes there without his wife he sits at the bar, tosses back shots of whiskey, then stacks the glasses in a pyramid."

Josh nodded. "I saw him. Big guy. Small eyes, thin mouth. You think he's the peeper?"

"Maybe. One of Virginia's neighbors couldn't sleep, so he went outside to smoke. He saw O'Toole walking in the area a little after one o'clock."

Josh rubbed his fingers over his stubbled jaw. One o'clock was about the time he delivered Etta's apple pie to Regan's apartment. "Have you questioned O'Toole?"

"Not yet." Decker's gaze went to the house next door. "I want to talk to Regan first. From what I hear, she has to boot O'Toole out of the tavern at closing time on a regular basis. If he's had too much to drink, she takes his keys and makes him walk home. I need to find out if that's what happened the night of the burglary. And exactly what condition O'Toole was in."

Josh nodded. "Does he live here full-time?"

"No, in Dallas where he owns a used car dealership. He and his wife first came to Sundown about three years ago so Seamus could compete in Paradise Lake's derby. When they're here, they rent the house that belongs to the widow Throckmorton."

"Does O'Toole have a record?"

"Two old arrests. For B and E and soliciting a prostitute."

"A burglary and a sex crime," Josh said. "If your theory's right about the Nash house, it's the same thing you've got going with the peeper."

"It's a tie-in I can't ignore. So's the fact that O'Toole has been in Sundown every time there's been a peeper sighting."

Both men looked up when a dusty brown pickup rumbled into view. "A.C.," Decker said. He rose, waved at Etta's fiancé, then handed Josh the manila envelope. "Do you want to sit in while I talk to Regan?"

Josh ran his fingertips over the envelope's flap while Regan's request that he keep his distance crowded in. If the sleepless night he'd spent was any indication of his involvement with her, he questioned his ability to stay away.

But that was on a personal level, he reasoned. He was now consulting on the peeper case, and his sitting in on Decker's interview was business.

He rose. "Lead the way, Chief."

"That sore looks dang ugly." Etta looked up from her unwrapped ankle. "Is it supposed to be so red?"

"It's still infected," Regan said, using gloved fingers to finish applying antibiotic cream to Etta's ankle. "The good news is it looks better than it did yesterday at the clinic."

"That's a relief."

"Your fever's gone, too." Regan tore open a pack of gauze, applied a pad to the wound, then taped its edges. "All done." She smiled. "You're a good patient, Etta."

"One who's kept you from your morning run."

"I'll get to it," Regan said.

Quite simply, she had put off jogging because she hadn't wanted to encounter Josh. She didn't know what to do about the fact that a cop now knew she was on the run. Hiding. Didn't know what to do if the little she'd told him about her past didn't satisfy him. She was confident her Regan Ford identity could withstand a cursory check, but what if Creath had posted information about her—including her picture—on law enforcement Web sites that Josh had access to? Just the prospect of him chancing onto one of those sites had her stomach in knots.

Then there was the matter of what had happened between them last night. Dammit, it felt as if her mouth was still on fire from his. And what, she wondered, was she supposed to do about the sexual buzz that had kept her system churning all night? Still had it churning.

"Folks here are saying you've got a real knack for medicine, Regan." The sunlight slanting through the windows gleamed on Etta's gray hair when she settled back in the pillows propped behind her. "They're right."

"I wish I could have saved Amelia." Regan placed a hand beneath Etta's calf, then positioned the cast back into place. "Her grandparents must be grief stricken."

"They are. And I feel bad I can't get into the kitchen and fix a casserole to send over." Etta sniffed the air. "Speaking of food, whatever it is you're baking has my mouth watering."

"It's a surprise," Regan said while gathering the paper that had held the gauze. "Move, Anthracite," she said, nudging the kitten aside with one foot on her way to the trash can beside Etta's pine vanity. "And you'll be in the kitchen, fixing that casserole before you know it."

"How? Doc Zink said he'll skin me if he finds out I've been on my feet."

"A.C.'s picking up the wheelchair that belonged to Howie's mother." Regan glanced at her watch. "He'll be here soon."

Etta's forehead furrowed. "A wheelchair?"

"It's a temporary fix to get you back in the kitchen," Regan said, patting Etta's thin shoulder. "I'll put the ingredients you need for the casserole on the table. You can mix it there."

"You're a godsend, Regan." Etta smoothed her pale yellow robe. "It was my lucky day when your car broke down in Sundown."

"You gave me a job and a place to live." Without warning, a ball of emotion wedged in Regan's throat, turning her voice raspy. "You saved my life."

Etta reached out a hand, her eyes clouded with concern. "Tell me what's weighing so heavy on you, child."

"It's…nothing." Settling onto the side of the bed, Regan gripped Etta's hand. "My hormones are stirred up is all."

Etta nodded slowly. "Seems to me they started getting stirred about the time Josh came to Sundown. If there's one man who can get a woman's hormones going, it's him."

"There's nothing…" Regan shook her head, thinking how

close she had come last night to lowering all her defenses. "I don't *want* there to be anything between us."

"That's your choice. But yesterday at the clinic, I saw how he looked at you." Etta patted her hand. "Mind you, I've seen him around more than a few women. He never looked at them the way he was looking at you."

"What way?"

"Serious."

Regan arched a brow. "I think the fever you had made you a little delirious."

Etta shook her head. "No. That man's plenty interested."

That man is a cop. And she was wanted for murder.

"Even if you're right, things wouldn't work out between us," Regan said. "I told him we should keep our distance."

"Do you mind me asking how he took that?"

"He agreed."

Etta pursed her mouth. "Doesn't sound like the Joshua McCall I know. Growing up, when he saw something he wanted, nothing slowed that boy down. I don't expect he's changed all that much."

A sharp rap on the front screen door brought Regan's head around. "That must be A.C." She slid her hand from Etta's as she rose. "We'll have you in the kitchen in no time."

"Can't wait," Etta said.

Regan headed out of the bedroom. She spotted A.C. Konklin standing on the other side of the screen door at the end of the hallway. Etta's fiancé was in his sixties, six feet of solid muscle with a linebacker's shoulders, a square-jawed face and a head as bald and shiny as a new dime. Regan adored him.

"Hi, handsome," she said, unlatching the screen.

"There's my girl," he said, engulfing her in a bear hug. "I brought the wheelchair and a couple of fellas with me."

"Who…?"

She peered around A.C.'s arm and met Josh's gaze. Then her eyes flicked to Chief Decker and she froze like a dazzled rabbit.

"Morning, Regan," Decker said, sending her a nod. "I need to have a word with you."

Warning bells shrilled in her head. "I… I'm busy with Etta right now."

"This shouldn't take long," Decker said. His voice was even, his tone all business. Despite the mirrored sunglasses shielding his eyes, she could tell he regarded her with a cool, assessing look.

The warning bells were lost under the thunder of her heart.

"You talk to the chief," A.C. said, sweeping her deeper into the hallway as if she weighed nothing. "I'll see to Etta. The chief and Josh did some heavy lifting, getting that chair out of my pickup and hefting it up the porch steps." While he spoke, A.C. took control of the wheelchair Josh angled through the door. "You have something cold in the icebox for them?"

"Lemonade." Regan said the word quietly, keeping her expression set as she forced herself to meet Decker's gaze. "What…did you need to talk to me about?"

"A case." He slid off his sunglasses. "I'd appreciate some of that lemonade. I imagine Josh would, too."

Regan flicked her gaze back to Josh while panic sliced through her. Had he gone to Decker, told the chief that she was running, hiding? Had Decker somehow found out her real name? Was he here to arrest her for murder?

Oh, God. Oh, God.

She clenched her fists, vaguely aware that her vision was dimming at the edges. "A case?" she managed.

Decker studied her with eyes that gave away nothing. "I need some information about one of your customers at the tavern."

Regan blinked. "A customer," she repeated, looking at Josh. "Why are *you* here?"

"Good to see you, too." He angled his chin. "I work sex crimes, so the chief asked me to sit in while he talks to you."

"Sex crimes?"

"Yeah," Josh said. "How about we adjourn to the kitchen?" He sniffed the air. "Think the chief and I can talk you into sharing some of whatever it is that smells so good?"

"Lemon tea bread." Knowing her secret was still safe, Regan felt something loosen inside her. "It's cooling. I haven't glazed it yet."

Josh's mouth curved. "I've got all day."

"I don't," she tossed back just as Decker's cell phone rang. He pulled it off his uniform belt, answered.

A streak of black whizzed by and landed on one of Josh's shoes. Chuckling, he scooped up Anthracite, ruffling her fur as he regarded Regan. "Want to go to the kitchen while the chief finishes his call?"

"I'm done," Decker said. "The mayor decided to schedule a meeting this morning and I have to be there." He looked at Josh. "I figure you know what questions to ask Regan. You and I can get together this afternoon and discuss things."

"Works for me."

"Regan, give my best to Etta," Decker said.

"I will." She waited for him to step out the door, then turned and headed for the kitchen. She could hear Josh following on her heels. Despite the relief she felt at Decker's departure, her nerves jittered over the prospect of spending time with the man who had her system churning.

She retrieved a glass from a cabinet while he settled the kitten beside her food bowl. Making himself at home, Josh opened the refrigerator, pulled out the pitcher of lemonade.

"Aren't you having some?" he asked when she handed him the single glass.

This close, Regan caught his faint scent, dark, musky, overtly male. The sexual awareness that had tormented her throughout the night began buzzing a little louder.

"I'm not thirsty," she said, her voice sharper than she'd intended. Wanting to put distance between them, she gestured toward the table in the kitchen's center. "Have a seat."

He glanced at the table, then back at her, watching as she pulled a mixing bowl from the dish drainer.

"Are you going to join me there?"

"No. I need to mix the glaze while the bread's still warm."

"Then I'll stand here and watch you work." He dipped his head toward the counter where a loaf cooled on a wire rack. "It looks like a pound cake, but that's not what you called it."

"It's lemon tea bread. For Etta." Regan sent him a pointed look. "She gets the first slice."

"Good thing there's plenty to go around."

He looked so…male, Regan thought, leaning back against the counter with his ankles crossed while he drank lemonade. He was dressed in jogging shorts, a gray T-shirt and running shoes. His dark hair was rumpled, stubble darkened his jaw.

The remembered feel of that stubble against her face sent a quick thrill racing through her. A thrill she needed to make herself immune to.

Her hands were ice-cold as she gripped Etta's cast-iron skillet and shifted it out of the way.

"Since you're working with Chief Decker he must not hold your criminal past against you," she said.

"I've redeemed myself. Want some help with the glaze?"

"I need fresh lemon juice."

"I'm ace at squeezing lemons." Josh retrieved a knife from a drawer, then snagged a lemon from a nearby bowl. "The customer Decker wanted to ask you about is Seamus O'Toole."

"O'Toole?" Regan paused in the process of dumping powdered sugar into her mixing bowl. "What did he do?"

"Decker doesn't know if he did anything. So you need to keep what we talk about between us."

"All right." She finished with the powdered sugar. "What about O'Toole?"

"Think back to his behavior three nights ago. That's the same night I came into Truelove's."

Regan nodded. "O'Toole sat at the bar. Had shot glasses stacked in front of him. I remember you giving him a look."

"I do that to anyone who tosses back that many shots of whiskey," Josh said, squeezing a lemon half over a small bowl. "How much juice do you need?"

"I never measure. Just do a couple of lemons." She furrowed her brow. "O'Toole sits at that same spot at the bar on the nights his wife isn't with him. She wasn't there that night, unfortunately."

"Why unfortunately?"

"Because he got loaded. More so than usual. He gave me a lot of grief when I tried to get him out the door at closing time."

"What sort of grief?"

"He kept insisting on us going upstairs to my place to party. When I turned him down he stabbed a finger in my face, accused me of being a man-hater. I gave the lamebrain's thumb a good twist and dropped him to his knees."

Josh slid her a look. "I'll keep in mind you know that move. What happened after that?"

"I made O'Toole give me his car keys and told him to walk home." Regan shifted the loaf from the cooling rack to a platter. "We'd been through that routine before so I reminded him the keys would be in a drawer behind the bar and he could pick them up when he was sober."

"So, he'd had a few too many. But not enough to where you thought he couldn't make it home on foot?"

"Right. Well, maybe." Using the back of a wrist, she pushed her bangs off her forehead. "I started worrying that O'Toole might be too plowed to get home. And that if something happened he might sue Etta since Truelove's is where he got drunk. Howie offered to drive O'Toole's route to make sure he hadn't stumbled over some curb and hit his head."

"Do you know if Howie did that?"

"He never said. And I didn't ask." She furrowed her brow. "What does your working sex crimes have to do with O'Toole getting drunk at Truelove's?"

"His pride would have taken a hit when you did that job on his thumb. A man gets dropped to his knees by a woman, he might hold a grudge. Want a little payback."

Regan nodded. She knew all too well about men who held grudges.

"Which," Josh continued, "could be why the peeper showed up on your balcony the following night."

Regan did a double take. "You think O'Toole's the Sundown peeper?"

"I think it's possible."

She blew out a breath. "What about the lightbulb from the fixture on my balcony? Did Decker get any prints?"

"No." Josh handed her the bowl of lemon juice. "The guy wore gloves."

"Too bad," she said, then checked the juice. "You did good, McCall. No seeds."

"I've been performing culinary chores all my life."

"Is that so?" Regan asked while adding juice to the powdered sugar. She retrieved a wooden spoon, began stirring.

"It is. Mom didn't want us to starve so she made sure all of us kids knew our way around the kitchen." He leaned a hip against the counter. "There wasn't much danger of starving for Bran, Nate and me."

"Because you learned to cook?"

"No, we learned early to bribe our sisters into feeding us. Especially Morgan. She's not only a cop, she's an awesome cook."

"What did you bribe her with?"

His mouth curved. "Boys."

"You bribed your sister with a guy?"

"That's right." Josh crossed his arms over his chest. "Her

first crush was on my pal, Stan Scoggins. She had it so bad that all it took was Stan rumpling her hair and grinning while he told her he loved her cooking. In no time she'd whip up some killer dessert for us. Then Stan and I would go off and ignore her until we got hungry again."

Regan laughed. "That's mean."

"That's being a brother."

She felt a pull inside her, as sensual as a touch, as tempting as a kiss. The love she heard in Josh's voice when he talked about his family attracted her every bit as much as his toughly handsome face.

Watching her, he smiled, a slow movement of lips that was both arrogant and charming. Smiled, she thought, as if he knew exactly what she was thinking.

"Come to think about it," he said, "I've had a lot of success getting women to cook for me. Like now."

"I'm cooking for Etta, slick," Regan said as she continued stirring. "Not you."

"This time," he murmured. Reaching out, he tucked her hair behind one ear.

When his knuckles grazed her cheek, Regan shivered. She knew it was something more than just his touch that warmed her blood. There was an undercurrent of emotion that she felt whenever he was near her. If she wasn't careful, there'd be a time it would simply sweep her away.

Wanting to focus on something else, she asked, "So how does a guy who got busted for skiing naked wind up working in Sex Crimes?"

He raised his brows. "You thinking along the lines of 'it's harder to catch a thief if you've never stolen anything?'"

"Maybe."

"Sorry to blow your theory, but I've never been a sex fiend on the prowl. It just happened that when I got promoted to detective, the only opening was in Sex Crimes." He sniffed the air again. "Does your lemon tea bread taste as great as it smells?"

"It's about as good as getting a big hug from your grandma. Makes you feel all happy inside." Regan froze, midstir. The comment had been automatic, said without thinking. And brought the emotions she'd been battling for days swarming dangerously close to the surface.

"Regan?"

When she didn't answer, Josh settled a hand on her shoulder. "What is it?"

She wavered against the urge to shrug him off, to add another lie to the myriad ones she'd told over the past year. Yet, the memory had been so intense, so sudden, so heart wrenching.

"This was my mother's recipe," she said, her voice barely above a whisper. "I used to sit in the kitchen and watch her make the bread. And she always gave me the first piece because she said she wanted me to feel happy inside. To always be happy."

And she had been years later when she baked the same bread for the man she loved. Since she'd gone on the run, she'd had none of Steven's things to touch and hold and weep over. She hadn't dared let herself think of him too much, and now she discovered she couldn't quite capture his face, or the sound of his voice.

Josh took the spoon out of her hand, laid it aside. He settled his hands on her shoulders, shifted her to face him. "Tell me about your mom."

She looked away. Talking about any part of her past could open a door into who she was. Still, standing there, surrounded by the warm scent of the bread that brought back so many memories overwhelmed her. After a year of running, she could no longer hide from what was inside her, every minute of every day.

"She worked in a bakery," Regan began. "When I was little she'd bundle me into the car at about three in the morning so she could get to work in time to make doughnuts."

"What about your dad?"

"He died when I was a baby. It was just Mom and me. She was my best friend."

"Was?"

"She died of cancer two years ago," Regan said, her throat tightening against the unremitting ache of her loss. She had met Steven during her mother's last hospital stay. Over time they'd fallen in love. And Payne Creath had killed him. Then her paramedic partner, Bobby.

Lifting her gaze, she stared up at the man whose strong hands now gripped her shoulders. Compassion played across his face, softening those dark eyes.

"I haven't talked about my mother in a long time. Not since…"

"You went on the run."

"I shouldn't have told you. I don't know why I did." When she tried to shrug away, Josh tightened his grip.

"Think maybe it's because there's something between us? Something that goes deeper than physical attraction?"

It wasn't the response she wanted or expected. The world was hard and cruel and unpredictable, and she wasn't going to make things worse by letting him know she was desperately afraid he was right. Acknowledging that would only make things harder when she left. And she would leave, as soon as Etta healed.

She gave her head a derisive shake. "Our libidos are singing some elemental duet, is all. A common occurrence between people who haven't known each other a week."

"Feels like it's been a lot longer. And after last night, there's no denying something's got a hold of both of us. Something more complicated than that elemental duet."

When the blood began to hum in her ears, she raised her hands, curled her fingers around his wrists. "That doesn't matter. Neither of us can let that matter." She had to use all of her self-control to keep the plea out of her voice. "I've told you all I know about O'Toole, so you should go. You gave your word you'd keep your distance."

"Not exactly."

"You said—"

"I said I'm not in the habit of forcing women, so you didn't need to worry about me keeping my distance." He lifted a shoulder. "That was a statement, not a promise."

"You're playing games."

He dipped his head, his mouth hovering just above hers. "I felt you flame like a rocket in my arms, then spent the rest of the night with thoughts of you churning in my head." His voice was as low and intimate as if he were whispering words of seduction. "Where a woman's concerned, that's a first for me. I intend to find out why. No way in hell is this a game."

"What happened between us was…" *Exquisite,* she thought, feeling heat rise up her neck into her face. If she thought it would help, she would have begged him to go. "I told you why nothing more can happen between us."

"Because the guy who abused you is dangerous. And if he finds you, he might come after me."

"If he finds me, he *will* come after you."

Josh kept his eyes locked on hers. "If," he repeated. "Last night you said he doesn't know where you are. How can you be sure?"

Regan's thoughts flashed to Langley. The only peace of mind she had was in knowing the P.I. was observing Payne Creath and would e-mail her if the homicide cop left New Orleans.

"I'm having him…watched."

"So, we can consider the coast is clear for now."

She tightened her fingers on his wrists as if holding back the strength of longing that threatened to weaken her resolve. "That doesn't matter—"

"Have you ever seen a moonstar, Regan?"

His sudden change of subject had her shaking her head. "I don't know what that is."

"Go with me tonight so I can show you."

"I'm working tonight." She stepped back from him. In her mind, the distance was much wider than the simple movement.

As if reading her thoughts, Josh closed the space between them. "When you get off, then."

"I have to check on Etta."

"Fine, come home and do that. I'll wait for you in my car. All you have to do is walk across the lawn, step around the hedge. It'll be dark, no one will know we're together. No one will see us."

"Josh—"

He held his palms up toward her. "No touching," he said. "No kissing. I just want to share something wonderful with you. Just you."

She tried to think, consider the consequences while temptation rose inside her like a gilded god from the sea. Caught between common sense and feelings, she didn't know what to do.

Turning to the counter, she reclaimed the wooden spoon with a hand that wasn't quiet steady and began drizzling glaze over the lemon tea bread. She knew whatever it was about Josh Mc-Call that called to her should frighten her, but right now it just left her…defenseless. And so very tempted.

"I have to think about it," she said without meeting his gaze.

"The decision's yours, Regan. I'll be in my car, waiting for you."

Chapter 8

Payne Creath munched on a sugar-covered beignet while he strolled through Jackson Square. Dressed in a lightweight suit, gold detectives' badge clipped to his belt, he mixed with the tourists braving a typical New Orleans summer day, the humidity almost as high as the temperature. With his internal radar pinging, the heat was only a nebulous irritant.

Someone was watching him.

Creath had no doubt he was under surveillance, although he had yet to spot his watcher. Hadn't figured out who had closed in on him.

He just knew someone had.

The feeling first hit him three days ago when his innate cop instinct sounded a warning. He had learned long ago that when a smoke alarm went off, that meant there was smoke somewhere. Even if it was the kind that couldn't be seen, it was still *there*.

As was his observer.

The minute he'd felt the surveillance he stopped talking to

his informants, to his acquaintances, to other cops. He was living in a self-imposed pool of isolation, but he didn't know why. He would find out. Eventually.

Meanwhile, he spent as much time as he could out in the open, waiting for the watcher to show himself.

Or herself.

After finishing the beignet, Creath reached into the plastic bag he habitually carried in his pocket, retrieved a peppermint, unwrapped it and popped it into his mouth. Beneath his suit coat, he felt the comfortable weight of the Ruger holstered against his left ribs. He paused near one of the square's itinerant artists whose hands flew across a pad as he sketched a caricature of a sloe-eyed blonde with a hotly painted mouth.

The blonde's murderous-red glossed lips threw a mental switch, shooting Creath back to his helpless, defenseless childhood. To the hours he'd endured in the dark closet. Day after day, year after year spent breathing air that held a woman's vile musky scent.

The sudden blare of brassy jazz jerked Creath from the past. He sliced his gaze to a nearby trio of dark-skinned street musicians while bitterness, lodged deep for years, burned like acid in his gut. Taking a controlled breath, he willed his system to level. Refocused on the business at hand.

His watcher.

Creath had been careful in all his past dealings, damn careful. He'd worked enough homicides to know he had left nothing to chance. So he was certain the watcher wasn't some rat squad flunky from Internal Affairs. Or from any other law enforcement entity, for that matter. Still, whoever had him under surveillance was experienced enough to stay hidden. So far.

His eyes shielded by dark glasses, Creath scanned the square, his gaze slicking over the throng of sweltering tourists, lines of vendors, the silver-painted street performer dressed like an angel who stood statue-still in front of the St. Louis Cathedral. He saw no sign, no hint of anyone surveilling him.

Forcing his mind to remain locked in the present, he looked back at the blonde, her red-glossed mouth now settled into a pout. He had no wife, no woman in his life who would have reason to hire someone to follow him.

No woman in his life, but one.

Susan. She'd gone to ground a year ago, was too smart to risk returning to New Orleans to check on his whereabouts. Yet human nature dictated that she would constantly be looking over her shoulder, eternally fighting the paranoia that clawed at the edges of her mind. No matter where she was, despite how well concealed, she would want some sort of assurance he hadn't caught her scent. Wasn't about to close in on her hiding place. To obtain that, she would have to hire someone to watch him.

The hope she had done just that sent the slow fire of anticipation spreading through Creath's veins. He was the supreme hunter. When he caught up with the watcher—and he *would* catch up—he was prepared to do whatever it took to get a lead to Susan's whereabouts. All he needed was one small tear in his quarry's cover, one hole he could peer through. Then he would find the bitch who, by leaving him, had turned something good into gut-searing, relentless pain.

Time and fate were on his side. No matter how long it took, he would find her. When he did, he would put the second murder charge against her into play. Then he would slap her in cuffs and lock her in a cell. A dark cell that over the days, weeks, years would fill with her vile, musky female scent.

Susan Kincaid would have the rest of her life to think about what she'd done. About how wrong she'd been to reject him.

Hours later, Josh stood in his upstairs bedroom window, watching the headlights of Regan's Mustang turn into the driveway next door. When she walked along the moonlight-bathed sidewalk toward Etta's house, his thoughts centered on the alluring swing of her slim hips encased in snug denim.

In the silver light she looked small. Vulnerable. Watching her, he felt something inside him clench. Whatever that something was, he in no way wanted to examine it too closely. Not while so many unanswered questions loomed about her past. About the woman herself.

He tugged his keys out of the pocket of his faded cutoffs, headed down the staircase, then eased out the back door into the warm, silent night. With the Corvette's top already down, he slid over the door into the driver's seat.

All he could do now was wait, and hope Etta's sexy, dark-haired bartender-caregiver took him up on his offer.

Whoever the hell she was.

Resting his head back against the seat, he watched a pair of fireflies hover over the windshield while he reviewed what he'd learned that day.

According to Nate, the check on the Mustang revealed it was registered to Regan Ford in Sundown, Oklahoma. Josh hadn't been surprised. Nor had he raised a brow when his own phone call to his IRS contact unearthed the fact the government had no record of a Regan Ford ever having paid federal income tax.

For Josh, it wasn't a giant mental step to connect the dots. She was hiding from the bastard who'd abused her—using her real name would be like painting a target on her forehead. So, she'd adopted an alias.

Since there were no fraud alerts issued on a stolen identity under the Regan Ford name, he figured she'd stopped by some newspaper's morgue or a cemetery and obtained the name of a female who'd been born around the same year she had. Then died young. A request at a courthouse would have gotten her a copy of the real Regan Ford's birth certificate. Having that enabled her to obtain a driver's license. Which was the type of ID required to register the Mustang.

For the most part, it had probably taken her only a few steps to become someone else.

Who the hell was the woman behind the alias?

He could maybe start finding out by running the aka through Internet databases of birth records. Regan, after all, was an unusual first name. Once he found out the state in which she'd created her alias, he could take things from there.

He scowled at the fireflies bombarding the windshield. Women were *not* a mystery to him. He knew what they were about; he always had. Inside an hour of a first meeting, he could usually find out about a woman's past, her family, her job—hell, even her bra size. With Regan, he'd gotten nowhere. Maybe the fact he couldn't figure up from down about her was why he was so intrigued. And why he wanted her to *tell* him about herself rather than him digging it out of a database.

He didn't think she was lying, but he knew she wasn't telling him the whole truth. Meaning the whole truth was probably big and bad. Which only made him want to help her that much more.

"Dammit," he muttered, shoving a hand through his hair.

He knew it was going to take some finesse on his part to get her to open up to him. Hiding out, being someone she wasn't, had to put enormous pressure on her. He didn't want to add more. But somehow, *someway,* he needed to get her to trust him enough to confide in him. Trust him, so he could figure out how to keep the woman he had begun to feel something for safe.

It was hard to believe they'd met less than a week ago. All he'd wanted when he'd stopped by Truelove's Tavern the night he arrived in Sundown was one of Howie's excellent burgers and a cold brew. The instant he'd spotted Regan behind the bar things had begun getting complicated. Always before, he'd made a point to avoid relationships that showed any sign of complications.

Now, avoidance was the last thing he wanted.

A faint scrape of footsteps had him turning his head. He caught the subtle lemony scent of Regan's soap an instant before she stepped around the hedge.

Silently, she opened the passenger door and slid into the seat beside him. She'd taken time to change into a black tank top and shorts. Her dark hair was tugged ponytail-style through the back loop of a gray baseball cap that was pulled down low. Sunglasses rode high on the bridge of her nose.

He didn't have to wonder about the reason for her attempt at disguise. This was the first time they'd been on what might be perceived as a date. If any of the locals glimpsed them driving together, Sundown's rumor mill would heat up with speculation. She was terrified her abuser would find her, might somehow get a whiff there was something between her and the cop next door, which would send her abuser after *him*. Josh felt his chest tighten at her attempt to protect him.

"How's your patient?" he asked quietly.

"Etta's sound asleep," Regan said, keeping her gaze focused out the windshield. "It should be only a couple more days before Doc Zink switches her from IV antibiotics to a pill form."

And only a matter of time until you leave Sundown. Josh blinked against a sudden clench in his gut. He knew next to nothing about the woman beside him, yet all he wanted to do was hold on to her.

"That's a great disguise, Regan. Can you see anything through those shades?"

"I shouldn't even be with you," she said, her whisper-soft voice thready with nerves. "I don't know why I'm here. Just drive, okay?"

He regarded her, overwhelmed with a need to protect he'd felt for no one before. He wanted to tell her he could help her if she'd just give him her real name. And the name of the bastard she was hiding from. But he didn't want her to stiffen up and climb out of the car, so he let it pass. For now.

He cranked on the key; the 'Vette's engine came to life, more like a powerful animal waking than a machine. He backed out of the driveway, then steered toward the lake, the headlights slicing through the darkness.

The night air flowed across his skin while earthy, mellow blues from the CD player filled the silence between them. When he steered onto the tree-lined road that edged the water, ghostly moonlight broke through the canopy of leaves.

Ten minutes later, he swung the 'Vette to the side of the road at the base of Sundown Ridge. When he cut off the engine, the heavy hush of night surrounded them.

Beside him, Regan sat scrunched down in the seat, the ball cap and sunglasses blocking his view of her face. He ached, he discovered. Just looking at her made him ache. He fought the need to pull her into his arms, feel again the press of her mouth against his, the hammering of her pulse at the base of her throat. He'd promised to keep his hands and his mouth off her tonight, and he intended to keep his word. Was determined it would be Regan who made the next move.

"Enjoy the ride?" he asked.

"I see the moon and the stars, but that's it." She inched the glasses down the bridge of her nose and peered at him. "You promised to show me a moonstar, whatever that is. Did I fall for some cheesy ploy to get me off somewhere in the dark?"

"One thing you need to learn about me is that I'm a man of my word." He climbed out, rounded the hood and opened her door. "We have to make a short climb, but it's worth it."

He waited until she stood beside him then he pulled off her cap.

"Hey—"

"We didn't pass one car on the way here," he said, tossing the cap on the dash. "No one else is around, Regan. It's safe for you to ditch the disguise." He dipped his head. "You're safe with me."

She hesitated, then pulled off her sunglasses and left them beside the cap.

With moonlight illuminating the way, he led her up a narrow graveled path to a clearing halfway up the ridge. There, he settled down on a slab of rock and patted the spot beside him. "Have a seat. This is the place to get the best view."

She eyed him, her face bathed in silver light and shadow. "This better be good, McCall."

"Good doesn't begin to describe it," he said as she sat beside him. He inclined his head in the direction of the huge butterball moon hanging low over the lake. Silvery light reflected off its surface like shards of glass. "What do you think?"

She followed his gaze, remained still for a moment. "It's beautiful," she said quietly.

"Moonstars. That only happens when the moon is full," he said, watching her. "Around this time of night."

She glanced up at the ridge, then looked back at him. "Wouldn't the view of the water be even better from the top?"

"Beats me, I've never been up there."

She pursed her mouth. "According to the locals, that's the premier make-out spot for teenagers. It's hard to believe the guy who once raided the Camp Fire Girls overnight jamboree has never taken a date up to Sundown Ridge."

"Believe it." He wanted to touch her so badly, he had to curl his fingers into his palms to quell the urge. "The ridge is cursed."

"Cursed?"

"That's right."

"I've been in this town for six months and I haven't heard about any curse connected with Sundown Ridge."

"That's because most people think it's a place of good luck."

She leaned back on her elbows, her body slim and sleek, her bare legs shimmering in the moonlight. He wanted those legs wrapped around him. Wanted *her*.

"I'm waiting," she said.

So am I, he thought with resignation. "There's a general belief around town that when a man takes a woman to Sundown Ridge, he'll wind up marrying her."

She swiped her bangs away from her eyes. "So, you view marriage as a curse?"

"Not so much a curse as something to be avoided."

"Why? Did some woman sink her claws into you and break your heart?"

"Not me. I've just paid attention to what my sisters and brothers have gone through when it comes to matters of the heart."

"For instance?"

"Nate got dumped by his beauty queen fiancée two days before their wedding. Bran's wife, Patience, died of an aneurysm. A few years later, he and Tory eloped and they went through some rough times before things between them settled down. Morgan's college sweetheart walked out on her while she was in a coma, and Grace's first husband died in the line of duty. I've seen the people I care most about totally devastated, all in the name of love. It makes me wonder if getting that close to someone is worth it."

"I take it where you're concerned, no woman has ever merited that kind of risk?"

"No." He let his gaze skim from her soft, angular profile, down her slender, delicate frame. For the first time in his life, he was beginning to think lowering the walls he'd erected around his heart might outweigh the risk.

"What about you?" he asked. "Has any man been worth taking a chance on?"

She pulled her bottom lip between her teeth. "I was engaged once."

"Things didn't work out?"

He saw emotion flicker over her face before she turned her head away. "He died."

"Sorry. I didn't mean to bring up bad memories."

"It seems like a lifetime ago." She lifted her chin, her gaze sliding back up to the top of the ridge. "So, to hedge your bets you avoid going up on Sundown Ridge."

"Location's important when you're talking real estate and gunshot wounds. Not so essential when it comes to finding a spot to conduct a little romance."

She turned her head so she faced him fully, her mouth curving. "Is this one of those spots where you bring women, McCall? Do you woo them into your arms by showing them moonstars?"

"No, Ford, I conduct my wooing elsewhere. *This* is where I come when I need to do some thinking and want to be alone." He angled his chin. "I've never brought anyone else here. Until tonight."

The intimacy in his voice was like a velvet glove against Regan's flesh, sending a tremor up her spine. She sat up slowly, her smile fading. "Why me?" she asked quietly. "Why bring me here?"

"You're on the run. Cut off from friends. Family. People you love. I just figured you might need a place to come and think about that other life you left behind."

She squeezed her eyes shut briefly. The fact he had even thought about that, considered how alone she felt had a myriad of emotions sweeping through her. Instantly she tried to block them, reminding herself she couldn't afford too many good feelings toward Josh McCall. *The cop*.

Yet, her heart wasn't listening to the strict common sense she had imposed on it. With the spicy scent of his aftershave filling her lungs, she felt everything closing in on her—the need to flee Sundown, her desperate desire to stay. Her growing feelings for Josh which, until this moment, she'd steadfastly refused to acknowledge.

"It has to be hard," he continued as he shifted his gaze back to the lake, "not to have someone to talk things out with. To share your feelings with."

Harder than you'll ever know, she agreed silently, achingly aware she'd opened herself up more with him than she had with any man since Steven.

Tears blurred her vision as she pictured the memorial service, her fiancé's coffin disappearing into his family's lichen-covered crypt in a New Orleans cemetery. His killer, Payne Creath, standing amid the mourners, offering her solace.

She kept her gaze locked on the moonlight glistening on the water like icy diamonds until the press of memories eased. Acknowledging that the hold she held on her control was tenuous, she diverted the subject away from herself. "When was the last time you came here just to think?"

Josh took a moment to answer. "About a month ago."

She looked back at him. "Etta didn't mention you were in Sundown."

"Etta didn't know. It was a turnaround trip. I drove down from the city, spent a couple of hours here, then I headed back for a session with Internal Affairs."

Regan kept her eyes steady on his. It was her own session with a New Orleans PD Internal Affairs cop that made her realize how effectively Creath had blocked her from getting help from anyone in law enforcement. "Internal Affairs," she said evenly. "Don't they investigate wrongdoing by cops?"

"Exactly. I'd been accused of several things."

"Such as?"

"Evidence tampering, attempting to frame a suspect." When she remained silent, Josh looked back at her. "Aren't you going to ask me why I did it?"

"Being accused doesn't mean you're guilty."

"I'm living proof of that," he murmured. He leaned forward, resting his elbows on his knees. "My partner and I were tracking a dirtbag who'd attacked six women. He raped and beat them, then forced them to take a shower to wash off forensic evidence. We pegged him the Shower Stall Rapist. An anonymous tip led us to a rich kid named Wahlberg. We gathered information on him that was enough to get a search warrant for his place, but not to make an arrest. Before we could serve the warrant, we got called to another scene where the MO matched the Shower Stall Rapist's."

Regan remained silent, studying Josh. He seemed lost in thought, his profile hard and unyielding.

After a moment, he continued. "My partner and I worked the crime scene while another team of detectives served the search warrant. I left my partner to wrap up things at the rape scene while I went to Wahlberg's apartment to help wind up the search. We were getting ready to leave when one of the detectives who served the warrant did a final walk-through of the place. He noticed a minuscule blot of white sticking out from under the bed. He thought it was strange no one had noticed it before."

"What was it?"

"A pair of women's panties. Forensics later matched them to the last rape victim."

"That's good, isn't it?"

"It would have been if any of the cops who'd already searched the bedroom had noticed the panties. The theory was they'd been planted. Since the crime-scene logs showed I was the only cop who'd been at the rape scene, then at Wahlberg's apartment, the suspicion fell on me."

Regan heard the bitterness tinged with frustration in his voice. "And so you wound up at Internal Affairs," she said quietly.

He nodded. "I've got a rep for being able to dig up evidence on dirtbags that a lot of cops can't get. That's mainly because I've made a point to keep in touch with some of the less-than-savory contacts I made during my rebellious youth." As he spoke, Josh trailed a fingertip along the thin scar winding out of his collar on the right side of his neck. "And I don't mind cutting corners to get what I need to take down a piece of scum. But I don't break the law to get it." He lifted a shoulder. "Even so, a lot of cops thought I'd planted the evidence in Wahlberg's bedroom. My own captain made noises about standing behind me, but I knew he thought I'd done it. After a couple of weeks of other cops giving me suspicious looks I got close to walking into the chief's office and tossing my badge on his desk."

"Why didn't you?"

"Two reasons. My family believed in me. And I was innocent."

So was she. Regan curled her hands into fists so he couldn't see them shake. "What happened?"

"I kept going over things, making lists of everyone I'd seen at the rape scene, then at Wahlberg's apartment, and comparing them to the scene logs. Nothing. Then I remembered something."

"What?"

"Like I said, Wahlberg was a rich kid, his family high profile. One of the TV stations had gotten wind we were serving a warrant on his place, so they set up outside and filmed sound bites. I went to the station and reviewed their tapes, over and over. I finally caught a glimpse of an assistant D.A. named Rhodd whose name hadn't shown up on the Wahlberg scene log. It wasn't until then that I remembered seeing him at the rape scene, too."

"Why was an assistant D.A. at either place?"

"Most all the A.D.A.'s show up at crime scenes occasionally, so it wasn't a big deal that he'd been there. Besides, his boss is retiring next year, and Rhodd had already announced he was running for the job as the 'tough on crime' candidate. He knew his prosecuting the Shower Stall Rapist, who'd had every woman in Oklahoma City looking over her shoulder, would cinch the election. After I saw Rhodd on the video, I asked around, and a couple of uniforms also remembered him showing up at the rape scene."

"Why wasn't his name on either log?"

"At the rape scene a rookie was filling out the log. There were detectives, CSIs, EMTs all over the place, and the rookie couldn't keep up. Rhodd just detoured around him and walked on in. He used the same type of move to get into Wahlberg's apartment. Just slipped in."

"So, he stole a pair of the victim's panties, then took them to Wahlberg's apartment and planted them under the bed?"

"That was my theory."

Regan had theories about Payne Creath, but nothing she could prove. "Since you're still a cop, I take it you figured out a way to prove Rhodd did that?"

"Actually, I got lucky," Josh replied. "The lab found one of Rhodd's hairs inside the panties. He'd have had to handle them in order for the hair to get where it was."

"And that put you in the clear?"

"After a month of suspension, yeah. Rhodd's now a former A.D.A., with felony charges pending against him."

With emotion flooding through her, Regan pushed off the rock and moved to the edge of the clearing. "Why did Rhodd want to set you up?" she asked, aware only after she'd spoken that her voice sounded thick. Tight.

"His intention was to cement the evidence against Wahlberg, not set me up. I just happened to get in the way of a power-hungry A.D.A.'s wrecking ball."

Wrapping her arms around her waist, she stared at the moon. "If Rhodd hadn't shown up on that TV news tape, you'd have lost your badge, maybe wound up in jail. Would you have just been able to accept that?"

"Hell, no. I was innocent. I'd have kept digging for evidence. Looking for a way to clear my name."

Langley, the P.I. she had watching Creath, had assured her the evidence Creath had manufactured against her was compelling and unbeatable. When her lips trembled, Regan gave thanks that Josh couldn't see her face. She just needed a minute, she told herself. Time to pull back, get a grip on control before she told him it was time to take her home.

Home. Whom was she trying to kid? Etta's house was just

a port in the storm in the roiling ocean that was her life. She didn't have a home, would never again have one. She pressed her fingertips against her lips and tried to will the moment to pass. She was so tired, *so scared*. Sick from knowing that any minute her secret might be revealed. Then she'd be in jail for killing the man she'd loved and planned to spend her life with.

A tear escaped and slid down her cheek. She dashed it away, then wrapped her arms tighter around her waist, aching inside.

Here she was, sharing a moment in time with another man she was very afraid she could fall in love with. A man whose life she risked just by going with him for a drive in the moonlight. Oh God, she felt so lost. Alone. She wanted—desperately wanted to have someone to share things with, to belong. She just wanted to feel normal again.

But her life was far from normal and she had no way to change things. It had been wrong of her to come here with Josh. Risky and careless and selfish. Using her fingertips to swipe away another tear, she dragged in a breath. Then another.

When she felt steadier, she turned. Only then did she realize Josh was no longer sitting on the rock, but standing only inches from her.

The dim light deepened the hollows in his face, casting his eyes into shadow. Even though they weren't touching, it was as if she could feel the strength in him. He could be fierce, she imagined, just as easily as he could be gentle.

She forced her mouth to curve. "I'm glad things worked out for you. That you got to keep your badge."

"So am I."

"And I appreciate you sharing your thinking spot with me, McCall. I might use it sometime. I'd better get back to Etta's."

"You'll get there in time. Right now you're on the verge of tears, and I don't figure it's because I told you about my brush with losing my badge." His dark gaze focused on her like a laser. "Talk to me, Regan."

She retreated a step back. "I'm not close to tears."

"I've got three sisters. I know when a woman is on the verge of opening the floodgates. They'd all tell you they highly recommend a good cry as a way to vent. Purge."

"I don't need a good cry. I don't need anything...." Except a life where she wasn't constantly in turmoil. Forever afraid.

Turning her back on him, she covered her face with her hands and broke.

"That's a good start," Josh murmured. His hands settled gently on her shoulders, turning her to face him. "Get it all out." He drew her close, stroking her hair. "All of it."

The tears came as if there was no end to them. It didn't matter that Josh McCall wore a badge. His arms were strong, his voice understanding. With her face buried against his chest, Regan sobbed out the grief, the frustration, the fear.

One of his hands slid up her back to close over the nape of her neck while the other continued stroking her hair. She kept her face pressed against his chest, relying on his strength now that her own had evaporated. His small gift of comfort meant more to her than she should have let it.

As the tears passed, she leaned back, wiping them from her cheeks with the back of her hands. "I'm sorry. Dammit." Her breath came out shaky and she would have pulled away, but he continued to hold her.

"Nothing to be sorry about," he said quietly. "It's not healthy to hold everything in."

"I got your T-shirt all wet."

"It'll dry." He skimmed his hand from her hair to her cheek. The tender, caring gesture sent a quick, sharp pang of arousal through her. She didn't want to want him. But she did. Standing there, his strong, sturdy arms around her and moonstars glittering in the distance, he was all she wanted.

"What's in your past, Regan?"

The question should have been enough to have her pulling

away. Instead she leaned toward him. It was only a hint of surrender, but it was enough to appall her, knowing for an instant she'd been tempted to tell him.

Too tempted.

Her heart took one hard, violent leap into her throat that was part fear, part long-suppressed desire. *He's a cop,* she reminded herself. If she told him the truth, he would lock her in a cage—no matter what was between them. He would do what had to be done. And it wasn't just her fear of going to jail that held her back. His arresting her would forge an undeniable link between them. She knew better than anyone how methodical, how thorough Payne Creath was. He would want to know exactly how a vacationing cop had gotten close enough to her to unearth her secrets. No, even if she wanted to tell Josh the truth, she couldn't. Not when doing so would risk his life.

"Tell me," he repeated softly.

Her throat was burning dry. Why was she drawn to him again and again, when all she should do was step away? "I can't."

"Regan—"

"I'm sorry." She slipped from his arms, but continued to face him. After the solace he'd given her she couldn't turn her back on him. "I've told you all I can."

His jaw set, Josh kept his gaze locked on her face. She'd paled, and he saw what was now a familiar glimmer of fear in her eyes when she took another step back. He clamped a lid on the frustration and edgy need that rippled inside him.

She swept a hand toward the lake. "Thank you for sharing your moonstars. And lending me a shoulder to cry on." She attempted a smile that didn't gel. "You're a good man, Josh McCall. I won't ever forget you."

The finality in her tone sent something hot and lethal spreading in his gut. Dammit, no woman had ever made him feel this shaky. Unsettled. "You sound like you're saying goodbye."

"I shouldn't have come here with you." She shoved a hand through her dark hair, leaving it tousled. "I can't do this, Josh. I can't be with you. Anywhere. I need to get back to Etta's."

"Fine." Her secrets were still her secrets, and his desire to unravel them was stronger than ever.

When she started to turn, he put a finger under her chin, stilling her movement. While she didn't jerk away, she did shoot up an invisible wall.

He slicked his thumb over her bottom lip, and felt her tremble. The reaction was enough to cement his determination. If he couldn't get over that wall of secrecy she'd erected, he'd damn well tear it down with his bare hands.

I want you, was all he could think.

"I'll take you back, Regan, but we haven't finished with each other," he said in a low, murmured challenge. "Not by a long shot. And we both know it."

Chapter 9

Because Seamus O'Toole had driven to Dallas to handle a business matter, Josh and Chief Decker had to wait a day to interview the used car dealership owner. They caught up with O'Toole early in the morning in the parking lot of a busy stop-and-rob convenience store a mile from Paradise Lake.

Since the peeper case was Decker's, Josh chose to stay in the background, leaning against the front of the patrol car. Already the June air was heating, raising a sheen of sweat over his skin.

Decker stepped up to the lemon-yellow pickup displaying a dealer's tag in the next parking space just as O'Toole used his remote to unlock the driver's door. "Mr. O'Toole, we need a word with you."

O'Toole turned, eyed Decker in his sharply pressed uniform before flicking Josh a look. "Who's he?"

"Sergeant McCall. We're working on a case where your name came up."

"Yeah? What case?"

O'Toole was approximately six foot two and weighed around two hundred pounds, Josh estimated. His face was round; thatches of gray edged the temples of the dark hair combed in a style that Elvis would have favored. He was dressed in olive pants and a stained T-shirt that strained over his gut. Two plastic bags dangled from his right hand, a twelve-pack of beer was clenched in his left.

"You were spotted out walking the other night around 1:00 a.m.," Decker said.

"There a law against taking a stroll?"

"A burglary occurred in the vicinity of where you were seen. We need to know if you saw anyone during your stroll."

"Nope." O'Toole shrugged. "Least I don't remember if I did."

Decker nudged his mirrored sunglasses up the bridge of his nose. "If you did see someone, why wouldn't you remember?"

"'Cause I was strolling home from Truelove's."

"You telling me you were drunk?"

"I'm saying I had one too many." O'Toole hoisted the beer and bags into the back of the pickup, then turned to Decker, his eyes telegraphing his annoyance. "I don't remember seeing nobody, so I can't help you."

"Someone mentioned you were talking to a nice-looking redhead at Truelove's," Decker said.

Josh sent a mental *attaboy* to the chief. His mention of Karen Nash, the woman whose black thong had been stolen during the burglary, was a bluff to see if O'Toole took the bait.

The puzzled look on his face told Josh he hadn't.

"I didn't talk to no redhead."

"Since you had one too many, how would you know?" Decker asked mildly.

O'Toole's face reddened. "I don't know nothing about a burglary or a redhead. You want to stop wasting my time and do some real police work? Find out who unlocked my back gate, unscrewed the porch light and scared my wife."

Josh pushed away from the patrol car while sharing a look with Decker. "When did that happen?" Decker asked.

"Hell, I don't know," O'Toole said. "Ask Yolanda."

"I will," Decker said. "I don't remember a report about this."

"I don't think she called the cops, either time."

Josh raised a brow. "It happened more than once?"

"Both nights I was out fishing." He checked his watch. "Which is where I ought to be now. I'm ahead in points in the derby and I intend to win."

Decker held up a hand. "Who else has a key to your gate?"

"Nobody."

"How about your landlord?" Josh asked.

"It's my lock. I put it on so no kids would let Kinsey out."

"Kinsey?" Josh asked.

"My wife's miniature Chihuahua."

Decker angled his chin. "Was Kinsey in the yard on the nights the gate got unlocked?"

"No, in the house."

"Why didn't your wife report the incidents?" Josh asked.

"Ask her. I told her to, but she don't listen to me."

"You're sure about the gate key?" Decker asked. "No one else has one?"

"Yeah, I'm..." O'Toole's eyes narrowed. "Except Regan. She's that dark-haired bartender at Truelove's."

Josh took a step forward. "Ms. Ford has a key to your gate?"

"She's taken my keys away a couple of times. Kept 'em overnight. She could have had a copy made."

"Why would she do that?" Josh asked.

O'Toole's mouth curled. "I was trying to be friendly and she about tore off my thumb. Maybe the bitch wanted payback, decided to scare Yolanda."

Josh set his jaw. It was all he could do not to plow his fist into the idiot's face.

"We'll check that out, Mr. O'Toole," Decker said. "You can go now."

Through narrowed eyes, Josh tracked O'Toole as he backed the pickup out of the lot and turned toward the lake. "If that bastard was the peeper, I doubt he'd have mentioned unscrewing lightbulbs."

"I agree." Decker paused. "Did Regan tell you where she puts his keys when she confiscates them?"

"In a drawer behind the bar. She said he comes by the tavern after he sobers up to get them."

"While the day shift is there?"

"That I don't know."

"I'll stop by Etta's and ask Regan. You want to come?"

Josh diverted his gaze back to the lake road. While a steady stream of traffic rolled by, his thoughts went to the previous night. The woman who'd sobbed in his arms was on the edge. Vulnerable.

How would he feel, he wondered, if he'd had to cut himself off from his family, his friends, his job? His life. By doing that, Regan had placed herself in emotional isolation, refusing to let anyone past the wall she'd erected around herself. A wall made even more inviolable by her insistence on protecting *him*.

Dammit, how the hell could he keep her safe when she wouldn't open up to him, trust him?

He could taste the frustration, the edgy need inside him. He ached for a woman who wanted only distance from him. And if he didn't give it to her, she might take off.

The thought of her leaving, of never seeing Regan again put knots in his gut.

As far as he was concerned, life was about acquiring what he wanted, not losing it. For the first time, he didn't just want a woman, he wanted *this* woman. And all of his senses told him his only chance for success was to give her the space she demanded.

Right now wasn't the time to try to stretch Regan's rules.

Shoving a hand through his hair, he looked back at Decker. "There's an order of supplies I need to pick up at the lumber-yard. I'll leave Regan to you."

Decker nodded. "Since I'm not paying for your help on this case, you're calling the shots."

No, Josh thought. Not yet I'm not.

"This is the biggest turnout yet for the annual fish fry," Etta commented.

"Since A.C.'s marina is the main sponsor, I imagine he's happy," Regan replied as she steered Etta's wheelchair along the walk that led toward the lake.

When they reached the grassy bank that fronted the marina, Regan swept her gaze over the crowd. People milled around rows of tables covered with red-and-white-checked plastic cloths. Some sat at the tables, others on the grass. Babies were passed from hand to hand. The old had found spots in areas where the massive oaks provided shade against the still-searing early-evening sun. The young raced around them.

A stereo had been set up at the farthest point of the marina. A group of teenagers were gathered there.

As Regan edged the wheelchair up to the table where several of Etta's female cronies had congregated, it occurred to her that she knew the name of almost every person there. Some she recognized from the tavern, others she'd met on the times she'd attended church with Etta. Still others she'd come into contact with while at the market and other shops.

Soon she would have to leave the people and the town with its yawning pace that she'd begun to feel a part of. Knowing that was like a dull-edged knife to her heart.

"Regan, are you okay?" Etta asked, reaching out to squeeze her hand. "You went pale all of a sudden."

"It's just the heat," she improvised. She gave Etta's hand another squeeze before setting the brake on the wheelchair. "How about some iced tea?"

"That sounds good."

Less than five minutes later, Regan was back with foam cups filled with icy tea.

Etta took a sip. "That hits the spot." With her gray hair smoothly brushed, her blue shirtwaist dress perfectly ironed and color back in her cheeks, Etta looked like the picture of health. "It's good to get out of the house and be around other folks. I was going stir-crazy."

"Doc Zink said he'd stop by tomorrow evening after he's done at his clinic," Regan said as she settled into the chair beside Etta. "I think he'll lift your home detention."

"Does that mean no more IVs?" Etta asked, her lined face brightening.

"Yes. Your temperature's been normal for days and your ankle's healing. He'll probably prescribe antibiotics in pill form." Regan smiled. "When he does, I'll have to reprogram your recorder."

Etta chuckled. "That's all I need is another voice coming out of my memory box, reminding me to take more pills." She nodded toward the area in the distance where platters of fried fish, hot corn-on-the-cob and vats of coleslaw were being set out. "Well, now, there's someone we haven't seen in a couple of days."

Regan looked up, and felt everything inside her go still at the sight of Josh hauling a tray of pies to one of the tables. He was dressed in snug jeans and a white T-shirt. His dark hair ruffled in the breeze; a day's growth of stubble shadowed his jaw. While she watched him, the smell of good food and sounds of laughter faded from her mind.

Although Etta hadn't seen Josh for two days, he was all *she'd* seen, Regan thought. In the mornings when she'd gone out to jog she'd spotted him working on the roof of his house.

Stripped down to only faded cutoffs and a tool belt, his tanned muscles slicked with sweat, he'd distracted her so that she'd had to force herself to stay her course. Both evenings when she left for work he'd been in his front yard, cutting boards stretched over sawhorses. This afternoon when she went for a swim, he'd been working on the engine of the speedboat moored at the dock behind his house.

Each time she'd seen him she'd barely managed to keep her distance, caught on the thin edge between temptation and common sense.

Each time, he'd barely given her a glance.

Which was what she wanted, she reminded herself. What she'd demanded of him.

She pulled her gaze from his strong profile and forced herself to focus on the infant someone had settled in Etta's arms. Still, her thoughts remained on Josh. On the sturdiness she'd felt when he'd held her. On his compelling scent. His taste.

She closed her eyes against the desire thudding in her stomach. Desire she didn't dare sate. She reminded herself of the sudden urge she'd felt to tell him the truth about herself. The fact she'd even entertained doing that had scared the hell out of her. It still scared her. And was ample reason for her to stay away from him. Even if all she wanted was to step back into his arms.

"Just the woman I've been looking for."

Burns Yost's voice had Regan's muscles clenching tight. She gazed up into the reporter's round, pleasant face, thinking how benign he looked, dressed in a red golf shirt and khakis, with a newspaper folded under one arm. She knew his unassuming countenance masked a sharp mind that went after a story like a pit bull after a hunk of steak. And she was the story he wanted.

"Hello, Mr. Yost."

"Regan." He touched an index finger to the brim of the ball

cap that shaded his eyes. "Etta." His gaze swept the length of the table. "Ladies."

"Nice to see you, Burns," Etta said, adding to the chorus of greetings he received. Grinning, she bounced the baby in her arms. "This here's Mildred England's new granddaughter. You ought to put this angel's picture on the front page of the *Sundown Sentinel*."

"She sure is pretty," Yost said, then sliced his gaze back to Regan. "I thought you might like an advanced copy of tomorrow's edition."

He dropped the newspaper, faceup, on the table in front of Regan. She looked down and said nothing.

There was a well-framed, very clear picture of her standing beside the car at the accident scene, her skin and clothes smeared with blood. The photograph had captured the agony she'd felt moments after Amelia died.

The column beneath it was brief, giving her name and a summary of the accident.

Her gaze locked on the photograph of herself, Regan felt her already tenuous hold on control slip further. Her lungs seemed unable to pull in enough air. She pressed a hand to her stomach and tensed against the emotions that were buffeting her like hurricane winds.

"Who…took this?" she managed.

"Quentin Peterson," Yost said. "He used his cell phone to call the paramedics, then stayed on it to relate information to them."

A wave of dizzy faintness swept over her. Sweat pooled beneath her shorts and cotton tee.

"Peterson's cell is a photo phone." Smiling, Yost tapped an index finger against the newspaper. "I've posted your picture on the *Sentinel*'s Web site. And made calls to a few of my contacts in the business. I'm hoping one of the wire services'll run the photo."

Someone hollered Yost's name and he glanced over his

shoulder. He waved, then looked back at Regan. "Even though you wouldn't give me an interview, I might make you famous. Have a good evening."

Regan sat motionless. She was outdoors, no walls around her, yet she felt everything closing in on her, getting tighter until there wasn't any air to breathe. One long, sick crest of nausea rolled through her stomach. "I've...got to go."

Etta stopped rocking the baby. "Regan, what's wrong?"

"I don't feel well." With muscles that felt like glass, she turned the newspaper over so her picture was facedown, then rose, her legs trembling. "Can you get...A.C. to bring...you home?"

"Of course. Regan—"

"I've got...to go."

Josh had seen Burns Yost approach the table where Regan and Etta sat. Since he was like most cops and entertained an active distrust of the press, he was considering rethinking his decision to give Regan a wide berth when he felt a tug on his jeans.

"Mr. Josh?"

He glanced down and grinned at the towhead with a short, turned-up nose and big ears he would hopefully grow into. "Hey, Tommy, what's up?"

"Have you ever shot a bad guy?"

Josh crouched. The kid had on dirt-streaked shorts and a T-shirt with a miniature badge pinned in its center. Wrapped around his skinny hips was a gun belt with a holster holding a toy pistol.

"I've never shot a bad guy," Josh said gravely. He skimmed a fingertip over the plastic badge. "How about you, Officer?"

"My brother was robbin' the bank yesterday, so I shot him dead."

"Is that so?"

"Yeah. Then my mom made me take a nap."

Josh stifled a laugh. "Catching robbers is tiring business."

Just then, another boy streaked by, knocking Tommy on the arm and yelling, "Tag, you're it!"

"Am not!" Tommy bellowed and took off in pursuit.

Chuckling, Josh rose and glanced again at the table. His eyes narrowed. Both Yost and Regan were gone and Etta was waving madly in his direction. The closer he got, the more pronounced the lines of concern in her face.

"Etta, what's wrong?"

"It's Regan. She just up and walked off. I don't know if she's sick or upset, or both."

The cop in him zeroed in on one word. "Upset over what?"

"This." Etta flipped over the newspaper lying on the table. "Burns brought her a copy of tomorrow's *Sentinel*. When Regan saw her picture on the front page she turned as pale as chalk. And she got even paler when Burns said her picture's on the Internet. And he's trying to get one of the wire services to pick it up."

Christ. Josh didn't have to wonder what was wrong. The last thing someone in hiding needed was publicity.

"Joshua, she shouldn't drive while she's in that state."

"She won't."

He spotted Regan in the graveled parking lot, stumbling toward her Mustang. He caught up with her just as she wrenched open the driver's door.

He locked a hand on her arm, pulled her around to face him. "Regan—"

She jerked back, tried to twist away. "Let go."

He grabbed her other arm, held her still. She was shaking, trembling; her skin felt clammy under his hands. Her face was colorless except for the deep pools of her eyes, which flashed with panic. He knew full well he was looking at a woman whose mind was racing to find a way out.

"Regan, I know about the picture. I know you're scared."

"Leave me alone." She shoved at him, sick and desperate.

Hands were squeezing her heart, making it pound in an irregular cadence. All she could see was Creath's face, smell the scent of the peppermint candy that hung on his breath. He would see her picture. *Find her.* Heat closed around her like a fist. She felt ill from the terror burning inside her.

"I...have to...leave."

"With me," Josh said as he swept her into his arms.

"No!"

"Yes." Using his thigh, he closed the Mustang's door, then carried her to his 'Vette. With the top down, he leaned over the door and settled her into.the passenger's seat. He skirted the hood, climbed behind the wheel.

She would have shoved open the door but her vision was dimming and there were bands around her head, around her chest. "I can't...breathe."

"Yes, you can." Setting his jaw, he put a hand on the back of her head and shoved it between her knees. "Take a slow breath." Although his gut was knotted tight, he forced a calmness into his voice. "Then let it out. Take another one." He skimmed his palm up and down her spine. "In and out. That's it."

The knots in his belly stayed clenched until her breathing evened out.

She raised her head. She felt far from steady, but at least the boulder was no longer sitting on her chest. "I'm okay now."

"You're better, but you're not okay," Josh bit out. He yanked her seat belt around her and fastened it, then fired up the engine, turned out of the lot and steered for home.

Still weak and half-nauseated, Regan put her head back against the seat. She felt incapable of doing anything but closing her eyes while the evening air cooled her heated flesh.

When Josh pulled into his driveway, she opened her eyes, took one long breath. "Thanks for the ride. I'm fine now."

With her system starting to settle she'd be able to think. Plan.

Oh, God, Burns Yost had posted her picture on the Internet. Had Creath already seen it?

She started trembling all over again.

"Fine, my ass," Josh grated. He was out of the car and had her door open before she could react.

She started to stand, felt her legs go wobbly. She lowered back to the seat. "I just need another minute. Maybe two."

"Take all the time you want," he said, then lifted her into his arms.

She had enough strength to press a fist against his rock-solid chest. "What are you doing?"

"Taking care of you," he said as he headed toward his house.

She could have resisted, she knew. Could have demanded he put her down. But her lungs ached and her head felt clogged with too many thoughts. Too many fears. And his arms were strong, his scent compelling. Just until she felt a little stronger, she told herself. She would stay with him until her mind cleared.

Josh carried her through the wood-planked hallway into the living room where walls of books flanked the leather couch and matching chairs. An oval area rug spread a bright pattern across the wood floor.

"I really do feel better," she said as he settled her into one corner of the couch.

He cupped her face in his hands and leaned in. For the first time she saw the turbulence in his dark eyes. "Tell that to the guy who can't see how pale you are. Or feel you shaking."

She curled her fingers around his wrists and felt something inside her stir that was far removed from the cold fear that held her in its grip. "Thank you for taking care of me."

He gazed into her eyes for a long moment. He couldn't stand to see her sitting there, trembling, her face white. From the moment he'd known she was on the run, he'd felt useless to help her. Totally useless. Now, Burns Yost had unknowingly upped the stakes and Josh wasn't going to let her push him away again. He just needed to figure out the best way to deal with her.

"You're welcome." He straightened, then headed across the room to the small wet bar tucked into one corner. He retrieved a snifter, splashed in a liberal amount of brandy, then strode back across the room.

"This should help the shakes," he said, offering Regan the snifter.

"Thank you."

She took the first drink as medicine. He could see that in the way she tossed it back then shuddered hard. Still, it didn't bring the color back to her face.

The frustration he'd held leashed for days surfaced. "I don't want your thanks," he ground out. "I want you to trust me. I want you to tell me who the hell it is you're hiding from. I'll deal with him so he can't ever hurt you again."

You're so wrong, Regan thought as she stared down into the brandy. If she told him about Creath, Josh would find out she was wanted for murder and lock her in a cell. And Creath would have his revenge. He would never stop hurting her.

She raised the snifter to her lips, took another long swallow. The brandy slid down her throat like hot, liquid silk.

Eyes grim, Josh stood beside one of the leather chairs, his gaze locked on her face. "Regan, tell me his name."

"I can't."

His mouth set in a grim line. "You won't."

She cupped the snifter in her palm, swirled the brandy. "Won't."

"Why?"

"Who he is doesn't matter."

"Let me make sure I'm understanding this," he said, his voice a cold snap. "You're terrified of the man who abused you. You won't have anything to do with me because you're afraid if he finds you, he'll come after me. But you won't tell me his name because *it doesn't matter.*"

Her thoughts slapped back to that terrible day in New Orleans when she'd walked into Steven's house and nearly stumbled over his dead body. Creath had killed the man she loved. And weeks later he'd shot her partner. All because of Creath's sick obsession to own her.

She closed her eyes. It was too easy to imagine Josh lying dead on the brightly colored rug. Dead because of her.

She drank more brandy. Thankful it had taken the edge off her shivering, she set the snifter on the table beside the couch, then rose. "I don't want you hurt."

"What hurts is that you won't trust me."

She walked to where he stood. "I do trust you," she said quietly. "To always do the right thing." In her case, that would be to arrest her and put her in jail. "I care about you, Josh. Too much." Because she couldn't help herself, she reached up, cupped her palm against his cheek. And felt the muscle knotted in his jaw. "I'm doing what I have to do. It's the only thing I *can* do. I'm asking you to accept that."

His response was to snake an arm around her waist and jerk her against him. The breath clogged in her throat as his other hand fisted in her hair, drawing her head back so that his eyes blazed down into hers.

"You think you're the only one whose feelings are involved here?" he asked, his voice dangerously soft. "Think again. I care about you, Regan. Too much for my own damn good."

His words, his touch sent need surging through her. Then his mouth was on hers and she spun from arousal to passion at the instant of contact.

Flames erupted inside her, fierce and intense. A liquid heat welled somewhere in the region below her stomach. Her heart was hammering again. Not from fear this time, but from need.

Her arms slid around him. She heard herself make a whimpering sound in the back of her throat. Not a sound of protest. Or pain. But of desire.

Keeping his mouth on hers he turned her, braced her back against the wall and covered her breasts with his palms. Against his hands, her body began to vibrate. He slid his knee between her legs, forcing them apart so that he could move closer. There was no mistaking the hardness pressing against her, aggressive and demanding. Wanting her, as a man wants a woman.

His mouth continued to plunder, his hands to explore. It wasn't until she began to feel herself go weak that she remembered to fear. He was taking her deep, where she'd have no control over the moment, or the outcome of it. The need she felt sped beyond the hot, frantic sex she knew they could share. She knew, too, if she let herself, she could be in love. And then she'd have nowhere to run.

Panic surged again inside her. She had to stop him…and herself. If he held her much longer, she would succumb, and succumbing, lose.

Gripping his shoulders, she dragged her mouth from his. "Let me go," she panted. "Josh…let go."

His mouth moved to her throat, tracing a path of fire to her shoulder while his hands slid down to cup her bottom. "Tell me, Regan," he murmured against her flesh. "You can trust me. Please just trust me."

Regret washed over her for what she could never give him. For what they could never have. "I've got to go. *You have to let me go.*"

Slowly he lifted his head. She could see it on his face—the struggle for control. And in his eyes the flare of desire yet to be fully banked. "How the hell am I supposed to step back with all that's between us?"

"There can't be anything between us." She fisted her hands against his chest. She needed space, but was trapped between the unmovable force of wall and man. She shook her head. "This is too much. It's all too much."

His hand came up to circle her throat. "It's everything."

"It can't be." She pushed sideways, shoved from his hold. "I have to step back. So do you." Her lips were burning from his and her entire body was shaking again. "This can't happen. *It can't.*"

With her heart ripping apart, she turned and walked out.

Hands fisted, Josh stood motionless until he heard the front door close behind her. He thought about going after her, but he didn't have a full grip on control, and didn't totally trust what he would do when he caught up with her.

Toss her to the ground? Rip off her clothes and bury himself in her? That'd put a cap on things.

Swearing viciously, he stalked to the bar, grabbed the closest bottle, splashed a shot into a glass and tossed it back like water. After repeating the process two more times, the slick, sharp flavor of bourbon had taken the edge off the need that had spewed through his system like molten lava.

He poured a fourth shot, but didn't drink it. He leaned against the bar, and stared down at the glass in his hand. There'd been a time when he would have said the desire he felt for one woman was much the same for another. When he thought needs could be sated by whatever warm body he currently shared a bed with.

But with Regan's scent on his skin, with her taste now a part of him and the feel of her flesh branded in his brain, he knew everything was different.

Knew that if he wasn't in love with her yet, he would be.

This time there was no strength behind the curse he vented. How the hell did a man deal with loving a woman who didn't trust him? Who wouldn't confide in him? A woman who needed his help in the worst kind of way, but blocked every effort he made to protect her?

He scowled into the bourbon. Maybe it had been the brush with losing his job that had made him realize he needed something more than just the badge to focus his life, to center it.

Maybe that was why it had been so important that Regan tell him her secrets instead of him finding out on his own. But she'd refused time and again. He knew for certain now that she wouldn't.

So, he was going to do what a cop did best: uncover secrets.

He held his drink up toward the window. Even with the waning daylight, he could see his fingerprints on the glass. His gaze flicked to the snifter Regan had left on the table. If her prints were anywhere in the various nationwide databases available to law enforcement, he would know a hell of a lot more about her by this time tomorrow.

Chapter 10

"You've done a good job," Orson Zink said the following evening as he followed Regan out the back door of Etta's house.

"Thanks, Doc." She slid her right hand into her shorts pocket and curled her fingers around the bills she'd secreted there that morning. The rest of her running money was in her suitcase, which she had packed for an early-morning departure. "I'm relieved Etta's on the mend."

"Mostly thanks to you." Switching his medical bag from one hand to the other, Zink studied her through the waning daylight. The brisk wind ruffled his brown hair. "If you weren't trained to administer IVs, I would have had to hospitalize her. As feisty as Etta is, that sure wouldn't have set well."

"True," Regan agreed. Her telling Etta she was quitting her job and leaving Sundown wasn't going to go over well, either. But with Burns Yost running her photo on the *Sentinel*'s front page and posting it on the Web site, leaving was the only sensible thing to do. The only thing that would protect the people she'd come to care about in this small town. Especially if Yost got one of the wire services to run her photo.

The possibility of that happening—and Creath spotting her picture—sent a shiver through Regan. Tomorrow, she thought. Tomorrow she would start adjusting to a new identity, a new life. She had no choice but to adjust.

As if pulled by an invisible force, her gaze slid to the neighboring house. Josh's red Corvette was parked in the driveway. Light glowed in several upstairs windows. Thinking about never seeing him again—just *thinking* about it—was the equivalent of having her heart ripped out.

How the hell was she supposed to adjust to that? To never being with him again? Touching him? Kissing him?

"Let's talk about you, Regan."

She sliced her gaze back to Zink. "What about me?"

"I'm concerned about how pale you look. Not to mention exhausted. And if I'm not mistaken, you're even thinner now than you were a couple of days ago. I'd like you to come by the clinic tomorrow for some tests."

"Thanks, but I'll pass." She forced a smile. "The heat's put a damper on my appetite. And I'm tired because I didn't get any sleep last night." Every time she'd closed her eyes, she saw her picture on the *Sentinel*'s front page. Which had been quickly followed by a replay of her encounter with Josh. His touch. His kiss that had turned her weak. The mix of hurt and anger in his eyes when she refused to confide in him.

"Well, if you change your mind, come see me," Zink said. "Make sure Etta starts taking those new antibiotics in the morning. The samples I left will get her through three days before she has to get her prescription filled."

"I'll see to it," Regan said, making a mental note to reprogram Etta's recorder.

While Zink drove away, Regan lingered in the advancing evening gloom that was slowly turning the sky a ghostly lavender. A few minutes, she told herself. She just needed some time alone to align her thoughts. And get a handle on control so she wouldn't start sobbing when she told Etta she was leaving.

Pulling her bottom lip between her teeth, Regan glanced at her watch. Etta was now probably glued to the TV, watching her favorite sitcom. A.C. had called earlier to say he was bringing dinner by after he ended his shift at the marina, so Regan didn't need to cook on her night off from the tavern.

Just as well, she thought as fatigue seeped through her. She was so tired, she wasn't sure she could stay awake long enough to put a meal together.

She wandered onto the wooden dock, where the breeze off the lake turned the air ten degrees cooler. With the lounge chair beckoning her, she settled onto its padded surface and stretched out her legs. Helplessly, her thoughts turned again to Josh.

After Steven's death, she had thought she would never want another man, but she did. Achingly. Desperately. A man she could never have. Would never even see again. All she could do was hope that after she distanced herself from Sundown she would be able to shut off the needs that were eating away at her.

She could *hope* that, but in her heart she knew that would never happen. She would think about Josh McCall for the rest of her life. And want him.

She closed her eyes against a throbbing sense of grief and loss and loneliness.

Minutes later, she dropped off the edge of fatigue into sleep.

Josh had just stepped out of the shower when the phone started ringing. Not his cell phone, which he'd left in easy reach on the bathroom vanity, but the landline phone downstairs.

"Hell!" He grabbed a towel, hitched it around his waist and headed for the stairs. He reached the kitchen just as the answering machine clicked on.

And swore again when he heard Nate's voice.

Josh scooped up the phone as he stabbed the button to turn off the machine's recorder.

"Dammit, Nate, I about broke my neck getting downstairs. Why didn't you call my cell?"

"Because using a cell phone is the equivalent of talking on a radio transmitter. Trust me, bro, you don't want anyone with the right equipment eavesdropping on what I've got to say."

Dread clamped a vise on Josh's chest. "You got something back on the run you did on Regan's prints?"

"I got plenty. Her real name is Susan Kincaid. She's a paramedic. Her prints were entered into the system when she went to work for a Louisiana ambulance service."

"Okay." Josh shoved a hand through his wet hair. He'd already known the Regan Ford name was an alias. And that she had extensive medical training. He'd also been on-target when he pegged a hint of the South in her voice. "What else?"

"Ms. Kincaid's got trouble. Or maybe I should say she *is* trouble."

Josh hesitated. "What sort of trouble?"

"She's wanted for murder out of New Orleans."

The comment caught Josh like a punch in the gut. He braced a shoulder against the wall. "Are you sure?"

"Positive. I had a lab tech do a second comparison of the latent prints you sent me off the snifter with those on the classification listed in the NCIC hit. It's her."

"Christ." Josh set his jaw against the pain that snuck through, fast as a razor-sharp blade, and pierced his heart. On the heels of that came a rush of realization that he cared about Regan, had *connected* with her in a way he never had with another woman. He squeezed his eyes shut and fought to steady himself. It took a couple of seconds to regain his mental balance. Later, he would let himself feel.

Now, the only way he could deal with this was to shift into cop mode. "Who did she supposedly kill?"

"Dr. Steven Vaughn. Her fiancé."

I was engaged once. He died.

Josh clenched his jaw tighter against the memory of Regan's words. "How?"

"She slipped him an overdose of drugs," Nate continued, "then set it up to look like suicide. That's all the info that came back on the NCIC hit, except that the New Orleans PD is willing to extradite. The contact at the NOPD is Detective Payne Creath."

"You have to figure Creath asked NCIC to notify him if her fingerprint classification got a hit," Josh commented, forcing his mind to focus on the facts. "Which means if you don't contact him, he'll contact you."

The silence coming across the line pressed like fingers against Josh's eardrums.

"Why the hell wouldn't I contact Creath?" Nate asked.

"Because I'll do it," Josh snapped. Dammit, his mind was already accepting what Nate said as fact. Why, then, was there another part of him sending the message to hold back? "After I find out what Regan has to say."

"Her name's Susan, bro, and I already know what she'll say. She'll swear she's innocent. Then she'll try to explain how changing her identity and hiding out from the law for a year shouldn't make her look guilty."

"Yeah," Josh agreed. There was no reasonable argument to that.

"Look, when I talked to you the other day it was obvious you have a personal interest in this woman," Nate said, his voice losing its hard edge. "If it'll make things easier on you, I'll call Decker and have him pick her up."

Josh stared unseeingly across the kitchen. There'd been so many contradictions in what Regan had said. The way she'd acted. So many things the cop in him had overlooked while emotionally he just let himself get sucked in deeper. Caring for her. Wanting her.

Have you broken any laws?
Not a one.

Dammit, he'd believed her. Would have banked his career on the fact she was telling the truth.

His career. Damn.

He hadn't known how much his badge meant to him until he'd spent an entire month living with the prospect of losing it. Just the thought had put the fear of God in him. And resulted in his resolve to toe the line a little closer from now on. If he was smart, he would call Decker and have the chief come and pick Regan up. *Susan,* he reminded himself. Decker could call Creath and deal directly with the NOPD cop.

And *he* could stay out of it, away from her, which is what she'd said she wanted all along. Not because some guy had abused her and she was afraid he'd come after her lover. No, she'd needed to put distance between them because *he* was a cop. And she was wanted for murder.

The storm of dark anger brewing in his gut had him curling his fist against the kitchen counter. Like hell he would stand back. They were playing by his rules now and the lady was going to have to deal with him face-to-face.

This time, there'd be no running away on her part.

"I'll notify Decker," he said, his voice clipped with anger.

"All right," Nate agreed. "What about Creath?"

Josh knew the standard procedure—contacting an officer who'd issued a warrant should be the first item on the list. Still, there was that something niggling at him, an uneasiness or maybe even an awareness that told him to hold back until after he confronted her. *Dared* her to look him in the eye and lie again.

"I'll contact Creath, too. After I get some answers from her."

Nate cursed. "You can get whatever the hell answers you think you need from her after you contact Decker and Creath."

"I'll handle this my way, Nate. I want twenty-four hours."

"Bro, *I* ran Kincaid's prints. As you've already pointed out, if I don't contact Creath, he'll probably call me, wanting to know how I got her fingerprints and where the hell she is."

"Right." Josh was well aware he was not only stretching rules for a woman wanted for murder, he was asking his brother to do the same. Still, there was that something in his gut.

"If Creath calls you, use the stolen car story."

"Dammit, Josh." Nate paused and Josh could almost hear his brother gnashing his teeth. "All right, you've got twenty-four hours, and the clock starts ticking now. If I don't hear from you by this time tomorrow, I'm getting Bran and our sisters and we're all coming to Sundown and kicking your butt."

Josh narrowed his eyes. "You're welcome to try."

"Whatever it takes to stop our rebel brother from tossing away his career over a woman he's gotten in too deep with."

"I'm not in *that* deep. And you'll hear back from me."

Josh slammed down the phone, stripped off his towel as he took the stairs two at a time. In his bedroom he jerked on a T-shirt and jeans, then wrenched open the drawer on the nightstand.

With his anger growing into a black heat that bubbled in the blood, he clipped his badge to his waistband, snagged his handcuffs, then stalked toward the door.

Asleep on the padded lounger, Regan dreamed she was in a clearing, with the woods, thick and green, surrounding her. The air was still, the bright sun warmed her flesh. She was alone, her secrets safe.

All at once, a green car slammed into one of the massive oaks that lined the clearing. The crash of glass, the horrendous rending of metal exploded on the air. She raced to the car, worked desperately, *futilely* to save the injured teenage girl. And while Regan worked, a man snapped her picture.

Suddenly the sun hazed over. The air went cold. Something moved stealthily at the edge of the darkened woods.

The shadows parted, and Creath stepped into view, his eyes glinting with the lust for revenge.

"No!" Frantic, Regan shoved at the hand Creath locked on her arm, jerked against the metal he snapped around one wrist. And then he snatched her up off the lounger.

A scream caught in her throat; her eyes flew open. This was no nightmare, she realized. It was real. But it wasn't Creath who'd picked her up. Not Creath who she stared up at through the waning evening light. It was the hard, angry face of another cop.

"Josh." His name came out in a raw gasp as he turned and strode across the dock. She craned her neck, saw he was carrying her toward his slick, high-powered speedboat. "What are—"

"Just shut the hell up."

"I—" The air hissed out of her lungs when his muscled arms locked around her, as hard as the steel he'd fastened around her right wrist. *Handcuff!*

Fear erased the last muddled dregs of sleep. "No." In wild panic, she fought against his hold, shoving a palm against his chest, the loose end of the cuff dangling from her wrist. "No!"

His hand shot up into her hair, his fingers clenching as he tugged her head back. His eyes were smoldering, his lips a thin, furious line. "Keep struggling, and I'll add resisting arrest to the charges against you. *Susan.*"

Paralyzing terror engulfed her. She knew her color faded. She could feel it drain and leave her face cold and stiff.

Her dazed mind cataloged Josh's movements as he stepped onto the boat, felt it sway beneath their weight. A second later he dropped her on one of the deep-cushioned benches that faced each other behind the control console. Before she could move, he locked the loose end of the handcuff onto a metal rail bolted to the boat's hull.

"That's just in case you get the urge to run from the law again." His voice was utterly flat, more frightening than the hiss of a snake. From behind him, the dim light from the dock enhanced the sheer physical power of his hard, broad shoulders and conditioned muscles.

She was Josh McCall's prisoner. And he was in total control.

Oh, God. Her mouth dry, lungs heaving, Regan watched in stunned silence while he cast off the ropes that moored the boat. That done, he dropped into the seat behind the control console. Seconds later, the engine roared to life; he kept the speed slow and steady as the boat curved away from the dock, then he hit the throttle and sent the boat slicing through the dark water.

While wind slapped at her face, fear speared into Regan's bones. Despite the heated night air that rushed across her flesh, a cold sweat misted her skin. For an entire year she had lived in dread of this moment. Had imagined it playing out in any number of scenarios, which always included a backup plan for escape. She jerked her right wrist, felt the bite of metal against her flesh and knew there'd be no escaping this.

No running from Josh.

The boat seemed to spin beneath her, and nausea crawled up the back of her throat. While she fought for control, she studied Josh's face, illuminated in the wash of light from the control panel. He kept his gaze focused out over the dark water, and never once looked her way.

Even through her fear, Regan ached. From the moment she'd met him, she'd known that whatever danger she faced from the outside, she was facing danger just as great from her own heart. And she'd been right, she thought. She had fallen in love with the man who would send her to prison.

She had no idea in what direction they were going, no clue how long the boat cut through the inky water. When Josh finally turned off the engine, she heard her own heart tattooing through the abrupt silence.

He lowered the anchor, then turned in his seat toward her, his face unreadable. The boat's navigation lights glinted off the gold badge clipped to the waistband of his jeans. She understood it was the cop she was dealing with, not the man.

"You know who I am." Her lips began to tremble, and she firmed them into a hard line. "So why did you bring me here instead of taking me to jail?"

"The first thing you need to understand, Ms. Kincaid, is that I'll be the one asking the questions."

She narrowed her eyes, welcoming the flare of temper that heated her cheeks. For a time anyway, she would use that anger to push back the debilitating fear clawing inside her. "Well, Sergeant McCall, would you at least tell me how you found out who I am?"

"I ran your fingerprints."

She blinked. "My prints…"

"Which I lifted off the snifter you drank from last night." His voice changed from dangerously soft to viciously sharp. "I watched a woman I cared about have a panic attack. I wanted to help her. Protect her. But I couldn't do that without knowing what she was up against. Which meant finding out what the hell she wasn't telling me. Now I know."

"You should have left it alone," she shot back, her temper building to match his. "You should have just left *me* the hell alone."

"Yeah, I can see why you'd think that." The hand he'd rested on the steering wheel clenched into a fist. "You had me convinced you were hiding from some badass who'd abused you. That you had to keep your distance to *protect* me. Lady, you deserve an Oscar."

"It was no act!" she shouted, because she was too frightened to do otherwise. "The badass is obsessed with me. He killed my fiancé and my partner because he viewed them as obstacles in his way to having *me*. And when I disappeared to get away from him, he set things up to make it look like I'd killed the man I loved. If you don't think all that's abuse, think again."

Josh studied her for a long moment, his eyes steady and measuring. "Since the New Orleans PD wants you for murder, it doesn't look like they bought your story."

"Why should they? He's one of them."

This time it was Josh who blinked. "Are you claiming some obsessed NOPD cop committed two murders?"

"I'm not *claiming* it," she said, tossing the word back at him. "I'm telling you he did. He admitted it to me." The wind whipped her hair into her face. In reflex, she started to lift her right hand, wincing when the cuff bit into her wrist. She used her free hand to shove at her hair. "It wasn't until after I reported him to his chief that I found out how effectively Creath had blocked me from getting help."

"Creath," Josh repeated mildly. "This would be Detective Payne Creath? The cop who issued the murder warrant on you?"

Regan's insides turned to ice. "Have you…" Fear settled over her like a vapor, rippling against her spine. "Have you talked to him?"

"Not yet."

"Don't. Josh…don't talk to him." The terror that clawed up her throat sounded in her voice. "No matter if you believe anything else I say, you have to take my word for it that Creath is dangerous." Her hands had begun to shake, and she curled her fingers into her palms. "You won't think he is, because he has a way of making people like him. Believe whatever he tells them. *I* did. So did Steven and Bobby. But something inside him is twisted. Evil. *He killed them.*"

Having deliberately positioned Regan on the end of the padded bench where the stern's navigation light would illuminate her, Josh had a clear view of her face. To his knowledge, a person could not intentionally make herself go pale, much less pale to the point that the skin seemed translucent and the lips looked like those of a cadaver. That's exactly what she'd done when he'd said Creath's name.

Seeing her looking so small and fragile—and terrified—tightened the knots in his gut. He conceded there was more than just cold anger inside him. His heart had also taken a couple of nasty slashes from the news Nate had give him. The realization he was powerless to keep his emotions totally at bay had him wanting to break something with his bare hands.

He forced his gaze past her shoulder. In the distance, lights dotted the lake where other boats were anchored. Around them there was only silence. Echoing, stretching silence.

He looked back at Regan, stared into the deep pools of her eyes. It hadn't just been a cop's refusal to allow a suspect to ask questions that had kept him from explaining why he'd hauled her into his boat and driven to the middle of the lake. He hadn't answered because he simply didn't know the reason.

Her name's Susan, bro, and I already know what she'll say. She'll swear she's innocent. Then she'll try to explain how changing her identity and hiding out from the law for a year shouldn't make her look guilty.

He appreciated the spirit of Nate's warning. But like Nate said, *he* was the rebel of the McCall clan and he'd never allowed others to make up his mind for him. No reason to start now. He had always trusted his instincts when it came to forming conclusions about people's character. Conclusions that were almost always confirmed—or disproved—by that person's actions and behavior.

Regan's hiding from the law and doing everything in her power to keep him from finding out who and what she was painted her in the worst light possible. And if he hadn't cuffed her to the boat, he wasn't entirely sure she wouldn't even now try to swim for shore and keep running.

He *knew* all that. But from the instant they'd met, he'd been conscious of a nagging certainty that there was more—much more—to the woman than what was on the surface. And it hadn't been his own blood-heating attraction to her that made him feel that, but the instincts he'd learned to trust.

So what was it? What lay beneath the layers of the woman using a fake identity and on the lam from the law?

The woman who hadn't hesitated to use her medical skills to tend victims at an accident scene, knowing that doing so would raise questions she didn't dare answer about her past. The woman who, despite those questions, had remained in Sundown to care for her elderly boss, even though staying might cost her her freedom.

The woman who was clearly terrified of the New Orleans cop who hunted her. During his police career, Josh had hunted countless suspects. None had ever had reason to be terrified of him.

Hell, he thought. Why the hell did it have to be this woman, *this one woman,* who had gotten through his defenses and clamped a hand on his heart? And now she was squeezing it.

He eased back in his seat, figuring he had about twenty-three hours left to find some answers.

"Start at the beginning," he said levelly. "And don't leave anything out."

Chapter 11

Regan eyed Josh, sitting in the seat behind the control console, one wrist propped over the steering wheel, his gaze fixed on her, his face unreadable. Around them, the quiet of the night was broken only by the soft lap of water against the boat's hull.

"You want me to tell you about Creath?" she asked.

"About him, and everything else you've been holding back. *Everything.*"

She slid her tongue across her parched lips. She'd watched Josh over the past minutes while he'd remained silent. There'd been a deep, unfathomable emotion in his eyes that she was at a loss to decipher. She knew his willingness to listen to her version of things wouldn't keep her out of jail, but if she could convince him she was telling the truth, she might be able to keep him alive. *Oh God, she had to protect him from Creath.*

"I first worked as a paramedic in a small town in Louisiana," she began. "Later I went to work for a New Orleans ambulance service. That's when I met Steven Vaughn, an E.R. doctor."

Shifting her gaze, she stared out into the dark night. For so long she'd held her secrets, her grief, close to her heart. Now, she had no choice but to reveal everything. It was a struggle to get over the first hurdle. "Steven…was a wonderful man, warm and caring and funny. I loved him." She looked back at Josh. *"I loved him."* She fisted her hands against a swell of pain. "We were going to get married, raise a family. And then *Detective* Creath came along."

There were tears in her throat now, tears welling in her eyes. She put a trembling hand to her lips. She didn't want to cry. Crying wouldn't help. Wouldn't convince Josh she was telling the truth.

When he remained flatly silent, she dragged in a deep breath. "The first time my path crossed Creath's was at a homicide crime scene. There were two victims, one dead, one alive. My partner, Bobby Ivers, and I transported the critical victim to the same E.R. where Steven worked. Creath showed up to interview the victim, but he'd already gone into surgery, so Creath asked Bobby and me if we wanted to have a cup of coffee in the doctor's lounge. We said yes—it was smart to get on good terms with the cops we sometimes had to deal with.

"Creath is a nice-looking man, big and fit, approachable, even though there's that cynical cop-edge to him. Peppermints," she continued, her stomach churning with the remembered scent she now detested. "He had a handful of those round, red-and-white peppermints and he offered me one. Later, I found out he was hooked on them, always carries a plastic baggy of them in his pocket. But that night all I knew was that he seemed okay while he sat beside me, drinking coffee. Bobby and I got a call, and we were on our way out of the lounge when Steven walked in. I gave him a kiss, told him I'd see him later at his place.

"A few days after that, I was at a mall and ran into Creath. He asked if I wanted to grab another cup of coffee. I was in a hurry to get somewhere, so I said no. Over the following weeks

I kept running into him—sometimes at the grocery store, coming out of the cleaners, the video rental shop. One evening, a girlfriend and I were buying movie tickets when Creath walked up. He said his date was supposed to meet him there, but she'd just called to say she'd gotten hung up at work. He asked if we minded if he joined us." Regan raised a shoulder. "We wanted a girls' night out, but didn't want to be rude. It was then, while sitting in the movie beside Creath, smelling peppermint, that I got this creepy feeling. That maybe the times I'd run into him hadn't been coincidence. But he'd never made a move on me, so I shrugged it off. After the movie, Creath insisted on buying our dinner. My girlfriend was cute and single and he was giving her the eye, so I figured he wanted to connect with her."

Josh measured her through narrowed eyes. "*Did* he?"

"He got her phone number, but never called. A week later was Steven's birthday, and I'd made reservations at his favorite restaurant. When we walked in, Creath was at the table next to ours. He was alone, and Steven asked him to join us. During dinner Creath kept brushing his knee against my thigh. I didn't say anything because I didn't want to cause a scene, but the next day, I called Creath at his office and arranged to meet him at a diner. When I got there, I told him I didn't know what his game was, but I wasn't interested."

"How did he react?"

Regan kept her gaze leveled on Josh's. Was he asking because he believed her? Or was he giving her more rope to hang herself with? Either way, she was determined to get through this.

"Creath just sat in the booth across from me with this patronizing look on his face. He said that from the moment we met he knew I was his *one magic person*—those were his exact words. I was his special someone, he wanted me, therefore he would have me." Regan shoved at her bangs. "At first I thought he was playing some sick joke on me, but then I saw in his eyes he was totally serious. I told him I loved Steven and there was

no room in my life for him, or any other man. Creath just nodded, like nothing I said mattered. He told me he'd give me a
couple of days to rethink things. I informed him I didn't want
anything more to do with him, then I left.

"A week went by. I didn't run into Creath anywhere, so I
thought he'd finally gotten my message and backed off. Then,
on a Friday night, I got off work and went to Steven's house
like I always did for the weekend. I found…him…." For a moment Regan saw it as it had been, the man she loved crumpled
on the floor, her desperate attempts to revive him, even though
she'd known he was gone. "I tried…to save him…but I got
there too late. Oh, God."

Struggling against a haze of remembered grief, she was
vaguely aware of Josh standing. He lifted a lid on one of the
boat's built-in coolers and pulled out a bottle of water.

"Take a drink," he said quietly, handing her the bottle.

"Thanks." Closing her eyes, Regan took a long, slow swallow of the cool water while willing back the horrible images
of that night.

"What happened after you found your fiancé?"

Only after Josh spoke did she realize he'd settled on the opposite end of the padded bench from her. He was close enough
that she could smell the clean, salty scent of his skin. Emotionally, she suspected he was a universe away.

"I called 911. A patrol cop showed up, then Creath and his
partner. After a while, cops started swarming through the house.
I didn't understand why they were all there because I thought
Steven must have had a heart attack. The next day Creath came
to my apartment and told me preliminary tests indicated Steven
had died of a drug overdose. Then Creath showed me a suicide
note he'd found on Steven's computer. In the note, Steven con-
fessed to battling a drug problem." She shook her head. "I was
stunned, I'd had no idea. Steven wrote that he was getting pressure to improve his performance on the job, pressure from *me*

to set a wedding date. That he'd tried to get off the drugs, but couldn't. He could no longer deal with the stress coming at him from all sides.

"I felt like a tank had rolled over me. There's no way I could have gotten through Steven's funeral if I hadn't had my partner, Bobby, to lean on." She narrowed her eyes. "I remember Creath there, standing apart from the other mourners, watching me. Just watching. I saw him a few days later at the E.R. A nurse gave me the things Steven had in his locker, and I just broke down, started sobbing on Bobby's shoulder. The next night, Bobby was killed in a drive-by shooting." Her throat raw, Regan took another drink, then set the bottle aside. "Bobby had a wife and a little boy and he died because of *me.*"

"Why do you think it was because of you?"

"Dammit, I don't *think!*" She spit out the words. "I *know.*"

"How?"

She fought a short, fierce battle to pull herself together. What she was about to say had already been discounted by the police. She had no reason to think Josh would react differently. Still, his association with her put him in mortal danger and she had to try to make him believe she was telling the truth.

"When I got home from Bobby's funeral, Creath was waiting inside my apartment. I don't know how he bypassed my security alarm, but he did. He grabbed me, kissed me. When I struggled away he told me I was the only woman who could fulfill him and complete his life. The sooner I accepted that the better. I was shaking, scared to death of him and at the same time furious. I told him I wanted him to leave me alone. Then I threatened to report him to his chief if he continued harassing me. In a finger-snap, I saw Creath's face change. It was like I finally saw the monster behind the facade."

The night air was steamy, yet the brittle cold had seeped back into Regan's bones. She wondered if she would ever feel warm again. "Creath told me that Steven and Bobby had been obstacles in his way to having me, and he'd removed them. That he would continue removing obstacles until I came to my senses and surrendered to him. Then he asked how much longer I was going to continue to disappoint him."

She let out a long breath, but it didn't steady her voice. "Right then, my minister and his wife knocked on my door and I opened it before Creath could stop me. He introduced himself as the cop working Steven's death, and he left.

"That afternoon I went to the police chief and told him what Creath had said. An Internal Affairs cop showed up at my apartment a few days later, saying he was investigating my 'complaint.' The IA cop told me Creath was claiming that I'd latched onto him emotionally after we met on the job. That *I'd* stalked *him* by constantly calling his house and showing up wherever he was. Creath told the IA cop he felt sorry for me, so he didn't report the harassment. He also said I'd made threats about what I would do if he refused to have a relationship with me.

"I kept insisting Creath had lied, that he'd admitted killing Steven and Bobby. Then the IA cop showed me a report he'd gotten from the phone company that listed numerous calls made from my home phone to Creath's." As Regan spoke, her fingers clenched and unclenched. "I never called him at home, not once. Then the IA cop played a tape of my own voice, telling Creath I loved him and wanted a relationship with him." She struggled to steady herself. Even to her own ears, her claims sounded unbelievable. "It was my voice on the tape, saying things to Creath I'd never said. Then the IA cop advised me that stalking is a crime. So is making a false police report and he had enough evidence against me to file charges."

"Did he?"

"No. He said Creath had asked him to hold off, to give me a warning because I was so emotionally distraught over my fiancé's suicide. That's when I realized how totally Creath had blocked any chance I had of getting help from the police. From any man, because he might perceive that person as a rival. And kill him."

Her breathing quickened, became a painful thumping in her ears. "You," she managed. "Josh, he will kill you if he finds out there is…was something between us."

Emotion flashed in Josh's eyes before the shutter came down. "When did Creath file the murder warrant?" he asked levelly.

It was crazy, she thought. Crazy that her heart should ache over his refusal to acknowledge the personal connection they'd forged.

"After I left New Orleans," she answered, struggling to keep her voice steady. "It got to the point that I couldn't concentrate. I couldn't function normally, so I moved to D.C. and got a job there as a paramedic. I used my real name because I thought all I needed to do was put distance between Creath and me and he'd get over his sick obsession. I'd been in D.C. nearly a month when I got off work one evening and thought I spotted him standing across the street. I kept telling myself I was hallucinating, but I *had* to know. I used a pay phone to call the NOPD and found out Creath was on his days off. When I got to my apartment, my bed was littered with pieces of peppermint candy. That night he called my unlisted number. He told me I had one chance to come to my senses. That if I moved back to New Orleans he would *forgive* me for leaving him. If I didn't, he would make sure I spent the rest of my life in prison."

Suddenly excruciatingly tired, she dragged an unsteady hand through her hair. "I hung up on him. I'd hooked a recorder to my phone, and turned it on when he called, and I just knew I'd gotten the proof I needed to make the police believe me. But when I tried to play the tape, it was blank." She shook her head. "Creath must have done something to the tape while he was in my apartment so it wouldn't record. Just like he'd done something to make my phone records look like I'd called him constantly. And then somehow manufactured the tape record-ing of me saying things to him I never said."

She studied Josh, his eyes dark and expressionless, the hard set of his jaw. "That night you took me to Sundown Ridge and shared your moonstars with me, you told me how one planted piece of evidence had Internal Affairs coming down on you. You almost lost your badge, and you didn't do one thing wrong. It's the same for me, Josh. Only there won't be a handy sound bite from some TV news footage that will clear me. Creath will have made certain of that."

Josh shifted his gaze from hers and stared out across the dark water. "What did you do after you hung up on him?" he asked after a moment.

"I knew the only way I was going to stay out of prison for something I hadn't done was to disappear. So that same night I packed what I could carry, told my neighbor she could have the rest of my stuff and I snuck down the fire escape and caught a train out of D.C. Then I rode buses." Regan shivered, remember-ing those cold, endless days. "I was afraid to go to sleep for fear I'd wake up and find Creath sitting beside me. I couldn't func-tion like that, so I called a P.I. in New Orleans whom I'd heard about. I hired him to find out if there was a warrant out on me. I wired him money, and gave him my e-mail address. The next day he wrote, saying that I was wanted for murdering Steven. I had no idea what evidence Creath had manufactured against me, but whatever it was, I knew it would stick. I arranged for the P.I. to watch Creath and to e-mail me if he left New Orleans."

"How did you come up with the name Regan Ford?"

"I saw it on a tombstone. She had been born two years be-fore me, and died while an infant. I got a copy of her birth cer-tificate, then a driver's license. I bought the Mustang and I ran for half a year."

"Then your car broke down here, in the middle of Main Street," Josh finished.

"I...didn't tell you that part."

"Etta did. She said you saw her card on the wall at the garage advertising a bartender's job."

Regan nodded. "That morning, I'd driven past this lake. It was a gray, icy day and I started thinking I could end everything if I just drove into the water. Doing that held more appeal than spending my life in jail." The emotion roiling inside her began to break through in her voice, but she could no longer help it.

"I detoured through Sundown," she continued, "trying to get my courage up to head back to the lake when my car died right in front of Smitty's Garage. I couldn't drive into the lake unless my car ran, so I used the last of my money to get it fixed. While I was waiting, I saw Etta's card on Smitty's bulletin board. It said the bartender's job came with room and board, and a bushel of TLC."

Regan could still feel the hopelessness that had raked at her soul that day. "The tender loving care part pulled at me. So, I walked over to Truelove's Tavern and met Etta. She started fussing over me, gave me a bowl of soup and hired me on the spot. She took me upstairs to show me the apartment, and she gave me a hug. Etta literally saved my life that day."

Regan stared at the metal cuff circling her wrist. "Being in Sundown, having a place to stay, a job, made me feel halfway normal again. Like I had a little part of my life back. There were times when I actually imagined myself living in Sundown for months, years, content and safe."

She paused, savoring the feel of fresh air against her flesh, knowing that soon her freedom would be only a memory. "Then you walked into Truelove's," she continued, looking back at Josh. "I knew instantly you were a cop. Deep down, I think I also knew you'd be the one to find out who I was and what I was hiding. But when you touched me, kissed me, that didn't matter because I'd never felt more alive. I wanted you, as much as you wanted me, but I couldn't make love with you because if Creath found out…" She shook her head. "He killed Steven and Bobby and I couldn't put you at risk, too."

"Dammit, Regan." Josh's eyes weren't cold anymore, but filled with the same hot, raw emotion she heard in his voice. He swept up the bottle of water, chugged its contents, then lobbed it onto the opposite bench. "Dammit to hell."

"I took someone else's name. Her identity. And I've hurt you. Those are the only things I'm sorry about. The only things I've done that I have to be sorry about. I'm not exactly in the position to ask a favor of you, but I have to."

He kept his eyes locked on hers. "You going to ask me to let you go?"

"I might if I thought you wore your badge for amusement. You don't. It's part of who you are. And your releasing a wanted killer would be a little more than bending a rule."

When he didn't comment, she said, "When you turn me over to Chief Decker, you can have him keep your name out of the report. He can tell Creath he'd spent enough time at Truelove's that he got curious about me or suspicious and ran my prints, something like that. You can go home to Oklahoma City and stay there until Creath takes me back to New Orleans."

Her emotions were rocking now, making it difficult to continue holding on to her thready composure. "Josh, you can't be here when Creath comes. He can't know that you found out who I am. He'd wonder how an out-of-town cop on vacation got close enough to me to do that. He'd figure out…" She was shaking; tears streamed down her cheeks, but she was past caring. "Creath is twisted. The truth, the facts don't matter, only what he perceives does. He'll see you as a rival, the same way he saw Steven and Bobby. Leave, Josh. Please leave so he won't know about you. Won't…kill you."

"Regan, don't."

"Promise me." She choked on her tears as if Creath already had his hands around her throat. "It doesn't...matter if you...believe me. Just promise...you'll take me to jail then...leave Sundown. *Just leave.*"

"The hell with this." Between one heartbeat and the next, Josh forgot the rules, forgot the consequences of breaking them. All he could see was her.

"Please, Josh."

"Stop." He moved beside her, dragged her onto his lap. "Stop now."

"I'll beg." She gripped his shoulder with her free hand. "If that's what it takes to get you to leave, I'll beg."

Any defense, any rational reason he may have had left quite simply crumbled. "Regan."

"Promise." With tears blurring her vision, she stared up at him. She didn't question why he'd pulled her onto his lap, didn't care. All she cared about was keeping him alive. "You *have* to leave Sundown before Creath gets here."

"I'm staying."

"No." She shook her head. "You can't—"

"I believe you." His voice was thick, unsteady as his thumbs slicked across her cheeks to wipe away her tears.

She felt her heart kick hard as she stared up into his eyes that looked like polished onyx in the dim light. "You...believe me?"

"Yes."

"Why?"

"A mix of things." He pulled a key from the pocket on his T-shirt, unlocked the cuff from her wrist. "Last year, I worked a case where a waitress was being harassed big-time by a trucker. All she did was smile at the guy and make a little conversation while serving him a piece of apple pie, and just like that he decided they were soul mates. I learned a lot about stalkers so I've got a good idea how they operate." He smoothed her hair back from her temples. "And there's the way you look and sound when you talk about Creath. About Steven and Bobby. Reactions like that can't be faked. Then there's me."

Feeling utter disbelief, she gazed at him through wet, spiky lashes. "What…about you?"

"I always listen to what my gut tells me. And I'm good at knowing when I'm being lied to. You're not lying." He skimmed his fingertips down her cheek. His eyes softened, as did his voice. "You've got a caring heart, Regan. Otherwise you'd have left after the accident when people started asking questions about your past."

"I *was* going to leave."

"And then Etta got sick." He pressed a palm against the side of her throat. "You chose to stay for her."

"I couldn't take off and let Doc Zink put her in the hospital. Etta needed me."

"Seems she's not the only one who needed you to stay in Sundown." Josh slid one thumb down to the hollow of her throat, stroked her flesh. "I felt something, too, that night I walked into the tavern and saw you. I was curious because you were so skittish. Your eyes," he murmured. "You had secrets in your eyes. But more than that, there was something about you that got to me in a way nothing or no one else ever has." He pressed a kiss against her temple, her cheek. "I can't shake it, Regan. I tried, but I can't shake you."

Even as she locked her arms around him, a dim voice inside Regan told her to pull away, reminding her nothing had changed. That no matter what had happened between them he would have no choice but to put her in jail. But that was the future. Here, now, she was too exhausted, too emotionally drained to fight off the wave of feelings that assaulted her. So, she pressed herself against the firm body that transmitted safety and, for the first time in over a year she felt no need to be on guard, no underlying compulsion to pack up and run. For the first time in so long she felt…normal.

She tilted her head back to look up at Josh, and all the misery, all the pain, all the bitterness she had carried with her for so long faded.

"I tried to stay away from you," she said, her voice whisper soft. "*Needed* to. But I can't shake you, either."

"We've both got the same problem," he said, then brought his mouth down to cover hers.

His lips were hard and demanding, his muscled arms like steel around her. She felt the rush of need, the hard, sharp-edged wave of it. Desires she'd ruthlessly buried broke the surface and heat flashed inside her where only ice had been.

Her system stuttered with pleasure, then roared into full raging life.

While they feasted on each other's mouths, she burrowed against him, offering more. Straining for more.

He fisted one hand in her hair, angled her head back and plunged his tongue between her parted lips. His kiss transformed into something raw and primitive.

Her tongue played with his, her hands slid up to twine around his neck. Need was too great a force to resist, the future facing her too bleak. Here, in the middle of the dark lake, with only the moon and stars to witness, she could steep herself in blessed oblivion of her problems and be with the man she craved. This one man. This one night.

His mouth left hers to trail kisses along her jaw, then down the column of her throat, sending a shudder of pure longing through her. Lights seemed to dance behind her eyes. Her muscles, so stiff before, began to melt with the warmth of desire.

Heat poured through Josh, molten, liquid heat searing his veins, pooling in his groin. The scent of her was lemon and nerves, and he wanted her, had wanted her from the first, this woman with her alluring combination of fire and vulnerability. He wanted her in a way he hadn't wanted any other woman—possessively, totally. He wanted her to be his in a way she had never been any other man's. *Dangerous thinking,* the lone spark of logic remaining in his brain warned.

He would think later, he told himself. Figure out how to deal with all this after his blood cooled and his brain kicked in again. Right now, all that mattered was having her.

The low, humming moan that sounded in her throat fired his blood even hotter, blasting a charge of lust straight to his belly. With every cell in his body burning for her, he jerked off her tank top, tossed it aside, then unhooked her bra.

"You're beautiful," he murmured, gazing down at her small, firm breasts slicked with silver moonlight and shadows. He slipped his hand up around the back of her neck then leaned her back in his lap. One strong arm supported her while he closed his mouth on one nipple, suckled, then let his teeth close softly while his free hand skimmed over her.

Regan couldn't make her breathing quiet, couldn't stop her body from shuddering. Arching her back in delicious pleasure, she tangled her fingers in his hair, pressing him closer, giving herself over to her madly churning needs while he fed. Explored. The heady combination of euphoria and pain had her half whimpering, half sighing. It had been so long, she thought dizzily, an eternity since she had felt anything this intensely. Wanted this passionately.

She moved restlessly beneath his hands, his mouth. Her flesh burned against his clever tongue while the soft wet pulse between her legs throbbed.

Her senses slashing one against the other in an edgy tangle of needs, Regan levered up on his lap and jerked at his T-shirt. "I want to feel you," she breathed. "Need to feel you."

He raised one arm and then the other so she could wrench his shirt off over his head. Her unsteady palms skimmed across his broad chest that was solid muscle. Winding one arm around his neck, she rubbed against him like a cat as her other hand slid down and fought the snap on his jeans.

Uttering a muffled groan, he scooped her up and stood. He released her legs but kept one arm around her upper body as the boat rocked against the movement. While she grabbed at his shoulders for balance he yanked down the zipper of her shorts, then peeled them off, along with her panties. He gazed down at her, his eyes glittering with hot need.

A thrill of dark pleasure rippled through her at that lethal spark in his eyes.

She was exquisite, Josh thought, drinking her in. Fine boned and angular, slender and sleek. Delicate.

"I want to touch you everywhere," he murmured as he traced his fingers down her shoulders, her back, caressing, exploring every dip and curve.

"It feels like you are," she managed as a thousand nerves sprang to life beneath his touch.

He tugged her against him, kissing her greedily, hungrily while he locked an arm around her waist. Pressed thigh to thigh, he let her feel his arousal, let her know how badly, how urgently he wanted her. Only her.

Her mouth tore from his and began a heady, intricate journey along his jaw, his neck as her fingers fumbled with the snap of his jeans, the zipper. When he felt her tongue dip into the hollow at the base of his throat, the flames of desire leaped, licking at his sanity. He slid his hand between their bodies, down the flat plain of her stomach, downward until he cupped her.

His chest tightened when he found her hot and wet, ready for him. Her body was vibrating against his like a string already plucked. It was tempting, knowing he could plunge himself into her and take them both into oblivion. But this time, this first time, he intended to sate her with pleasure until there was nothing and no one else but him in her universe.

He dragged the cushions off the benches, nesting them together at their feet, then he shucked the rest of his clothes. They dragged each other down onto the cushions, he sprawling beside her, wedging his hand between her legs.

When his fingers speared into her, Regan moaned, beyond thought, beyond everything but need. He murmured her name against her throat, his mouth savoring, exploiting, plundering while he made love to her with his hand, driving her toward the steep rise of desire.

Her heart lurched when the jarring explosion of pleasure shot through her. She sank into the climax, everything fading around her until the only focus of her existence was the intense pleasure.

"Josh…" His name was nothing more than a soft, throaty sob on the still night air, yet it beat in his blood like a primal chant.

Propped on one elbow, he gazed down at her, taking in the flush along her cheekbones, the glazed, sultry look in her eyes. The faint lemon tang of her soap mixed with the musky scent of her arousal. Every muscle in him quivered with the strain of holding himself back.

"Again," he whispered through clenched teeth.

"No, I…"

He stroked his fingers deeper, then eased slowly out of her, opening her, stretching her. The sound she made seemed to claw up from her throat and was every bit as feral as the need that raged through him.

"Oh, God." Her hips arched, urging him back into her.

"Again." His breath sawed in and out of his lungs while he watched her ride the peak and a hungry, possessive tide rose through him, knotting his stomach, churning his already hot blood. *Mine* was all he could think as she writhed beneath his touch. *Only mine.* With that dark, powerful thought fueling him, he moved over her, levered her hips high and drove himself into her. To claim. To mate.

He hissed out a breath when her muscles clenched around him. Her nails scraped at his back while he nipped the side of her neck, murmured her name as they moved in sync, a quick piston of hips.

And when the explosion rocked him, he buried himself to the hilt, his consciousness dimming in the hot rush of fulfillment.

Chapter 12

Regan woke just as dawn began to light the sky. She was curled on her side with Josh a solid wall behind her, his legs tangled with hers. One of his arms was a heavy weight over her hip. His breath felt warm on her shoulder.

She stirred softly, having no idea how many times they'd made love, drifted to sleep, then made love again on the cushions positioned on the boat's deck. Sometime during the night he retrieved a pair of beach towels, one of which was still partially draped over her. Except for that, and the occasional visit to the small, enclosed head compartment, they had remained in each other's arms.

She lay quietly while the warm dawn air caressed her flesh, wishing she could slip back into sleep before her mind began to work.

But it was too late. Already she was thinking about the future, knowing that the freedom she'd been so terrified of losing would be gone by the end of this day. She closed her eyes briefly, then opened them again. She couldn't bring herself to regret becoming Josh McCall's lover, but already she felt the aching sense of what it meant to lose him.

Even though he believed Creath had killed Steven and Bobby and set her up to take the fall for Steven's murder, that didn't make the warrant for her arrest go away. Josh was a cop, he'd run her prints, she was sure there would be a record of that. He couldn't just ignore the fact she was on the run from the law. He had to go by the book and turn her in to Chief Decker. And even if Josh tried to help prove her innocence, she knew too well how thorough Payne Creath was. No weak link would exist in the evidence he'd manufactured against her.

There was no way to sidestep Creath's sick need for revenge. No way to prevent him from coming to Sundown. Coming for her.

Along with the fear that feathered up her spine, the determination she'd felt last night to obtain Josh's promise to leave before Creath showed up returned with a vengeance. She would do whatever it took to keep Josh out of harm's way.

Just then, his lips brushed the back of her neck, sending an altogether different kind of shiver up her spine.

"Morning," he murmured.

"Morning." She nuzzled against him, sighing. It had been so long since she'd awoken, held close by the man she loved. *Loved,* she thought, but could never have. His mouth skimmed her shoulder and her lips trembled against the hollow aloneness she knew awaited her.

"You've been lying here awhile, thinking," he said quietly, the words hot on her skin. "About what?"

His comment caught her off guard. She hadn't realized he'd been awake that long.

"You." She twisted around. In the weak dawn light, his face was all hollows and shadows. She cradled his cheek in her palm, day-old stubble prickling her flesh. "I was thinking that you still haven't promised me you'll leave Sundown."

"You're right, I haven't."

"Josh—"

"That's one promise you won't get." He sat up, dragging her with him as he propped his shoulder against one of the boat's built-in benches. "We need to talk," he added. "About a lot of things."

"One being Etta."

His brows rose. "What about Etta?"

"I should have asked you to call her last night." Regan shoved a hand through her tousled hair. "She'd have been worried when I didn't come home."

"Her house was my first stop when I started looking for you. She told me you'd walked Doc Zink outside, so she knew I went to find you. I imagine Etta figured you and I wound up together."

But only for one night, Regan thought. She'd had the time with Josh she'd so desperately craved, and their future was now the past. It was no longer practical to think beyond the overwhelming present.

Suddenly conscious of her nakedness—and needing to shore up her defenses—she scooted from his hold, snagged one of the beach towels and wrapped it around herself, sarong-style. "I want to talk to Etta," she said evenly. "Explain to her about…who I am. Everything. I'd like to do that before you take me to Decker."

Josh studied her in the advancing dawn light. He saw the tension in the way she held her smooth, shapely shoulders, the strain in those exotically tilted cat's eyes, the paleness in her cheeks. And he was very aware of what her edging from his touch and covering herself with the towel symbolized. Seeing her drawing in on herself, pulling back physically and emotionally had fresh emotion surging through him.

She had no way of knowing that throughout the night, while she'd drifted to sleep during the intervals between their love-making, he'd stayed awake, staring at the star-studded sky. He'd spent those sleepless hours trying to get a handle on how to best deal with her problems. As well as a few of his own.

Specifically, what was it about Regan Ford aka Susan Kincaid that had him turned inside out from the start? And why—before he even heard her side of things—had he brought her to the middle of the lake instead of transporting her to jail?

While he'd listened to her delicate breathing, he'd realized that somewhere over the short time they'd known each other, he had fallen in love. His descent had not been a gentle one onto a soft surface. No, he'd crashed down a cliff and landed on jagged rocks. Now he was helplessly, irrevocably in love.

He'd decided it had probably happened the moment he caught up with her jogging along the lake road and she'd whirled on him, looking strong and fierce, intent on taking him down with a tiny canister of Mace.

How could a man not love a woman who made thunder roll and lightning strike inside him?

In retrospect, that moment had opened his eyes to something about his own family. He'd stayed firmly footloose partly because of the emotional turmoil he'd seen his brothers and sisters go through all in the name of love. But he now understood what put the bedazzled look in his father's eyes whenever his mother was near. It was the same look he'd seen in the eyes of each of his newly married brother and sisters. And more recently in Nate's eyes whenever he talked about Paige. Josh knew now what caused a man or woman to fall so deeply in love it never ended.

It was finding that unique someone. That *only* someone. For him, that was Regan. This woman, to whom he'd given his heart.

This woman, who was worth any risk.

She was his, and he had no intention of letting Payne Creath win the sick game he'd drawn her into. So for now Josh had to put aside his own wants and needs and be a cop. To keep her safe, he had to be what Regan feared most.

"We need to talk," he repeated. Reaching out, he skimmed a hand down her gloriously messy hair. "After coffee."

She tilted her head. "You have coffee on this fancy speedboat?"

"Yeah," he said, slicking his knuckles along her jawline. "The McCalls consider caffeine one of the essential food groups. So there's a coffeepot onboard that hooks into the battery." He rose, grabbed his jeans and hitched them on. "I'll have it brewing in a couple of minutes."

Seeing the gold badge still clipped to his jeans reminded Regan all over again of what lay ahead of her. The only way she could get through this was if she locked down her emotions. To do that, she needed to keep distance between them. Well, as much distance as one could manage on a boat.

While Josh dealt with the coffee, she hurriedly dressed. She dragged the cushions onto the built-in benches, then settled onto the one Josh had dropped her on last night. She avoided looking at the handcuff still locked on the rail beside her.

"Sorry, there's no cream or sugar onboard," he said when he handed her a mug.

"Black's fine." She blew across the coffee's steaming surface then took her first sip while he settled on the opposite end of the bench from her. There was enough light now she could see a cop's intense assessment in his eyes as he studied her over the rim of his own mug.

"I have a lot of questions, so let's get to them," he said quietly. "The most important being, did you kill Steven Vaughn?"

Her heart kicked, and she slowly lowered the mug from her lips. "I told you I didn't. You said you believed me."

"I do. Which means I'm not arresting you or taking you to jail."

"But…you ran my fingerprints. Surely there's some system in place that Creath would find out about that. And know I'm in Sundown."

"I didn't want to alert anyone you were here, so I bypassed

the Sundown PD's computer. My brother Nate ran your prints from Oklahoma City."

"Won't that lead Creath to him?"

"Probably." Josh glanced at his watch. "Nate won't get in touch with Creath on his own, but Creath might have already contacted him."

Regan slid her tongue over her lips. "Nate knows I'm wanted. Won't he tell Creath I'm in Sundown?"

Glancing across the lake, Josh saw that the sun had almost totally cleared the horizon. He knew Nate would keep his word not to contact Creath. Just as Nate would wait the full twenty-four hours they'd agreed to, then—if necessary—he would make good on his promise to show up with the rest of the Mc-Call siblings in order to get their rebel brother out of hot water in his dealings with a woman wanted for murder.

But Regan hadn't killed anyone. And even if his entire family believed otherwise, Josh wasn't going to turn his back on her. He would do what had to be done.

"Nate will tell Creath your prints were pulled out of a stolen car recovered near one of the interstates in Oklahoma City. Your prints being *only* on the passenger side means that you aren't wanted for the car theft. And that doesn't necessarily put you in Oklahoma, since you could have hitched a ride anywhere and the thief ditched the car later." Josh raised a shoulder. "Creath won't have any reason to think Nate's covering for you."

Because just talking about Creath made her hands unsteady, Regan set her mug aside. "But his contacting your brother puts Creath one step closer to you. Josh, please…"

He held up a hand. "The instant I was accused of planting evidence in that rapist's apartment, I started trying to prove my innocence. I'm doing the same where you're concerned."

"You weren't intentionally set up." She fisted her hands in her lap. "I was. By a cop who investigates *homicides*. Creath knows how to kill people and get away with it."

"Every homicide cop worth his salt knows. It's just that the smart ones also know there's no such thing as the perfect crime." Leaning back, Josh rested an ankle over his knee. "Which explains why the cops catch so many bad guys. And why I need to know as much about Creath as possible."

Seeing the steadiness in Josh's eyes, hearing it in his voice gave Regan the first glimmer of hope she had found in a very dark tunnel that was over a year long. "What do you need to know?"

"At first, Creath was obsessed with having you in his life. He was so sure you were his 'one magic person' that it doesn't sound like he anticipated you would bolt. Even after you did, he found you in D.C., gave you one last chance to return to New Orleans and set up house with him. You wouldn't have been free to do that if he'd already set you up to take the fall for Steven's murder. Which means he had to do things in two phases."

"I hadn't thought of that," Regan said after a moment. "Everything's all knotted together in my mind. I never tried to analyze what happened step-by-step."

"It's hard to reason out a nightmare when you're living it." Josh sipped his coffee. He'd worked out a lot of it during the night, and he knew things would solidify even more while he talked to Regan.

"Do you know what drug Creath used to kill Steven? How he administered it?"

She nodded. "Because I was a paramedic, I knew all the assistants in the New Orleans coroner's office. One of them gave me copies of Steven's autopsy and tox report. Steven died from an overdose of fentanyl."

"Fentanyl?"

"An opioid, probably one of the most addictive there is. It gives a bigger high than heroin. It can be injected or taken orally. There are even fentanyl lollipops to help kids relax pre-op."

"Pre-op, meaning it's used a lot in hospitals?"

"Yes." Regan paused, collected her thoughts while she

shored up her emotions. "The night…I found Steven, there was an open bottle of scotch and a glass on the coffee table near his body. Lab tests later showed the scotch in the glass had been spiked with enough fentanyl to kill someone five times over."

"Were there track marks on Steven's body?"

She closed her eyes. "No."

"The suicide note you told me about that was found on Steven's computer talked about his battling a long-term drug problem. But Creath would know track marks can be used to date how long someone's been using drugs. By spiking the scotch, he created the impression Steven always ingested the fentanyl orally. And unless the investigating officer, in this case Creath, asked for a special tox screen on the liver which could show how long the victim had been abusing a drug, the usual tox screen would have been done on blood or urine. That screen would show only how much drug was in Steven's system at the time of death."

"True."

"Then Creath sees Bobby comforting you at Steven's funeral. A few days later he spots you at the E.R., crying on Bobby's shoulder. That may be when Creath realized as long as Bobby was around you wouldn't turn to him for solace. So, he took Bobby out of the picture." Josh paused, a sudden thought narrowing his eyes. "Did Creath ever threaten to set you up to take the blame for Bobby's murder?"

"No. I guess he thought Steven's would be sufficient."

"Okay, at that point Creath had cleared the way for the two of you to be together. Instead of cooperating, you threaten to go to his chief and tell him Creath killed Steven and Bobby. That would have sent the message to Creath he was going to have to play hardball to get you to go along with his plans. So by the time Internal Affairs interviewed him, he'd dummied up your phone records and had you on tape swearing your eternal love."

"I don't understand how Creath did either of those things."

"His coming up with the tape wouldn't be hard, especially if he carried a hidden recorder and taped your conversations from the time he first started those chance encounters with you, which were anything but chance. He was obsessed with you—it makes sense he'd want his true love's voice on tape. And don't forget the session where he met you at that diner. You said you told him 'I love Steven.' All Creath had to do was splice the section of tape with you saying 'I love' onto one where you say 'you.' Suddenly, he's got you on tape saying, 'I love you.'"

Regan shook her head. "It must have been so easy for him."

"That part," Josh agreed. "Your phone records are another matter. I'm not sure how he pulled that off. But OCPD's got a techno whiz on board named Wade Crawford who might be able to shed some light."

Josh paused, thinking. "After the IA cop's visit, you knew Creath had totally blocked you from getting help, so you left town. Which couldn't have done much for his ego. Still, his ultimate obsession was to have you, so he came to D.C., broke into your place and left peppermint candy—another obsession of his—on your bed. He would have seen the tape recorder hooked to your phone. By then he'd have been wary about what you might do. So he replaced the tape in the recorder with one that had been degaussed."

"I don't know what that means."

"Subjected to a strong magnet so it wouldn't record. What did you hear when you tried to play back the recording you made of Creath's phone call?"

"The hiss of a blank tape."

Josh nodded. "Which made you think your recorder screwed up. Chances are, if you'd put that cassette in a different machine and tried to record something, you would have still wound up with a blank tape."

"All I knew then was Creath would always be one step ahead of me. And if I didn't go back to New Orleans with him he would make good on his threat to make it look like I killed Steven."

"So you skipped out on Creath. Which probably zapped that twisted love he felt for you into deep-seated hate. That takes us to phase two."

"The murder warrant?" Regan asked.

"Right. No cop gets a warrant without presenting a halfway decent case to a D.A. Which includes at least some damn good circumstantial evidence. Any idea what Creath came up with to use against you?"

"No. When Langley told me I was wanted for murder, I didn't ask questions. I was too upset. Too scared. And I knew there wasn't any way for me to fight Creath."

"Who's Langley?"

"A New Orleans P.I. He watches Creath for me."

Leaning, Josh set his mug on the boat's deck. "Why Langley? Had you used him before?"

"No, I remembered Steven mentioning a doctor he worked with had hired Langley. The doctor had been on the verge of a divorce and suspected his wife was having an affair. He knew he needed proof of that so he could block her taking him to the cleaners for alimony. The doc got the name of a P.I. whose license had once been suspended over a run-in with cops. Word was, Langley would do whatever it took to get the goods on someone."

"Meaning break a few laws?"

Regan raised a shoulder. "I didn't care what it meant. He sounded like someone who wouldn't have qualms about keeping track of a cop's whereabouts."

"Did you ask Langley to do more? Maybe check out Creath's background?"

"I didn't have money for that." Regan stared down at her

hands, still clenched together in her lap. "In a couple of e-mails Langley said Creath had snagged his interest, but he never said why. All I wanted to know was if Creath left New Orleans."

Josh nodded, a plan forming in his mind. "If Langley's watched Creath for a year, then the P.I. must know a lot about him."

"Like what?"

"Who he hangs with. What he does, where he goes. Everyone has an Achilles heel—I want to know what Creath's is. I can check some things from a distance, but they can't help me get a fix on who Creath is. *Understand* who he is. I need to talk to Langley."

"Except for when I called and hired him, we've always communicated by e-mail. I trust Langley, but I don't want him to know where I am. Or to be able to trace my calls."

"What about your e-mail?"

"I have it set up to go through an anonymous remailing service. That makes it a lot harder to track e-mails to their true origin."

"Sounds like you've got yourself covered, and we want to leave things that way. So you and I are going to drive to Dallas this morning and use a pay phone to call Langley. You can tell him it's okay to talk to me, then I'll let him know what I need him to do." Josh's lips curved a little. "And don't worry about the cost, this is on me."

"No. I'll pay you back. It will take time, but I'll pay you." Feeling the pressure building in her lungs, Regan let out a slow breath. "Going to Langley just gets you in deeper."

"That's where I want to be."

"Josh, what if Creath doesn't believe Nate's story about finding my prints in a stolen car? What if he shows up in Nate's office, wanting to see that evidence?"

"Then Nate and I will figure out how to handle things without clueing Creath that we know where you are."

"He'll find out," she said, as if it were already a reality. "Somehow he'll find out you're protecting me. Then he'll come after you, just like he did Steven and Bobby." She rose, knowing if she sat still a moment longer, she'd explode. "Since you're not arresting me, I should leave Sundown. *This morning.*"

Josh was on his feet in a heartbeat. He advanced on her, framing her face with his hands. "That's not an option."

She reached up, curled her fingers around his wrists. "If Creath figures things out and comes here looking for me, he won't stay if I'm gone. He'll try to catch up with me."

"Meaning, if he's focused on you, he won't have time to look too hard at me."

"He'll kill you."

"Listen to me." Josh was tempted to shake some sense into her, but he knew she was running on pure emotion, so he held back. "Steven and Bobby weren't cops. *I* am. I know how cops work, how they think. I also know what it takes to set someone up, the steps that have to be gone through to make someone look bad. From both sides."

Her ice-cold fingers tightened on his wrists as she stared up at him, her eyes both brilliant and tormented. "Creath can't find out about you. If I leave Sundown, he won't find out."

"Dammit, Regan, if you run now, Creath wins. You'll have to run for the rest of your life. You'll never be sure he won't find you. Is that what you want?"

"What I want is not to be afraid anymore. I want to wake up and find out this has all been a nightmare and my life is as neat and tidy as it used to be. But that's not going to happen."

"It *can* happen. But only if you give me time to dig into Creath. Unearth whatever the hell mistakes he made when he set up what he believes is the perfect crime." Josh's fingers tightened against her face. "I want your word you won't run. That you'll trust me to take care of this. Of you. Promise me, Regan."

Her throat was so dry, she wasn't certain she could answer. With an effort, she swallowed. "Why are you doing this? You've got nothing but my word about what happened. I can't prove I didn't kill Steven. I can't prove *anything*. Yet, you're putting your job, your life at risk for me. Why?"

He gave her a long look that was close to grim. "I'm in love with you."

Shock flashed into her eyes an instant before she jerked back.

He set his jaw. "I see that thrills the hell out of you."

"Josh, I…" She *was* thrilled. And terrified. Filled with regrets and hammered with longings. She wanted desperately to tell him she loved him, too. But a dark, icy premonition held her back, whispering at the edges of her mind that if she voiced her feelings, Creath would somehow know. And come after Josh.

When she continued to stare at him, lips parted, eyes wide, Josh held up a hand. "Let's just deal with my feelings later," he ground out. "Right now, I want you to promise you'll stay in Sundown."

"I'll stay as long as Creath is in New Orleans." Her voice held a thread of desperation, but she didn't care. "If he leaves there—the *minute* he leaves—so do I."

Driven, he grabbed her arms, dragged her against him. "That's not good enough."

"It has to be," she said dully. She pressed her palms against his chest while emotion twisted inside her. "I can't lose anyone else, Josh. I won't sit around here waiting for Creath to show up and…" Her voice cracked. *Kill you.* She couldn't bring herself to say those words again. "I'll run for the rest of my life if it means keeping you safe."

On an oath, Josh wrapped his arms around her, wanting to soothe, needing to reassure. Wishing this closeness could last forever, he stroked her hair while searching for words to penetrate her fear, her grief. But there was no place for logic here, no place to be calm and rational. So he held her. Just held her.

And he knew that if she ran, he would never get over it. Never get over her. So he would hold tight to what he loved and figure out a way to take Creath down before the bastard picked up her scent.

Chapter 13

Hours later, Josh stood in a Dallas phone booth talking long-distance to the P.I. Regan had hired to watch Payne Creath. Concurrently, the subject of that conversation left his car parked out of sight off a rutted dirt road on the outskirts of New Orleans, and crept toward the rear of a house that looked to be a leading candidate for termite bait.

Vaguely aware of the heavy feel of his holstered Ruger against the small of his back, Creath unwrapped a piece of peppermint and popped it into his mouth. Mindful that a stray piece of evidence could trip up the most brilliant plan, he slid the cellophane wrapper deep into the pocket of his khaki pants.

With no breeze stirring, the row of tall cypress trees on the opposite side of the ragged backyard stood as still as death. Although it wasn't yet noon, the intense heat of the Louisiana sun had upped the humidity level, making the air nearly thick enough to swim in.

His hands sweating inside the latex gloves he'd pulled on,

Creath edged closer to the rear of the house, noting that every grimy window and door stood open.

He had spotted his watcher for the first time the previous evening as the man ducked into an aging Chevy. The car's tag had led to a Daniel Langley with a rural route address. Moments later, Creath and his partner had gotten called to a homicide scene, so he'd had to put off tracking down the exact location of the address until this morning. And running a background check on the Chevy's owner.

Daniel Langley, private investigator.

After a more in-depth check, Creath knew that Langley was small change, a camera for hire. Earned a living doing low-rent surveillance. Maybe running drug or gambling money when he was desperate for cash. Several years back, an arrest for assaulting a cop had resulted in Langley's P.I. license getting suspended until a technicality got the charge dropped. Since then, Langley had kept his nose clean.

Until he'd started watching Creath.

For who? Creath wondered, stepping silently onto the cement back porch that held only a pink metal lawn chair. Who the hell had an interest in him?

"Before today, I only spoke to Miss Kincaid once, the day she hired me."

It wasn't just the rough-as-pine-bark voice coming through the patched screen door that stopped Creath cold. It was hearing *her* name.

"She sounded scared spitless," the voice continued, mixing with the faint, rapid click of a keyboard. "Considering what I've dug up since then, I don't blame her. Not that I can *prove* anything, mind you. But considering he lived in the system since he was born, it's no wonder he learned how to manipulate it and everyone in it to his advantage."

Easing beside the door, Creath did a quick peek through the screen. The dark-haired, rail-thin man he'd spotted last night now wore a plaid shirt and brown slacks, and was sitting alone at a kitchen table. He had a phone wedged between his cheek and shoulder while he typed on a laptop.

"Okay, I just e-mailed the info I put together on Creath to Miss Kincaid. And I attached that article I told you about. Let me know if you need me to do more than just keep the bastard under surveillance."

Susan.

Pain sliced through Creath, just as sharp after a year's passage. Hate instantly followed, its vicious claws scrabbling up his throat at the thought of how she'd turned her back on him. Rejected him.

Tossed him away.

The merciless heat and humidity pressed in on Creath, jumping his mind backward in time. He remembered the stifling dark closet with only the thin band of illumination at the bottom. He had huddled, a small boy, on the bare floor near the light, near the air. He could see the woman's feet coming his way. Hear each step. The closet was ripe with her musky scent.

She had driven, like a spike into his brain, the knowledge that she'd never wanted him. That she kept him only because the state paid her money to do so. Money she used to buy booze and drugs and men. Men who abused her and, on occasion, the boy who cowered in the closet, unable to make himself small enough to go unnoticed.

Despite his young age he understood she wasn't to blame for his misery. He spent hours every day locked in the matte-black sweltering hell because another woman had tossed him away.

His mother.

Even after so many years, his hatred for her was liquid and cold, like mercury flowing through his veins. He felt the same hatred for Susan Kincaid.

Creath forced his breathing to even. Willed back the icy fury in his blood. He deserved to savor the taste of the hunt, of closing in, of cornering his prey.

His prey. Lifting his chin, he breathed deeply, like a dog seeking the scent of her.

He flexed his gloved fingers, unflexed them. The air of expectation thickened around him like mist hovering above the still, black waters of the bayou. The holstered Ruger pressed against the small of his back like a hand urging him to jerk open the screen door and rush in.

But Creath was not a man who allowed his impulses to control him. Fools did that all the time, and they got caught. He was smarter. More clever. Disciplined. He would wait until the P.I. ended the phone call.

Then he would make his move.

And finally, *finally* Susan Kincaid would be his.

"That had to have been a hellish childhood," Regan said late that afternoon as she sat on a stool in Josh's kitchen, her laptop before her on the granite-topped cooking island. She continued to scroll through the information Langley had e-mailed during his phone call with Josh.

"You feeling sorry for Creath?" Josh asked, handing her a glass of lemonade.

"For the child whose mother stuffed him in a garbage bag when he was less than an hour old and tossed him in a Dumpster," Regan qualified. "For the child who got fished out of that dumpster and wound up with a foster mother who was later convicted of abuse and fraud."

Josh settled onto the stool beside her. "Problem is, that little boy grew up to be a monster."

"Yes." Her throat dry, Regan sipped lemonade while her gaze moved down the monitor's screen. "And five years ago, he dated a woman who disappeared without a trace."

"Two days after she broke off their engagement," Josh added.

Regan's mind cataloged the information they'd learned from Langley who, after finding out about Creath's missing ex-fiancée, had dug into the cop's background all on his own.

One aspect of that information was like an ice pick stab to Regan's heart. "I had no idea Creath had Steven's body exhumed."

"Which supports the theory that when you disappeared, Creath had to backtrack to set you up. Like Langley said, after you split, Creath conducted a search of your apartment in New Orleans. Your former roommate still lives there, so it's not like everything got cleared out when you moved to D.C. During his search of what had been your bedroom, Creath claimed he found a hidden cache of fentanyl, the same drug that killed Steven. That was enough for Creath to get the exhumation order and request a quantitative tox report. The report would show the exact impurities, cutting agents and precise percentages of each in the fentanyl Steven ingested. Creath knew an analysis of the fentanyl he planted in your bedroom would show it was from the exact same batch that killed Steven."

"Which made it look like I murdered him."

Josh nodded. "You were Steven's fiancée, you found his body without a witness around. You skipped town secretly after attempting to harass and distract the detective investigating your fiancé's death and in your haste to flee you left behind some of the exact same drug that killed the doctor. At that point, Creath had enough to make a circumstantial case against you and get the murder warrant issued."

"It must have been so easy for him. So simple," Regan said, struggling to stay calm. "And there's no way to prove I didn't do any of those things."

"There's a way." Scooting her glass aside, Josh wrapped his hand around hers. "We just have to figure out what it is."

Regan looked down at their joined hands, then slowly lifted her gaze. The night she'd first set eyes on Josh at Truelove's Tavern, he'd looked both dangerous and competent. Now, sitting beside her, dressed in gray slacks and a black pullover, the thin scar winding up his throat, he looked just as dangerous. Just as competent.

Yet the thought of all that could go wrong had dread curling in her stomach. "You sound so sure of yourself."

"I am." He sent her a quick, smug look. "Have I mentioned that during my rebellious youth, I operated three-card monte games? Hawked designer knockoffs of expensive watches? Forged IDs so my pals and I could buy beer and get into clubs?"

"Quite an impressive résumé," Regan said and shook her head. "Are there any laws or rules you haven't broken?"

"A few." His thumb did a slow caress over her knuckles. "My point is, I mostly got away with that stuff. But there was always someone—usually someone wearing a badge—who knew enough to spot the weak link in my scams. Setting someone up to take the fall for something they didn't do is just a different kind of scam. And, trust me, that weak link is there. The trick is to dig in the right place to unearth it."

"The problem is finding that place."

Josh thought for a moment, his forehead furrowing. "As a paramedic you had knowledge of what drugs do what, and you were Steven Vaughn's fiancée. Meaning you had the means and opportunity to kill him. What would have been your motive?"

"Money," Regan answered instantly. "Steven's grandfather and father were both prominent doctors. His mother's grandfather made a killing in oil and real estate. Neither of Steven's parents had siblings. Steven was an only child. When his parents died in a plane crash, Steven inherited millions."

"Millions," Josh repeated. Crossing his arms over his chest, he studied Regan. Before they'd left for Dallas, she'd changed into narrow white jeans, sneakers and a soft white blouse, tied at her waist. Her sleek, black hair was anchored in a ponytail. He tried to envision her as a New Orleans socialite, married to a wealthy doctor, but the image wouldn't gel. The only man he could picture her with was himself.

"Hypothetically," he said, "if you wanted Steven's money, wouldn't you need to wait to kill him until you were married?"

"No. After we got engaged he set up a trust fund in my name, which I could access in the event of his death. I told him to wait until after the wedding, but he said he loved me and wanted to provide for me in case something happened to him."

"Creath happened," Josh said quietly.

"Yes." There were no tears in her eyes, no fear. Just an unbearable weariness. "My life is balanced on that single point in time. I can't remember what it was like to wake up and not be afraid. To wonder if that would be the day someone found out the truth."

"That day's past. And we're looking for a different truth." He slid his hand down her ponytail. "What will Susan Kincaid do when her nightmare ends and she's free to collect the money in that trust fund?"

"I don't know." Considering the question, she took a long, slow drink of lemonade. "I'm not that same woman anymore. And New Orleans seems so far removed it might as well be on another planet."

That geographical distancing was to his advantage, Josh thought, since he intended to make her a part of his life. After he dealt with Creath.

He looked back at the laptop's screen. "Let's check the attachment Langley sent with his e-mail."

"You said it's a newspaper article?" Regan asked as she typed in commands. "About Creath receiving an award from some civic organization?"

"Cop of the year," Josh said dryly. "Now there's a scam."

When the article blipped onto the screen, Josh got his first look at Payne Creath. He was good-looking in a mildly beat-up way. A big man with broad shoulders, big hands, a nose that had been broken a couple of times. He had a heavy tan, like a beach bum, but he was too old for that. Late thirties, Josh judged.

"I can't stand to look at him," Regan said, her voice a shaky whisper.

"Then don't." Settling his hands on her shoulders, Josh swiveled her sideways on her stool, their knees bumping. Just seeing Creath's picture had turned her face as pale as ice and put the haunted look back in her eyes. She was trembling, yet poised to move, he noted. To run. Slicking his hands down her arms, he firmed his grip and locked her thighs between his.

She wasn't going to take off on him. He'd be damned if he let her. "I've never been in love," he said quietly. "Never even close. I am now. I want to make a life with you."

She shook her head. "Don't."

"Don't what?" he asked firmly, though his hands remained gentle on her arms. "Notice you're on the verge of taking off? I want a future with you, Regan. If you bolt that can't happen. If you want promises—"

"No," she said quickly. "I don't want anything I can't give back." She dragged in a shuddering breath. "My life is a mess. I may never be able to give you anything."

He bit down on his frustration. He wanted her to tumble into love with him, as quickly and completely as he'd tumbled into love with her. He wanted that, even knowing how unreasonable he was to expect a woman who was adrift, afraid and in trouble to focus on what was going on in her heart.

"You can give me your trust," he said levelly. "Trust me to protect you. To find the evidence that will clear you. You can give me your word that you'll stay in Sundown."

"I do trust you." *And love you.* She could hardly bear knowing she was hurting him by denying him her promise not to leave Sundown. But that was preferable to his winding up dead. "Creath is another matter. If he finds me here, I don't trust that he will just put me in jail and be done with it. I *know* what he's capable of. And maybe you won't be the only one he'll perceive has blocked his way to having me. He might focus on Etta because she gave me a job and a home. Then there's Howie and Deni, my coworkers. I worked with Bobby, and he's dead."

At that instant, Josh's cell phone trilled. Regan took a deep breath while he checked its display.

"Decker," he said. "Probably calling about the peeper case."

While Josh answered the call, Regan eased off the stool and moved across the kitchen. She dumped the remainder of her lemonade in the sink, then lifted her gaze and stared out one of the room's expansive windows. As always, she found the panorama of rolling, tree-lined hills and the lake of crystal-blue water staggering.

As was the knowledge that Sundown felt more like home to her than New Orleans ever had.

With Josh's phone conversation a murmur in the background, she clenched her hands on the counter. After over a year of hiding, of holding her secrets close, it seemed surreal that she had revealed everything to Josh. And that she'd stood just outside a Dallas phone booth listening to him talk strategy with Langley. If it was foolish to allow herself one bright pinpoint of hope that this nightmare might end soon, then she'd be foolish. But also realistic. And she would do whatever it took to prevent one more person from dying on her account.

"Since you're tied up, I can interview the next person on the list this evening," Josh said.

Regan turned, frowning when she saw how somber his expression had turned.

"In that case I'll do the interview tomorrow when she gets back to town," Josh said after a moment. "I just need one of your cops available in case something about jurisdiction comes up."

When Josh ended the call, Regan asked, "Is there something going on with the peeper investigation?"

"Maybe." He laid his cell phone on the counter, then crossed to her. "Decker isn't going to be able to deal with it right now. This morning, the sheriff who had jurisdiction over Sundown

County and a few others died of a heart attack. Decker's been named acting sheriff, so he's got his hands full."

"I'm sorry to hear about the sheriff. The ladies in Sundown will be on edge until the peeper's caught."

Josh angled his chin. "Right now, there's only one lady in Sundown on my mind," he said, tugging her forward.

While he'd talked to Decker, Josh had studied Regan, wondering what thoughts were going through her mind while she stared out the window. He had not missed the tenseness in her shoulders or the way she gripped the counter until her knuckles turned white. Realizing she'd looked fragile enough to break had him ratcheting back his emotions. If he continued pushing at her, she might just shove him away. "How about we agree to take things one day at a time?"

"I've got a lot of experience at that." Inching her head back, she framed his face in her palms. "You can't know what your believing in me means. There's no way I can ever repay you for that."

"I can think of a way," he murmured, then settled his mouth on hers.

And ravished.

Her heart kicked hard in her chest, driving the breath out of her body. Instantly, all the emotions that had been roiling inside her honed down to one: desire. Her hands slid down his throat to his shoulders and gripped, as much for balance as for the sudden need that shot from him to her and fused them together.

His fevered mouth raced over her face, streaked down her throat. On a moan, she pulled his lips back to hers.

She wanted him, as she had never wanted before. It made no difference they had spent the previous night making love. The ache of wanting him was so huge it left no room for reason. No doubt.

But she forced away the need and fought to regain her sanity while she still could. "I have…to leave for work in about five minutes." She gazed up at him, her hands still locked on his shoulders, her lungs pumping. "I don't think that's enough time to repay my debt to you."

"Not nearly," he agreed, nipping her bottom lip. "So we'll get back to that later. You might be interested to know there's another way you can work on that repayment."

"Oh, really?" She leaned back against the counter, trying not to pant. "What?"

"The next day or two, you can come here and make lemon tea bread." He curled a finger beneath her chin, nudged it up. "I imagine we could figure out a creative way to pass the time while it's baking."

She gave him a look from behind her lashes. "So, lemon tea bread will pay off my debt?"

"Hell no, that first loaf would be the *initial* payment on your installment plan." He arched a dark brow. "We haven't even talked about the interest that'll accrue. Compounded daily."

"Sounds to me like the rate you charge is exorbitant."

"You have no idea. It might take the rest of your life to pay off your debt."

More than anything, she wished she could look into her future and see Josh there. In truth, she saw only Creath. Felt only a vivid premonition of disaster.

She drew in a slow breath, let it out, then pushed away from the counter. "If I don't leave now, I'll be late for work." She gestured toward her laptop. "Do you want me to leave my computer here?"

"Yeah. I'll take it upstairs and print off what Langley sent."

Sliding a companionable arm around her waist, Josh walked her down the hallway, thinking how right it felt to hold her against him. How right it felt for her to be in the house that he considered his second home.

Holding the screen door open, he followed her out onto the

front porch into the long shadows of the late afternoon. The air was hot and still, heavy with the scent of the yellow roses spilling out of the multitude of pots. "So, can I expect you here after you get off work?"

She glanced in the direction of Etta's house before looking back at him. "I don't know. With Etta off the IV, I'm thinking I should move back into the apartment over the tavern."

"Which translates into your wanting to put space between you and Etta. You and me."

"I'm being careful. There's nothing wrong with that."

"I agree. But Langley's watching Creath. If the bastard leaves New Orleans, we'll know. It's the same arrangement you've had with Langley the past year." He cupped his palm to her cheek. "The only thing that's changed is that you're not alone in this anymore."

She laid her hand over his. "I know." He was right, she conceded. Langley had assured them he'd seen Creath the previous night. If Creath left New Orleans, Langley would sound the alarm. So there was no reason she should say no to Josh. No reason to turn away from comfort, from passion. From the man she loved. "I'll see you later, then."

"I'll be waiting."

Josh leaned a shoulder against the nearest porch column, watching as she steered her Mustang out of Etta's driveway. The night he'd walked into Truelove's and spotted Regan, he had somehow known she was going to be a huge complication. He'd never been more right in his life.

He narrowed his eyes. One of the stops they'd made while in Dallas was to have lunch. When Regan excused herself to go to the ladies' room, he'd phoned Nate. As they'd anticipated, his brother had gotten a call about the run he'd done on Regan's prints. Only it had been from Creath's partner, who mentioned Creath was out of the office, wrapping up another case. As far as Nate could tell, the partner had been satisfied with the prints-found-in-a-stolen-car explanation. So maybe, just maybe, they'd dodged that bullet.

Personally, Josh hadn't been so lucky. When he told Nate he had no intention of arresting Regan and turning her in, Nate's curses had turned the air blue. Josh was well aware of the risk to his career, even without Nate's vehement reminders. Josh hadn't even attempted to explain to his brother what Regan meant to him. Wasn't sure he *could* explain.

He just knew she was worth every risk to his heart, to his job. His life. And he couldn't walk away from her.

He pulled open the screen door and headed back to the kitchen. There, he settled on the stool in front of the laptop and studied Payne Creath.

Josh had been a cop for a decade, yet in the course of his career, he had never confronted true evil until now. For a split second, he got the image of Creath with Regan, his hands… *No.* He couldn't think like that. If he did, he would go nuts.

So, he would concentrate on taking Creath down. And while he was at it, figure out the best way to keep the woman he wanted safe and firmly in his life.

Chapter 14

"These your thong panties, Howie?" Josh asked the following afternoon while leaning against the front of Chief Decker's desk.

Wearing a white T-shirt and green fatigues, his sandy hair overdue for a haircut, Howie Lyons sat stiffly in the visitor chair. He eyed the evidence bag in Josh's hand as if it were a snake ready to strike. "Don't know why you think they are."

"I found them in your nightstand."

Astonishment crossed Howie's sharp-boned face. Replaced by uneasiness. "You got no right snoopin' in my apartment. You're not even on the Sundown police force. Where's Chief Decker?"

"Dealing with county business." Josh laid the bag aside. "A warrant gave me the right to 'snoop.'" He flicked a look at the tall cop who stood near the closed door, his arms bulging under the short sleeves of his uniform shirt. "Officer Steed, who is on the Sundown PD, assisted in searching your residence." Steed had also Mirandized Howie when he picked Etta's night cook up at his favorite fishing spot, but Josh didn't make a habit of reminding suspects they had the right to remain silent.

"Want to tell me about the thong, Howie?"

"Belongs to a lady friend. Her name's private."

"So is what people do in their own homes. But you've been creeping around Sundown, looking in windows."

"Who says?"

Josh crossed his arms over his chest. "Late last year, the police began getting prowler reports. That's about the same time you started staying out after your shift at Truelove's ended instead of going home."

"You been talking to Cinda," Howie scoffed. "Don't know why you'd listen to a woman who went off the deep end gettin' religion and tossed her husband out—"

"You're right, I talked to your soon-to-be-ex when she got back to town this morning from visiting her sister. Cinda told me religion has nothing to do with your impending divorce. You stopped going home. The final straw was her finding a pair of women's panties in the glove box of your pickup."

"I found them panties outside the Laundromat. And you'd start staying out, too, if your wife barred you from her bed, saying she'd had enough sex to last a lifetime."

"So, you decided to get your kicks by peeking in windows. Scaring women." Josh narrowed his eyes. "I work sex crimes, Howie. That's why Decker asked me to consult on this investigation. I know that voyeurs don't stop with peeking in windows. They break into houses like you did when you stole that black thong. Commit rapes."

"Whoa, whoa." Howie held up his hands, palms toward Josh. "I ain't ever raped no woman."

"Ever thought about it?"

"Hell no! Dammit, Josh, you've known me since you was a boy. You *know* I don't go around rapin' women."

"No, I don't know." But Howie had been a part of Etta's life for as long as Josh could remember, so he settled into the chair beside the man's and warmed his voice up a couple of notches. "This is serious."

Howie eyed him warily. "Didn't mean no harm. It's just when Cinda cast me out I was so damn mad. Hurt. So, I started driving around Sundown after the tavern closed. Sometimes I'd walk. Peek in a window or two."

"Why did you unscrew porch lights?"

"Well, hell, I didn't want nobody to *see* me and get upset. Anyway, what harm is there in unscrewing a lightbulb?"

"Did you see any harm in breaking into Virginia Nash's house? Stealing her granddaughter's thong?"

"I didn't *break in.* Everybody knows Virginia don't lock her doors. In fact, her back door was standing open that night 'cause it was so hot out. I looked in the window and seen them thongs in the laundry basket. So I just opened the screen door and snagged 'em. A man's got a right to his fantasies."

Josh gave Howie a level look. "Were you fantasizing when you crept up on Regan's balcony and watched her sleeping?"

"I wasn't there 'cause of no fantasy. Mind you, Regan's a fine-looking young woman, but I've been worried about her. She looks so…I don't know, *scared* sometimes." Howie shrugged. "That night at work, she was jumpy, kept her eye on the door like she was expectin' someone she didn't want to see walk into the tavern. After closing, I snuck upstairs on the balcony and looked in her window to make sure she was okay."

Giving Howie credit for being perceptive, Josh tapped his fingers against the chair's arm while his thoughts slid to the previous night. When he'd heard Regan's car pull in after she got off work, he'd stepped out onto the porch. He could still feel the way her mouth had scorched over his, slicing a jagged line of need straight through him while her scent slithered into his system. And that was even before they got inside the front door.

But even the hungry, possessive tide that burned through him couldn't totally mask the deep, intuitive disquiet that had settled inside him. A disquiet that still hung on. He glanced at the wall clock, thinking Regan was probably busy right now in his kitchen, whipping up the loaf of lemon tea bread she'd promised to bake.

After a futile attempt to tweak the tenseness out of his shoulders, Josh shifted his gaze back to Howie. The sooner he dealt with the man, the sooner he could get back to Regan.

"Let's talk about why you took Seamus O'Toole's keys from behind the bar. Then unlocked his back gate, unscrewed the porch light and got an eyeful watching Mrs. O'Toole."

When Howie slid his gaze away, Josh continued. "That's how we got you, Howie. Chief Decker interviewed all the tavern's employees and vendors who had access to those keys. He whittled down the list until your name was the only one left. What Cinda told me cinched the deal. You might as well come clean."

"Well, hell, O'Toole brought his wife to the tavern a couple of times. She's an impressive woman." Howie shifted in his chair. "I admit to wantin' a closer look at Mrs. O'Toole."

Josh shook his head. "Howie, you're going to have to answer for what you've done."

"What have I got to answer for? The Sundown city council ought to hire me for keepin' an eye on things during the night. You want to know how many people's pets I've found wandering around and taken back home to keep 'em from gettin' run over? And I've lost count of the number of sprinklers I've turned off that people left running and water was gushing down the street. Saved 'em a pot of money on their utility bills, I expect."

Josh raised a brow. "That's quite a spin job. Maybe you should go into public relations."

"There you go," Howie said comfortably. "I could be the eyes and ears of the police, being as how the only cop on duty at night has to double as dispatcher. I also keep watch on all the hotels in Sundown *and* the ones on the other side of the lake."

Flicking a look at Officer Steed, Howie leaned closer to Josh. "If I wasn't so discreet I'd be naming folks who've been sneakin' over to those hotels to meet each other. A certain officer's girlfriend being one of 'em. And I haven't breathed a word about that cop I seen at the Sundown Inn last night, 'cause he might be on some secret undercover job."

Josh felt himself go still. "What cop?"

"Don't know. He's not one of our local boys."

"How do you know he's a cop?"

"Well, I didn't at first. I was strolling around the inn when I spotted a car pulling in that had a rental sticker on the back bumper. It was about an hour after Truelove's closed, and I wanted to get a better look at the man just to see if he'd been at the tavern earlier. The curtain over the window in his room was closed, but there was enough gap at the bottom for me to see in. He emptied his pants pockets onto the table in front of the window. Then he laid a gun and a shiny gold badge there, too."

Josh could feel the disquiet inside him ratchet up. "Could you read the name of the department on the badge?"

"Didn't pay no attention to that."

Josh's mouth was as dry as dust. Langley had assured him he would send Regan an e-mail if Creath left New Orleans. Langley hadn't, so Josh had no firm reason to think the cop Howie had seen was Creath. Still, the deep, intuitive disquiet that swept through Josh told him it was.

He was on his feet and on the other side of Decker's desk without being aware of having come up out of his chair. "If you saw a picture of the cop would you recognize him?" he asked as he booted up the chief's computer.

"Might. The gap in the curtain wasn't that wide so I never got a real good look at him."

Thanking the fates he remembered what newspaper had run the article Langley e-mailed, Josh accessed the archives, typed in Creath's name. When the article blipped onto the screen, Josh swiveled the monitor toward Howie. "This the cop?"

Howie leaned forward. "I think so. I'm not sure."

Josh waited for Creath's picture to print, grabbed it out of the printer. He gave Steed a quick look as he headed for the door. "Hold Howie."

"On what charge?"

"Public nuisance."

With adrenaline charging through his blood, Josh jerked his cell phone off the waist of his jeans. He had to get to Regan before Creath.

"Time to take two pink pills."

The voice coming out of nowhere had Regan fumbling the pan of batter she was about to slide into Josh's oven. Her heart thumping, she realized it had been her own voice.

Coming from the pocket of her shorts.

Etta's memory box, she remembered, expelling a shaky laugh.

After popping the pan into the oven, she dipped her hand in her pocket and pulled out the long, slim recorder. This morning, she'd helped Etta fix her hair so she would look "fittin'" when A.C. picked her up so they could spend the day at his daughter's house. Since Etta had finished taking all the antibiotics Doc Zink had prescribed, Regan had intended to delete the message before she left Etta's, but had forgotten.

Sliding the recorder back into her pocket, Regan made a mental note to return it next door after the lemon tea bread finished baking.

While a CD of low, bluesy music played in the background, Regan rinsed the mixing bowl she'd used, then replaced the flour in the pantry. She imagined she was the picture of domesticity—a woman baking, waiting for the man she loved to come home.

Home. She took in the expansive kitchen with its solid granite counters and up-to-date appliances. She felt so at home here. So loved. Last night, Josh had carried her to his bed and made slow, sweet love to her until she clung to him, feeling drugged and dizzy.

If only, she thought. If only.

When the phone rang, she paused, hoping it was Josh calling to tell her he'd finished his interviews on the peeper case and was on the way there. The answering machine clicked on, and his voice flowed out, instructing the caller to leave a message.

"Josh, it's Nate."

Regan went as taut as a bowstring. She'd never spoken to Nate McCall, but she recognized hot fury when she heard it.

"I just got a call from Creath's partner. Your Susan Kincaid pawned a gun that was used in a homicide in New Orleans. Victim's name is Bobby Ivers. Josh, you thinking what I'm thinking? Kincaid might be able to claim that being accused of one murder is a setup. But two is becoming a habit. A nasty one. She conveniently—or maybe I should say stupidly—listed her address on the pawn ticket as the apartment over Etta's tavern. Creath is on his way to pick her up."

Nate paused, uttered an oath. "Josh, you're in way over your head. Bran and I are on our way to Sundown to make sure you haven't lost all your mental capacity over this woman. Not to mention figure out how the hell you're going to keep your badge."

Trembling, her legs jelly, Regan gripped the edge of the counter. Creath had found her. She had no idea when. But it had been long enough for him to learn her address in Sundown, then pawn the gun he'd used to kill Bobby in order to set her up for her coworker's murder, too.

A mix of fear and panic stormed through her. All of her senses screamed the warning that Creath's arresting her would in no way appease the sick hatred he felt for her. No, he wouldn't rest until he stripped her of everything. Her freedom, the people she loved.

Josh.

The thing Creath wanted most was *her,* she reminded herself, struggling for calm. He couldn't track her and go after Josh at the same time. So, she would run. And if there was any light in the world, the man she loved would stay out of harm's way.

Holding on to that hope, Regan raced down the hallway. She needed to grab her running money, her computer and clothes from Etta's, then she'd be gone.

She punched open the front screen door and dashed outside. Her heartbeat battering her ribs, Regan shot across the porch, then the lawn without looking back.

"Regan!"

Josh was still on his front porch when he yelled her name. He shouted it again as he advanced down the hallway, the smell of burning food growing stronger the closer he got to the kitchen.

He didn't know why the hell he was calling for her. She was gone, and he knew it. Had known it the minute he steered into the drive and saw that her Mustang was gone. Had known it when he raced into Etta's house and discovered her laptop and her clothes missing from her bedroom.

"Dammit!" He turned off the oven, yanked open its door and got blasted by a cloud of thick, black smoke. He grabbed hot pads, jerked out the pan. She'd been gone long enough for the lemon tea bread to have baked to a black blob.

He lobbed the hot pads across the kitchen. He'd gotten a busy signal when he'd tried to call here while he sped to the Sundown Inn. After the clerk looked at Creath's picture and verified the New Orleans cop had been the man who'd paid cash for a room the previous night and checked out early that morning, Josh had tried to call Regan again. The phone had rung that time, but his prompting her to pick up had gone unheeded.

Standing in the center of the kitchen, his hands fisted, he became aware of the husky notes of a saxophone drifting on the air. Clenching his jaw, he forced back emotion, forced himself to think like a cop.

He knew that if Creath had gotten to Regan, he wouldn't have given her the chance to pack her belongings. So, logic told him she'd taken off on her own. And the only reason she would do that was if she'd found out Creath was in Sundown.

How would she know?

Whipping around, he strode to the answering machine. Saw there were two messages. One would be his, Josh thought as he hit the play button.

"Josh, it's Nate."

He listened to the message while the sax wailed and his gut knotted. It was easy to envision Regan standing here, listening to Nate. Realizing she was now wanted for a second murder and that Creath was closing in. Josh could almost see the fear in her eyes, feel her panic.

He swore viciously. Then again, quietly. Stalking out of the kitchen, he retraced his steps along the hallway. Despite the fear she'd surely felt, the panic, he knew the reason Regan had run wasn't to save herself, but him.

She'd forgotten to take the bread out of the oven.

Less than an hour had passed since Regan sped past the Sundown city limit sign; she was still trembling, shaking. Yet the thought blipping in her brain was that if Josh hadn't gotten home by now, the lemon tea bread might have already burst into flames and burned down his house.

Because of her, he could lose his house, his badge, *his life*.

Standing in the grimy bathroom at the rear of the mom-and-pop convenience store on an isolated country road, Regan stared into the wavy mirror. Her face was pale, her eyes half-glassy with fear. She wanted desperately to talk to Josh, tell him she trusted him. Loved him. But she didn't dare contact him. Not when she could almost feel Creath sniffing at her heels.

Still, that was where she wanted the NOPD cop. Sniffing at *her* heels, not Josh's.

She'd taken precious moments at Etta's while cramming her laptop and clothes into her suitcase to phone the tavern. She told the day bartender that she'd quit her job and was leaving town. Since Creath had used the address of the apartment over the tavern when he pawned the gun he'd used to kill Bobby, surely *that* would be the first place he would look for her. And hearing that she'd just left town he would come after her, thinking he could catch up with her. He wouldn't stay in Sundown long enough to find out about her close ties to Etta. To Josh.

Regan splashed cold water on her face, dried it, then took a deep breath when she felt despair rising inside her. She'd already pumped a full tank of gas into the Mustang and she needed to get back on the road. Needed to put as much distance as possible between herself and Sundown.

Dipping her hand into her shorts pocket to retrieve the key to the restroom, her fingers brushed across Etta's recorder. Regan shook her head. When she returned the key to the clerk, she would see if the small store sold padded mailing envelopes so she could send the recorder back to Etta.

Turning, Regan tugged open the door. The long rays of the afternoon sun had her squinting as she stepped out into the skin-soaking heat.

The door was still swinging shut behind her when a heavy hand seized her wrist and hauled her sideways.

"Got you," a gruff voice said.

Chapter 15

The instant the hand locked on her wrist, a jolt of sheer terror shot through Regan. She thrashed, struggling to get free, until she was jerked around and collided with a solid wall of muscle.

"Hold still, dammit."

Her head whipped up. Her breath whooshed out as she stared into Josh's face. "What…are you doing here?"

"Keeping you from making the biggest mistake of your life."

He loomed over her, his broad shoulders all but blocking the sun, his dark eyes glinting, anger showing in every tense line of his body.

"You shouldn't be here. Shouldn't be anywhere near me." Fear for him crimped her voice. "How did you find me?"

"You wouldn't give me your word to stay, so I put a tracking device in your laptop." His voice could have sharpened a razor. "You might ditch the Mustang, but you need the computer to stay in touch with Langley."

"You had no…" She shook her head. Going toe-to-toe with

him wouldn't get her the distance she desperately needed to put between them. "Surely you've talked to Nate by now. So you know that Creath is on his way to Sundown. You should leave here and go home to Oklahoma City—"

"Creath spent last night at the Sundown Inn."

Regan felt the blood drain out of her face. "I stayed at your house," she burst out. "He could have seen—"

"Us. Together." Josh's fingers tightened on her wrist as his eyes hardened. "If he did, he already knows you and I are involved. So your running away *to protect me* won't do a damn bit of good. It will only piss me off more and—"

"Police, freeze!"

Regan jerked toward the sound of Creath's voice at the same time Josh yanked her halfway behind him. While fear arrowed into her bones, her gaze flicked to the gun holstered against the small of Josh's back. His right hand, still locked rock steady around her wrist, was only inches from the weapon.

Looking past Josh, she watched Creath with a sick sense of dread. He was maybe ten feet away, standing on the hard-packed dirt in a legs-apart-cop-stance, gun aimed in their direction. The gold badge clipped to the waistband of his khaki pants glinted in the sun.

Behind him, she could see only a slice of the convenience store's parking lot, but no cars. She couldn't even see her Mustang, which she'd left parked at the gas pump. At the side of the building where they stood, they were out of view of almost all customers who stopped at the small, isolated store.

All potential witnesses.

Josh raised his free hand waist high while saying, "I'm a cop, too. I'm a cop."

Creath's chin lifted minutely. He was big and imposing with dark brown hair and brown eyes that were currently hidden behind mirrored sunglasses. "Don't see a badge."

"It's in my back pocket," Josh answered levelly. "I'll be happy to show it to you."

"Keep your hands where I can see them," Creath ordered. "*Both* hands."

Regan felt Josh hesitate before he gave her wrist a reassuring squeeze, then released it. Slowly, he moved his right hand into Creath's view.

Terror clawed into Regan's chest. With no witnesses, Creath could do whatever he wanted and no one would question the outcome. She slowly edged her hand into the pocket of her shorts, slid out Etta's recorder and clicked it on.

Despite Creath's mirrored sunglasses, she knew the exact moment he shifted his gaze to her, could almost feel his eyes crawl across her flesh. His mouth curled. "There's two warrants on the woman out of New Orleans. For murder. I'm taking her in."

Josh inched his elbows back. Regan tensed, sensing he was waiting for an opening to go for his gun.

"I know about the warrants," he responded. "In fact, right before you got here I placed Kincaid under arrest. Meaning she's *my* prisoner. You can follow me when I transport her to the county jail. Start your extradition paperwork there."

"Sure thing," Creath said, and pulled the trigger.

The deafening blast muffled Regan's scream as the bullet slammed into Josh. He staggered into her, knocking the recorder from her hand.

"No!" He was too heavy for her to support, so Regan went down with him, breaking his fall with her own body. She landed on her side, he on top of her, knocking the breath out of her.

"Josh!" Lungs heaving, she struggled from under him, scrambled to her knees. He was on his back wheezing, hand gripping his chest while he fought for air. Already, blood was soaking into the upper right side of his shirt. His eyes were narrowed, pain already overtaking the fierceness she'd seen there earlier.

Biting down on her lip, she forced her years of training to kick in and ripped open his shirt. The sucking sound and frothy bubbles of blood coming from the entrance wound told her the bullet had punctured the chest wall. Air entering the wound could cause his lung to collapse. It was urgent she find something airtight to seal the wound.

"Hold on, Josh. Hold—"

Creath's fingers twisted into her hair. She had a split second to press Josh's hand over the wound before Creath jerked her to her feet.

"Think I'm going to let Little Miss Paramedic save her latest lover?"

She lashed out at him with her hands, her feet, kicking at his knees, his shins, any part of him she could hit.

When he slammed her forward against the building, she grunted in pain. Pressing the length of his body against the back of hers, he trapped her against the rough concrete wall. He clenched his fingers tighter in her hair, angled her head sideways, forcing her to look at him. With his face only inches from hers, she smelled the cloying scent of peppermint on his breath. Her stomach roiled.

"Thought you could hide from me forever, didn't you, Susan?"

"Let me help him," she pleaded. Creath's mirrored sunglasses reflected back the desperation in her eyes. She wanted to lunge at him, scratch his eyes out, but with both of her arms trapped between her body and the building, and his full weight pressing against her she could barely breathe, much less move.

"Last night I was outside the tavern where you work." Creath's voice was cold, filled with malice. "I thought you'd go upstairs to that apartment after you closed, but you climbed into your car instead. I tailed you, wanting to see exactly what you'd been up to." He jerked his head toward where Josh lay. "Saw you on the porch with him. Figured since you had a job and were whoring yourself, you weren't planning to leave that armpit of a town anytime soon. So I drove to Dallas this morning, took care of some business for you."

Somehow using her name to pawn the gun he'd used to kill Bobby, Regan thought.

"I'd just gotten back to Sundown and was on my way to reunite with you when you sped by in the opposite direction," Creath continued, his breath hot against her skin. "I followed you. Hung back to see if lover boy would show up." Creath smiled. "He did."

"Let me help him," she pleaded. "He's a cop. Even you can't get away with killing a cop."

"But *I* didn't kill him, *cher*," Creath countered as his fingers tightened in her hair. "You see, I used a throwaway to shoot your lover. Before we're done here, that gun's going to have only your prints on it. And with me claiming I witnessed you shoot him, McCall'll be just one more man you killed."

"*You* killed!" Regan shouted. Josh was still alive—she wouldn't let herself think otherwise. She had to make sure he stayed alive. If anyone heard the gunshot, they hadn't dashed around the building to see what was happening. She had to get help. Had to try to make enough noise to attract someone's attention and get Josh help.

"You killed Steven and Bobby," she yelled. "You thought getting them out of the way would make me want you. I never wanted you. *Nothing* could make me want you!"

"Defiant bitch, you'll pay for leaving me." Creath shoved forward, pressing her so hard against the wall she could breathe only in painful pants. The rough concrete bit into her cheek, her arms, her legs. "You're going to sit in a cell for the rest of your life, thinking of me," he said with heavy satisfaction, then licked the side of her face.

She shuddered, trembling with revulsion as much as fear. "You're the last person I'll think of."

"Wrong, *cher.*" His mouth curled. "You'll wish a thousand times you'd turned to me after I took your pathetic Steven and Bobby out of the picture."

"That's what you did to your missing fiancée, isn't it? She broke up with you, *rejected you,* so you killed her, too."

"No one rejects me!" When Creath dragged her head back, Regan's cheek scraped across the concrete wall. She whimpered as pain exploded in the side of her face, jagged and sharp. Blood pooled warmly on her cheek.

Creath's fingers dragged from her hair to clamp onto the back of her neck. "I caught up with that P.I. you hired to follow me." His lips pulled back against his teeth in a feral snarl. "After I killed him I read the report on my background he e-mailed to you. That two-bit slime had no hard facts. *No evidence.*"

Langley, Regan thought, her heart clenching. So many dead on her account. And Josh lying just feet away, shot and bleeding and her unable to help him.

She had to *do* something. Had to get away from Creath long enough to get to Josh, find something to use to seal his wound.

"You soulless bastard," she hissed, seizing her anger and hate and using them as shields to beat back her terror. "You're sick, Creath. Twisted. I'd rather go to jail for the rest of my life than have you touch me!"

"Shut the hell up!" Enraged, he jerked her away from the building. The back of his hand exploded against the side of her face, snapping her head to the side and sending her reeling.

The blow brought a burst of stars behind her eyes and the taste of blood to her mouth even before she landed hard on her palms and knees. Gasping, Regan shook her head, trying to clear it. *Get to Josh,* she told herself, but the ground was spinning beneath her and nausea crawled up the back of her throat.

"You're going to have a whole lot more bruises on you, *cher,* by the time I get you to jail," Creath said, advancing on her. "That's to be expected when a fugitive felon resists arrest."

Seeing his right leg tense, Regan braced to absorb the kick she knew was coming.

The next second, a thunderclap blasted the air, and Creath crumpled beside her.

Wild-eyed, she jerked her head sideways. Josh was sitting up, blood covering his chest, his gun clenched in both hands. On a strangled cry, she pushed to her feet and raced to him as he did a slow-motion slide sideways.

She caught him before he hit the ground, eased him onto his back.

"Had...to wait...till...you were clear...to get a shot," he managed.

"You got him." Her heart drummed impossibly hard, impossibly loud. Tears rose to burn the back of her eyes. "You're going to be okay. Relax now. Don't talk."

The sucking sound from the wound continued; his pulse was weak and there was a bluish tint to his lips now. She slid her hand beneath his shoulders, checking for blood, but there wasn't any. No exit wound meant the bullet was still inside him. She couldn't be sure what angle it had entered his chest, had no idea how much damage the slug had done. If she didn't seal the wound to keep oxygen from entering the chest cavity, it was possible both lungs could collapse and he would suffocate.

"Creath." Josh kept his eyes closed. "Dead?"

"I don't know." She pressed her palm against the wound while she frantically patted his pockets with her free hand. His cell phone wasn't clipped to his waistband, it wasn't in his pockets. God, he must have left it in his car. She had to call for help, but she didn't dare leave him for that long.

"Get...Creath's gun." Josh winced, pain flickering across his face. "Kick it away...don't get your...prints on it. Make sure...there's not another...gun."

She didn't want to deal with Creath. But Josh was right—if the bastard wasn't dead he could take another shot at them.

"All right." She lifted Josh's right hand, pressed his palm over the bullet hole. "It will be easier to breathe if you can keep your hand here. You're going to be okay, Josh. I'm going to make sure you're okay."

Her legs barely supported her as she dashed toward Creath's body. He'd landed on his back, still wearing the mirrored sunglasses. There was a single, neat bullet hole in the center of his forehead. His right arm was outstretched, the gun a foot from his hand.

Regan kicked it away. Setting her jaw, she touched fingers against the pulse point on Creath's throat. As she confirmed he was dead, the scent of peppermint assaulted her.

Peppermint, she thought, desperation rising inside her like a flood. Creath habitually carried peppermints in a plastic bag.

Swallowing a sob, she stabbed her hand into his pants pocket, jerked out the bag and dumped the mints.

"Whoa, what's going on?"

She whirled. Two teenage boys wearing T-shirts, jeans and cowboy boots stood at the corner of the building, gaping. One had the keys to the men's restroom dangling from his hand.

Regan stabbed a finger at the boy on the right. "You, call the police," she ordered. "Tell them a cop has been shot. He needs to be airlifted to the nearest E.R. Have you got that?"

"Uh, yeah."

She aimed her finger at the other boy. "You, run into the store and bring me gauze and a roll of duct tape. Now!" she screamed when they both continued to goggle at her.

They took off like rockets. Praying they followed through, Regan dashed back to Josh.

She dropped beside him, clenched her jaw when she discovered he was now unconscious, his face pale as wax. "Hold on."

Shaking almost uncontrollably, she folded the empty plastic baggy, then moved his hand away from the wound and replaced it with the baggy. Once the kid returned with the gauze and duct tape, she would dress the wound then seal the bag over it on three sides, creating a flutter valve.

She kept her bloodstained fingers pressed around the baggy's sides and top. With no medical equipment, this was all she could do for him. All she could do to try to keep him alive.

"Hold on," she repeated while tears rolled down her cheeks. "You're not going to die. I won't let you die." Fear that he might do just that crimped her voice. "I love you, Josh. Please hold on."

"Well, Regan...guess I should say *Susan,* your turning on Etta's recorder when you did goes a long way to backing up your story about Payne Creath."

Gripping her hands together until her knuckles ached, Regan stared numbly across the scarred table at Jim Decker, clad in a sharp-pressed county sheriff's uniform. "I forgot all about the recorder after Creath shot Josh," she said, her voice a thin rasp.

Since the deputy who'd transported her from the convenience store and booked her into the county jail had confiscated her watch, she had no idea how long she'd sat alone in the small, gray-walled interrogation room before Decker arrived. No idea how long he'd spent questioning her.

It seemed like an eternity had passed since Decker told her Josh had survived the trip to a Dallas E.R. Was he still in surgery? Out of surgery and resting in ICU? *Was he even alive?*

She shifted her gaze to the dark-haired man leaning against the far wall who'd arrived with Decker. Dressed in chinos and a hunter-green shirt, Nate McCall was tall and rangy with black hair and a complexion swarthier than his brother's. But the dark eyes watching her were so much like Josh's she wanted to weep.

Decker tapped his pen against the legal pad he'd filled with notes. "That recording doesn't cancel the murder warrants. There's a lot of legalese and red tape that has to be dealt with.

So I have to keep you in custody until things get worked out with the New Orleans PD."

Nate's cell phone chimed, and both she and Decker jerked their heads his way. Barely breathing, Regan watched him shift to face the wall while he conversed with the caller.

When Nate finally ended the call he hesitated, then turned. "That was Bran," he said. "Josh made it out of surgery. His condition's guarded, but he's expected to recover."

"Thank God," Regan managed in a thick, trembling whisper.

"Damn good to hear." Decker gathered up his pen and legal pad, then rose. He paused to study the scrapes and bruises marring Regan's left cheek. "You're pretty banged up. I'm going to have you put in the infirmary instead of a cell."

She nodded, dangerously close to tears. "Thank you."

"Being the acting sheriff has its perks." Decker turned to Nate. "You coming?"

"I've got some things to say to Miss Kincaid," Nate said, moving to the table. "Mind if we use your room awhile longer?"

"Take as long as you need," Decker said before walking out.

Nate placed his palms on the table and leaned toward her. What Regan saw in his eyes wasn't a cop's stony hardness, but a brother's torment.

"When Josh first told me about you, I thought I should come to Sundown and haul you to jail."

She kept her gaze locked with his. "I wish you had. I wish…" She struggled to keep her tears at bay. "That bullet should have hit me. Not Josh. *It should have been me.*"

Nate closed his eyes, opened them, then he eased away from the table. "The doctor told Bran if you hadn't treated Josh's wound right after he was shot, he would have died before he made it to the E.R."

Nate swiped a hand across the back of his neck. "You knew the police were on the way, knew you still had two murder warrants out on you. You could have left my brother bleeding in the dirt and kept running."

"No, I couldn't." Regan scrubbed away a tear. "I couldn't leave him."

She saw a change in Nate's eyes. A softening. "All along I've questioned whether you were good for my little brother."

Regan stared at her reflection in the one-way glass set into the wall. "Believe me, so have I."

"The thing is, Josh never questioned that. So while the rest of the McCalls hang at the hospital, Bran and I are hopping a plane to New Orleans. We're going to firmly insist that the NOPD Internal Affairs boys take another look into Creath's activities. And we're going to make sure they do it right this time."

When Regan didn't comment, Nate angled his chin. "If things work out like I think they will and you're cleared, what happens between you and Josh?"

She closed her eyes. All along, Josh had asked only one thing of her: to put her trust in him. Trust him enough to stand and fight instead of run.

But that's just what she'd done. She'd run. Peel all the layers away, it wouldn't matter why. All that mattered was that she'd run.

And when Josh caught up with her at the convenience store he'd been furious. Beyond that fury had been hurt. He'd risked his career for her, his life.

He'd physically shielded her from Creath and she'd risked nothing for him. Given him *nothing*.

She met Nate's gaze. "What happens will be up to Josh."

Chapter 16

Music drifted through the open door of the nurses' station as Regan moved soundlessly along the dim hallway that was ripe with a sterile scent. While a paramedic, she'd learned a few tricks about sneaking in to see a patient after visiting hours.

She had spent nearly four days in the county jail before being released—cleared of all charges—earlier that evening. Since Decker had arranged to have her Mustang waiting for her there, she'd driven straight to the Dallas hospital.

And because it had been too unsettling to think about facing members of the McCall clan when she wasn't sure that one particular member—the most *important* member—would welcome her presence, Regan had waited past the time all visitors would have been shooed out by the nurses before making her move.

Not that she hadn't met plenty of McCalls already. She hadn't seen Nate since her first day in jail, but the McCall sisters had dropped by the jail's infirmary at various times. Morgan, Carrie and Grace had each been friendly. Kind. Yet they were all cops, and Regan hadn't missed the sharp assessment in their eyes.

Scoping out the woman who'd nearly gotten their youngest brother killed.

They were right, and Regan felt horribly responsible. She'd gotten little sleep over the past days and nights since every time she closed her eyes she saw Josh lying on the ground, bleeding. She couldn't think about how close he'd come to dying without her heart wrenching. And she thought about that every other minute. If she was ever going to find any peace, it would be after she faced him and told him how sorry she was.

For everything. And to thank him for believing in her. For risking everything for her when she'd risked nothing for him.

The fact that none of his sisters had delivered any sort of message to her from Josh was a message in itself. One that Regan clearly understood. Why would a man want a woman who'd given him nothing when he'd given her everything? A woman who'd spent most of her time trying to push him away?

Reaching the end of the dim hallway, Regan sidestepped an empty gurney then did a quick check of the sign that listed the direction of patient rooms. She turned right into another dimly lit hallway.

The silver lining to the McCall sisters' visits was they'd kept her apprised of Josh's condition. He'd been moved the previous morning out of the ICU. If he continued his rapid improvement, he would be home in a couple of days.

Home, Regan figured was Oklahoma City. Considering how angry, how hurt, Josh had been when he caught up with her at the convenience store, she wasn't expecting an invitation to visit.

Still, she was determined to see him this one last time. And after she made her peace with him, she would decide what to do with the life that suddenly stretched before her. She wasn't the same woman she'd been a year ago. Would never be her again. Her future was a blank slate, and she had no idea which way to turn.

She paused outside Josh's room, took a steadying breath, then slid soundlessly inside. And saw he was asleep. Her heart clenching at the sight of him, she moved across the room, the weak light over the small sink tucked into a built-in vanity illuminating her way.

His head was turned slightly toward the door; from what she could tell, his skin tone looked normal. His dark hair was close to the shaggy stage; several days worth of stubble shadowed his jaw. She noted the IV in his left forearm, then raised a brow when she realized the chest drainage instrument on the far side of the bed was sitting idle, with no tube running under Josh's hospital gown. His being unhooked from that told her he was well on his way to recovery.

Thank God.

Because she needed to touch him, to touch him and know he was whole and safe, she brushed unsteady fingertips across his brow. Only now, seeing him, being able to judge his condition for herself, did she feel a slight easing of the tension that had held her in its grip since that horrible day.

Although his eyes were closed, Josh wasn't asleep. He'd been lying there, concentrating on building up his strength so he could get out of the damn hospital and deal with a vital piece of business. He'd known the instant that piece of business stepped into the room, even before she brushed her fingers across his skin.

You're finally here, he thought, then opened his eyes and met her gaze.

Regan jerked her hand back as if she'd been stung. "I…didn't mean to wake you." Her eyes softened and she lowered her voice. "How are you?"

"Doing okay." One of the last clear images he had of that day was of Creath smashing the back of his hand against her cheek. A cheek that, even through the dim light, he could see was scraped and sported a bruise in healing shades of yellow-gray and green. Josh clenched his jaw, wishing he could kill the bastard all over again. "How about you?"

"I'm fine." The fingers of one of her hands played over the strap of her purse. "Decker sprang me a couple of hours ago."

Josh knew the exact time she'd walked out of jail because Decker had called to let him know. Since then, the uncertainty of whether she would come to him had kept his gut in knots. Good thing she had, because he didn't think he could have managed to check himself out of the hospital and go after her. Not yet, anyway.

Regan slid her tongue over her bottom lip. She'd practiced endlessly what she would say, but now that she was facing him, she felt her courage waver. "Look, you're probably ready to go to sleep. I can come back in the morning."

"All I've done since I got here is sleep," he said, snagging her wrist. No way was he letting her get away again. He punched a button on the bed's remote; a quiet hum sounded as the upper half of the mattress eased him into a sitting position. "Sleep, and get updates," he amended. "From Decker, and Nate's called a couple of times each day." Josh shifted, hid a wince when he felt the pull of the stitches in his chest. "He and Bran are flying back from New Orleans tomorrow."

"Decker didn't tell me what the police there found. He just told me I was free to go."

"Have a seat and I'll fill you in."

When she glanced at the chair at the side of the bed, Josh tightened his fingers on her wrist. "I won't have to strain to look at you if you sit on the bed."

Even after she set her purse aside and slid a hip onto the mattress, he kept his hand locked on her.

"Nate said that after the NOPD cops heard the recording you made, they got a warrant and tore Creath's house apart," Josh began. "That took an entire day and they didn't come up with anything incriminating. They did find a set of keys that no one could figure out what they went to. Nate was vague on details, but someone finally got a lead on a storage facility Creath rented under an alias. The unit had a concrete floor, but one section looked newer than the rest. They dug it up, and found the body of Creath's fiancée."

Regan shoved a hand through her hair. "Poor woman."

"That applies to any female the bastard set his sights on," Josh said while stroking his thumb against the soft pulse-point on her wrist. "The cops found Langley's laptop there, too. And a stash of fentanyl from the same batch that killed Steven. The search also turned up ammo the identical caliber as that used to kill Bobby Ivers. The NOPD cops used the murder weapon to do some test fires. That ammo showed the exact same markings as the slug the M.E. took out of Bobby."

"I'm not sure I understand how Creath managed to pawn the gun in my name."

"Since he's not alive to explain, it's mostly theory. But everyone agrees Creath was a whiz at computers. Once he locked onto Langley and figured out his connection to you, he killed him, got his laptop and found his e-mails to you. It probably didn't take Creath long to zero in on Sundown. And a guy who gets away with as much as he did isn't the type to rush in without a plan. In his twisted mind, he perceived you'd rejected him because of both Steven and Bobby. He'd already set you up for Steven's murder. He would have also wanted you to pay for slighting him because of Bobby. What better way than to have you pawn the murder weapon that killed your coworker?"

"When you pawn something, don't you have to show an ID that matches the name you put on the pawn slip?"

"Yes." Josh continued the soft strokes of her wrist while he studied her. Her face was about as pale as the white blouse she wore, and fatigue shadowed her eyes. She was the most beautiful thing he'd ever seen.

"Nate said the *Sundown Sentinel*'s Web site was accessed

on Langley's laptop the same day he was murdered," Josh continued. "You have to figure Creath is the one who accessed it. Once he knew you were in Sundown, it would be in his best interest to research the town. A good place to start would be the local newspaper. So he pulled up a few editions and presto, there's a picture of you using your paramedic skills plastered on the front page."

"The story Burns Yost wrote identified me as Regan Ford, the night bartender at Truelove's Tavern. That's the address Creath used on the pawn slip."

"Right. So Creath, like every cop in the universe, knows the lowlifes in his city who churn out phony IDs. The ID guy Creath went to probably snagged your picture off the *Sentinel*'s Web site, then made up what looked like a legal Texas driver's license. At that point, Creath called his lieutenant, said he had urgent personal business to take care of and needed some time off. That left Creath free to head to Sundown."

"He told me he waited outside the tavern, thinking I'd go upstairs to my apartment after we closed. Instead, I drove to your house." Regan fisted her hands against her thighs, suppressing a shudder. For the rest of her life she would regret going to Josh that night. "He saw us on the porch, kissing. That's why he shot you. Because he saw us together."

"He shot me because he was a sick, evil bastard," Josh reminded her, wishing he could brush away the lines of worry on her face. "From what Creath saw that night, he knew you had a job and a personal life in Sundown. You showed no sign you were about to take off in the next twelve hours, so he checked into the Sundown Inn for the night. The next morning he drove to Dallas.

"My guess is he hired some hooker to put on a black wig and dark sunglasses, then pawn the gun using the phony ID, which by law the pawnbroker would have had to make a copy of. About an hour later, the Dallas PD got an anonymous phone tip that a gun used in a New Orleans homicide was at that pawnshop. The cops picked up the copy of the ID and gun, test fired the weapon and entered the results into the FBI's Drug-fire firearm database. A hit came back and Creath's partner at the NOPD was notified."

"Your brothers learned all this for me?" she asked.

Josh nodded, his fingers still circling her wrist, holding her to him. "The partner called Creath to tell him about the hit and that they had a lead on your location. Creath's response was he just happened to be within driving distance of Sundown so he'd pick you up and transport you back to New Orleans. Since Creath's partner had talked to Nate already about your prints, he called Nate to let him know they'd located you. That was just in case you'd been pegged as a suspect in any crime in Oklahoma City since they last talked. Then Nate called me about Creath, which is the phone call you heard over my answering machine."

Regan closed her eyes, opened them. "Looking back, it all seems like such a nightmare."

"It *was* a nightmare."

"One you took on willingly." She met Josh's dark gaze. "You saved my life."

His brain had locked in the hazy image of her kneeling over him, a ruthless determination in her eyes while she worked to keep him alive. "I'd say it was the other way around."

"No." She struggled to keep her voice steady. "The minute you walked into my life, you saved me. You believed what I told you about Creath. You knew I was wanted for murder, but you didn't take me to jail even though it might have cost you your badge. That day outside the convenience store, you were so angry with me for running. So hurt. Still, you shielded me from Creath." Her voice had turned rough with emotion, but she forced herself to continue. "You took a bullet because of me."

"I took a bullet because an obsessed cop shot me. You're not responsible for what Creath did."

"He was obsessed with me. He shot you because of *me* and you almost died. You risked everything for me, and I gave you nothing. Risked nothing."

She couldn't have looked more guilty if she'd shot him herself, Josh thought. If they were going to get anywhere, he was going to have to nudge her past the self-recrimination.

"Seems to me your taking off to purposely lure a homicidal cop to come after you is plenty risky. But it's clear you and I could debate that issue into eternity and never agree." He studied her face, her shadowed eyes, the emotion in them. "So, you walked out of jail tonight. You could have driven to Sundown. To Etta. There's the million-dollar trust fund Steven set up, waiting for you in New Orleans. But you came here. Why?"

I followed my heart, she wanted to say, but held back. "To apologize for almost getting you killed. For everything."

"Frankly, Regan, I'm not interested in hearing your apologies."

That brought her chin up with a jerk and a quick sheen of tears to her eyes. "Oh. Well, then, I'll go."

When she started to pull away, he tightened his fingers on her wrist and gave her a pointed look. "*Because* I've found more interesting things to listen to over the past couple of days. Things you said."

Her forehead furrowed. "I've been in jail the past couple of days. Maybe your sisters mentioned they came to visit me?"

"Yeah, they mentioned it." They couldn't wait to scope Regan out after he told them he intended to make her a permanent part of his life. "Decker dropped by to see me and brought Etta's recorder with him. Since I was mostly out of commission after Creath showed up, I wanted to hear exactly what went on."

Her lips parted. "Didn't it bother you to listen to that?"

"More than you'll ever know." He would always remember the desperation in her voice while she pleaded with Creath, not for her own welfare but for *his*. "But it was worth listening to when I heard what you said toward the end of the recording."

"The end?" She gave him a blank look. "I was a little pre-occupied. I don't remember anything I said."

"You told me you weren't going to let me die. Then you said you loved me." Josh angled his chin. "Why is it you waited until I was unconscious to tell me?"

She blinked. "I was afraid if I told you, Creath would some-how know. And come after you."

"You kept your feelings to yourself and he came after me anyway. Now that we've got that out of the way and I'm conscious, what's holding you back?"

"I wasn't sure you wanted to hear how I felt. That day at the store, when you caught up with me, you were so angry that I'd run. So hurt."

"I was plenty of both," he agreed. "Knowing you took off because you thought Creath would be too busy tracking you to come after me made me want to throttle you. I *still* want to throttle you for that."

Increasing the pressure on her wrist, he drew her closer, his voice raspy. "Do you know what it did to me to have to lie there in the dirt and watch Creath smash you against the side of that building? To use his body to trap you there while you begged him to let you help me? I watched that, waiting for you to get clear so I could get a shot off, knowing at any minute he might decide to kill you instead of hauling you to jail." Lifting her chin with his fingers, he gazed into her dark eyes that had held so many secrets. "I knew before then I was in love with you. I just didn't know how much."

Regan's heart fluttered into her throat. "And I didn't know how much I loved you until you were bleeding under my hands and I thought I might lose you." She pressed her palm to his cheek. "I love you, Josh McCall. Wildly. Completely."

He went very still, and the fingers on her chin tightened. Emotions poured through him, sweet and potent as wine. "Took you long enough to get that out," he said softly.

"I know." Her pulse was hammering now in a hundred places. "And even if you don't want to hear it, I'll tell you again how much I regret putting your job at risk, not to mention your life."

"Speaking of my job, we need to talk about that." He shifted his hand from her chin, slid his palm down her dark, glossy hair. "I turned in my badge."

"Josh, no." Alarm streaked across her face. "Did it get out that you knew I was wanted for murder and didn't turn me in?"

"No, I skated on that. I got offered a job that suits me better."

"But you're a cop. That's who you are." She shook her head. "What job could suit you better?"

"I should have said a job in a *place* that suits me better. Sundown's mayor came to see me yesterday. Turns out, Decker's got the county sheriff's job on a permanent basis now. After I recuperate, I pin on his former badge."

"You'll be Sundown's police chief?" Regan stared at him while it all sunk in. "You're staying in Sundown? For good?"

"That's right. I have the family house here. Etta. Sundown's always been my second home." He gave Regan a slow head-to-toe study. "Plus, I've got this thing for the hot bartender who works the night shift at Truelove's Tavern."

Regan linked her fingers with his. "I happen to know she's got a thing for Sundown's hot police chief." She studied his face, the rugged lines and angles. "Nearly everyone in your family is an OCPD cop. How are they going to take your giving that up?"

"Don't forget, I'm the rebel. They're used to me pushing the envelope. Testing rules to see just how bendable they are." He lifted a brow. "Falling in love with a woman wanted for murder."

"You do that often?"

"I plan to do that only once." Emotion thudded into his chest, flooded into his heart. "You changed things for me, Regan. Made me see things, *feel* things I never have before."

He traced his fingertips along her jawline. "The timing's good, since the entire McCall clan is in Sundown."

"Timing for what?"

"A wedding." He lifted her hand to his mouth, pressed his lips to her knuckles and felt everything in his life snap into place. "I want it all with you. Marriage, family, everything."

"Josh…" Rocked by emotion, she could only stare at him while he gazed at her over her hand, flashing that grin she'd known was trouble the first night he walked into Truelove's Tavern.

"Come on, Regan, take a risk," he urged with soft irony in his voice and a tantalizing sparkle in his eyes. "Live dangerously for once in your life."

She brushed a fingertip along the scar that ran the length of his throat while her heart did a lovely bounding leap. "Well, *that* will be a new experience for me," she murmured.

"Is that a yes?"

"Yes, Josh, that's a yes. A huge yes." A wave of love swamped her. They would make a home together. A present. A future. "You know, Chief McCall, when I walked out of jail this evening, I thought I was free and clear of the law."

Josh's grin turned smug. "Think again, sweetheart. You're *always* going to be wanted by the law."

* * * * *

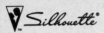

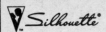

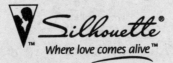

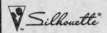

COMING NEXT MONTH

#1399 PENNY SUE GOT LUCKY—Beverly Barton
The Protectors
When an eccentric millionaire leaves her riches to her beloved
dog, Lucky, girl-next-door Penny Sue Paine is assigned as his
guardian. But someone wants this pooch dead…and fast. Enter
Vic Noble, gorgeous ex-CIA operative hired as Lucky's protector.
Suddenly Penny Sue starts thinking *she's* the one who got lucky!

#1400 THE SHERIFF OF HEARTBREAK COUNTY—
Kathleen Creighton
Starrs of the West
A congressman's son is murdered and all fingers point to
Mary Owen, the mousy newcomer to Hartsville, Montana…
but Sheriff Roan Harley can't quite make the pieces fit. At first
he's interested in Mary for purely investigative reasons. But
where will the lawman's loyalties lie when he realizes he's in love
with the suspected criminal?

#1401 AWAKEN TO DANGER—Catherine Mann
Wingmen Warriors
Nikki Price's world comes crashing to a halt when she wakes next
to a dead body. Added to this ordeal is the man sent to solve this
mystery, Squadron Commander Carson Hunt, who broke her heart
months ago. Carson is certain she's in danger and vows to protect
her. Will Nikki be able to trust Carson with her life…and the
passion threatening to consume them?

#1402 ENEMY HUSBAND—Nina Bruhns
FBI agent Kansas Hawthorne won't rest until the criminal that
betrayed her father is brought to justice. Only her archrival,
Stewart Rio, a tough-as-nails agent, could make her falter on
this top secret operation. Posing as newlyweds, their pretend
romance turns to real love. Will their new relationship survive the
past so they can have a future together?

SIMCNM1205